This special edition of

A GAME IN THE SUN

and other Stories

is limited to

750

signed and numbered copies.

This is number _567_.

John Coyne

A
GAME
IN THE
SUN
AND OTHER STORIES

A GAME IN THE SUN

AND OTHER STORIES

JOHN COYNE

CEMETERY DANCE PUBLICATIONS

Baltimore

2018

Cemetery Dance Publications
132-B Industry Lane
Unit 7
Forest Hill, MD 21050
www.cemeterydance.com

First Cemetery Dance Printing

ISBN 1-58767-630-7

Cover Artwork Copyright © 2018 by Elderlemon Design

Interior Design © 2018 by Desert Isle Design, LLC

TABLE OF CONTENTS

FLIGHT

My son slept. He slept without moving, without breathing it seemed, and several times i reached over in the dark front seat of the car to feel for the tiny warm puffs of his breath on my palm. My terrifying fear was that he would die right there and then, on the back roads of Virginia, after everything i had done to steal him from his mother.

It was three A.M., but still he slept. He hadn't even awakened when I leaned over his small crib, wrapped him gently in the wool blanket, and lifted him into my arms. His weight had nearly staggered me, there in the dark house. It wasn't his fifteen pounds, that I knew. It was my fear of taking him from his crib, taking him from his mother.

She could have the house, have everything we owned together, have everything I'd owned before we were married. But she couldn't have my son. Timmy was mine, now and forever. I had told her so when I walked out of her life.

It might have been different, I guess, if we had had a girl. Lynne had been expecting, planning on a girl. "What do I know about boys?" she had said, once she got pregnant.

7

A girl would have made everything a lot easier, all the way around. Women know about girls. I would have been happy with visiting rights. But a boy belongs with his father. That's what I think. That's what I told her. Told the judge. Told everyone. It's only right, whatever the law says. Her mother called me crazy. And then Lynne wouldn't even let me see my kid. She said I had no rights, not after what I had put her through.

Okay. I'll give her that much. I had gone a little crazy after she sprung it on me. I mean, she thought it was wonderful, great news, her getting pregnant. She phoned me at work with the news on the same day I was let go from TGRA.

McClintock had just come down to my cubicle and told me. With the cutbacks in the federal budget, there wouldn't be any more funding for our solar-energy research. Our task force was the first to get the federal axe. Bob felt bad about it, sorry, he said. Sure! But he wasn't out of work. I went a little wild thinking of where my next job would come from. Not in Washington, that was for sure, not while the Republicans were in office.

So I was in no mood to learn that Lynne was pregnant. A few of us went out and tied one on. I admit it. I told the judge that much. And when I got home, there she was, grinning and telling me, "Well, Nelson, I guess you weren't shooting blanks after all."

I swore at her, broke her favorite vase. That sort of thing. And I'm sorry about it. But that had more to do with getting the pink slip than her having a kid. I mean, I think I wanted a kid. We never talked about it, but heck, after six years you stop thinking of having one, about it being your turn. You get a little careless when it comes to preventing one. I hadn't expected it would happen to me. Having a family, I mean.

FLIGHT

I glanced at the dashboard clock and saw that I would have to stop soon. The baby should have been fed at 3:00. I knew that from the notebook Lynne kept on his feedings. I had taken that with me, too, slipped it into my belt before I reached down into the crib and picked him up. When I lifted him, he turned, like, into my arms. It was as if he suddenly knew he was being held by his old man.

I held my breath and listened. Lynne was only a dozen feet away, on the other side of the wall. But she was bad when it came to hearing anything. I was the one who always heard Timmy. He'd turn over in his bed and I'd hear him. It didn't matter how tired I was, I was the one who got out of bed and went to him in the middle of the night. After the first few weeks, Lynne said she couldn't. She just couldn't function without a good nine hours of sleep. Poor Timmy, I thought. He must have learned to live with a wet diaper.

Well, those days were over, I told myself. He was with his Dad now. For the rest of his life. And I knew how to take care of him.

It had felt wonderful, holding him. I hadn't held him, or seen him, since October. He wasn't even eight weeks old when I left. It was one o'clock and we were all up screaming: the baby, Lynne, me. It was a dumb thing, fighting in the middle of the night, yelling about her going back to work, and how dumpy she looked since having the kid. And she was yelling at me for not getting a job, for feeling sorry for myself and never helping with the baby. "We're going to lose this place, Nelson. Don't you understand? And I'm not going to ask my parents again for the mortgage payment."

I don't know what was wrong with us, but it seemed as if we could only fight late at night. I kept thinking that it must have to do with the tension building up all day, thinking of how hurt and rotten we felt toward each

9

other, and then—wow!—it had to come out, and with us, it was always the middle of the night, feeding Timmy.

I was sitting in the rocker trying to make him take the bottle, but he kept screaming, red in the face, gasping in that helpless way he had, as if he couldn't get his next breath. I kept thinking: he's going to die on me. I worried about that a lot. Lynne wouldn't shut up. She kept talking about the mortgage, about my getting a job. Kept pacing through the baby's room, and talking about what some of the guys had done. "You saw how long it took Logan to find work! He went straight off to Chattanooga and got hired by TVA. No, don't tell me you can't find anything. There are plenty of jobs in the paper, but you won't take anything less than what fits your goddamn qualifications. Oh, God!" She kept pacing, straightening up the nursery as she went on ranting. She always tidied things up when she got mad. It was an obsession.

I just snapped.

I didn't hit her or throw anything. I just took Tim—he was still scream-ing—stood, and went to her. She looked up, suddenly frightened, I think, after blaming me for everything, and she shouted over his noise, "Can't you even feed your child?"

I didn't say anything. I just gave her Timmy. I went back to our room, dressed, tossed a handful of clothes into my gym bag, and left the house. I could still hear Timmy crying. I never heard a kid with such lungs. It made me kinda proud, hearing him scream.

I know Lynne didn't hear me leave. She even said so. I drove out the Pike awhile, stopped at an all-night diner, had something to eat, then called Stan downtown in D.C. and asked if I could crash for the night.

"What happened?" he asked, trying to pull himself awake.

FLIGHT

"I left my family," I told him. But it wasn't true. I left Lynne. I didn't leave Timmy. I knew it then, even as I gave Timmy to Lynne. I would never leave my son. Never. And now they all know it.

That night, two months later, in the dark kitchen, on the way out the door with my baby, I stopped at the fridge and took out the bottles. I can't believe I was that casual. I mean, it's one thing to sneak back into my house after leaving my wife, and take my child from his crib, but then to remember the bottles...It made me feel good, knowing I hadn't panicked. I had to get through the first twenty-four hours, I told myself. After that I'd know his feeding schedule. I could start my own notebook and know how many ounces of formula he had taken.

I reached over and touched his thick body and he cried.

He was suddenly awake in the front seat, screaming with hunger. I felt beneath the wool blanket, felt the warm wetness of his stretch pajamas. He needed to be changed. Diapers I had. I had stopped at Toys 'R Us on Rockville Pike and filled the trunk with Huggies, plastic baby bottles, cans of Enfamil, a traveling crib, some toys. I had already stopped at a drug store for Tylenol, wipes, Desitin, cotton balls, everything Lynne had had neatly arranged on the shelf over Timmy's changing table.

I paid for it all with our Mastercard. That was it for the card, I knew. I had reached the credit limit, and once Lynne and the police realized what I was using to finance my escape, they'd have every cop in the Middle Atlantic looking for that number.

From now on it was cash only, and no expressways with tolls. I had to keep to the back roads, and I had to keep moving, at least until I got to North Carolina. In the mountains I'd be okay. In Blowing Rock, I could stop worrying about Lynne catching up to me. Stop worrying about the police.

I wasn't too worried about the cops. Lynne wouldn't be smart about that. She'd tell them I had taken Timmy. That would do it. A family matter, something for the divorce courts. The cops had more to worry about than some father taking his son. Besides, they were men. They'd understand. The kid was in no danger, not if he was with his father.

Kramer vs. Kramer proved that. And *Ordinary People*. It was the fathers in those movies who hung in there when the going got tough; the fathers who took care of their sons while the mothers split. It's all a lot of nonsense that mothers make the best parents. I told the judge that in family court. But I knew I didn't have a chance, not when I saw the judge was a woman. Forget it. There'd be no appeal. No throwing good money after bad. The odds were stacked against me. I didn't have a chance at custody after that judge heard I had hit Lynne.

Let them find me. Even with back roads, and stopping to feed Timmy, I'd be two hundred miles from Rockville by daybreak. By evening, I'd be hidden away in the Great Smoky's. Hidden away in one of those hollows that don't even appear on maps.

The car hit a bump and the baby screamed, flared his arms, his tight little fists.

"Okay, son, I hear you, I hear you," I said gently as I eased off the gas and with one hand reached forward and searched through my gym bag for the bottles. I could change him later, once I had a place to park. But I didn't want to stop here, on the side of the road, in the middle of nowhere. It would just be inviting trouble. I realized it was almost as if men, even fathers, were suspect if they were caught alone with an infant.

The last sign said Warrenton was ten miles ahead. I could stop in town and buy gas. A full tank would take me into the North Carolina Mountains.

FLIGHT

"When you're older, Timmy, we'll go fishing in these mountains. And white water rafting. How'd you like that?" I kept talking over his screams.

The bottle was cold and I wondered if Lynne was still warming them up first. I remembered those first weeks, getting up every two hours, rushing into the kitchen to get a bottle out of the fridge, then heating it while the baby kept screaming. We'd both gotten up those first weeks. We had a little routine between us, and even with us both half asleep, she'd get him changed while I warmed the bottle. Then Lynne would sit in the rocker with the baby and feed him. She'd always test the milk first against her wrist, as if she didn't believe me when I told her the formula wasn't too hot. She never totally trusted me with the baby. That was just another one of our problems.

And I'd stand there watching them, like some sort of intruder. It didn't seem he was alive at all, not those first weeks. I kept thinking: where did he come from? It was as if he was really *ET*.

"Okay, son, here we go." I kept one hand on the steering wheel as I slipped the bottle nipple into his mouth. He began to choke at once, formula spilling from his mouth. "Oh, God!" I hit the brake and bounced the car off the country road and onto the grassy apron, skidding to a stop. I was holding Timmy down with one hand. His tiny body was trembling beneath my palm as he screamed.

I slid over to the passenger side, lifting him up. "Please, sweetheart, be still. Shhh." I pulled him in a tight embrace. He was hungry and cold. No wonder he was screaming. "I'm sorry, Timmy. I'm sorry. But everything will be okay soon. I'll have you safe and sound again."

I set him down on the seat beside me and stripped off the blankets, the stretchy, and his diaper. I flipped on the reading light and worked fast, as if

13

he were a small bomb ready to explode, and stripped him naked. His face was scarlet and twisted as if in pain. I knew he didn't know who I was. I had read how babies know their parents by their smell and touch. I had been gone half of his life, over two months. Who did he think I was? Would he remember any of this? Our midnight escape?

I kept whispering to him, bent down over his tiny, trembling body as I taped on the Huggies. I never heard the county cop until he tapped his flashlight on the car window and then shone it in my face as if I were some sort of pervert.

I hadn't locked the door; when he spotted the naked baby, he jerked open the door and shoved his service revolver in my face.

"What the fuck are you doing?" he shouted at me.

Timmy screamed and I picked him up, and said softly, to answer the cop without upsetting the baby more, "He's mine. My son."

"What are you doing?" he asked again, but lowered his voice. Now he wasn't sure what to do.

Before he could say any more, I went on quickly. "I'm simply changing his diapers," I whispered. I told him that the baby had wakened, I had to change him, give him a bottle. "Do you have children, officer?" I asked nicely.

The man nodded, still staring at Timmy. I had gone back to diapering the baby, as if to show the cop I knew what I was doing.

"Well, you know how it is when they need to be fed. He's only four months old. My wife..."

"Where's she?" the cop said quickly, seizing on her absence. He was a big, Southern boy, with the sharp, clean features of a kid.

I stopped diapering, held a tube of Desitin in one hand, and looked up at him. "She died. In childbirth. It was a C-Section, and there were

complications. The baby was early—it was our first—and Sue, my wife..."
I looked away.

"Oh, man," the cop said. The breath went out of him. "That's tough, you know..." He stopped, not knowing what more to say. I knew I was safe then. Lynne hadn't gotten to the police, no alarm had been issued for my arrest, the missing child. I suddenly thought she probably didn't even know Timmy was gone. I felt bad then, imagining her coming into the dark baby's room and seeing the empty crib, Timmy and his blanket gone. She'd go wild at first, not realizing what had happened. Only when she thought about it for a moment would she know it was me and not some crazy nut.

"You take care now," the cop spoke up, backing off. He had snapped off his flashlight, and was embarrassed by his intrusion, my story. "I mean, there's not anything I can do for you, is there?"

"No, Officer. Thank you." I had Timmy changed and was wrapping him up again in his blue blanket. I slipped my hands underneath his head and body and lifted my sleeping son to my chest.

It was the only evidence this cop needed, seeing the sleeping child snuggled against me. He tipped his cap and hurried to his car. I waved, kept being friendly, and wondered what he'd think when he heard a baby boy was missing in Rockville, Maryland.

He'd know it was me, that there had been no mother lost in childbirth. I felt a small satisfaction at how easily the story had come to me. I began thinking I could get away with it. It was just that the notion of taking Timmy from Lynne was more frightening than the fact of it was. The baby was fine with me.

And then he threw up again.

The formula gushed out in a milky flow, wet his clothes and the blue blanket, and soaked my shirt.

"Dammit, Timmy!" My voice startled me on the empty back road. "Okay! Okay!' I kept talking, reassuring myself, trying to quiet the baby. He was screaming, frightened by me and the cold wind that was shaking the car. And he was hungry, I knew.

I had to get off the road. I had to get going. At home, Lynne would be waking, wondering why the baby wasn't crying. She would be going to his room right about now, I judged, glancing at my watch. I could almost hear her cries of alarm.

I tried to force the bottle into Timmy's mouth. If he got the taste of the formula he would drink again. I knew that from the first month of his life. But now he turned his head away, his little body squirming in my arms.

"All right! All right!" I shouted. "Take the goddamn bottle!" My nerves were shot. I couldn't keep going like this. I was exhausted. And it was doing no good screaming at Timmy.

I slid back into the car, strapped Timmy into the baby seat, then ran around the car and got in behind the wheel. Timmy kept screaming, his cries bouncing off the interior. I couldn't hear myself think.

On the road again, I raced the car as if I was trying to speed away from his screaming. I had forgotten how loud it was, how insistent. I hadn't lived at home for two months. I hadn't had to get up every night at his waking. I had forgotten what it was like.

Still racing the car, I gave Timmy the bottle again, but this time he reached up with his tiny hand and knocked it away. It was involuntary, I know, but I smiled, pleased at his anger.

FLIGHT

"That's a boy, Timmy, you don't let anyone push you around. You're my boy, okay. No one fucks with you."

That was part of Lynne's and my problem. Our personalities. Our stubbornness. We had gotten married late, both of us over thirty. And even then we didn't know each other. It would have been better if we had lived together for a while, gotten to see if we could get along.

It was a crazy time right after Lynne came home with the baby. Lynne was sick and crying a lot, and I couldn't get a job. Any couple, I guess, would start thinking of splitting. But it was worse with us. We didn't have any reserve of good will, you see, between us. Things started getting bad as soon as Lynne learned she was pregnant, and then she was always sick. She told me she would have quit her job at the Office of Education if I had been working. She held that against me, my getting fired.

Timmy stopped crying, as if the life had gone out of him. My heart seized up and I let the car coast to a stop as I leaned over in the seat. He had fallen asleep again, exhausted from crying. It wouldn't last long, not without a bottle. The poor kid. I had to get something into him.

I stepped on the gas. Warrenton was ahead. I could see the lights of a gas station at the intersection. I'd fill up there, I thought, and park, get Timmy to take a bottle. When I left home, he was only taking four ounces, but now, I saw, Lynne was using eight ounce bottles. When did that happen?

That's what drove me crazy. Every day he was changing on me, and I was cut out of his life.

Well, not any more.

He started crying again when I pulled up to the station. It was deserted. I could see a man, a kid really, inside the office. He looked up, but didn't move from behind the desk.

17

This had to be quick, I told myself. I didn't need more people seeing Timmy, remembering my car. I jumped out and pulled the gas nozzle from the pump and filled the tank while I watched Timmy in the front seat. He was still crying, struggling to get free of the car seat.

I was torturing my son, putting him through all this. I hated to have him crying. I just couldn't stand it, seeing him suffer.

"He's all right, Nelson! He's all right!" Lynne would yell at me when I complained.

"He's not okay if he's crying," I'd shout back. And I was right. But what drove me nuts was that neither one of us knew how to shut him up, once he started. I got into a pattern, first his diaper, then a bottle. I'd try to get him to sleep, rock him in the chair. Still he cried. For a while I thought it was that his tee-shirts were too small for him.

I topped off the tank then walked over to the station office to pay.

When I pushed open the door I could hear the CB radio. The kid had it tuned to the highway patrol. The radio crackled with static.

"Morning," the attendant said. He was wearing a John Deere cap that he pushed up on his head when he reached for my cash.

I nodded and held my breath as I listened to the police band. They were putting out an alert for my arrest.

"That's eleven twenty," the kid said, not picking up on the state alert. WHITE BLOND MALE, AGE 37, HEIGHT 6'1". GLASSES. DRIVING A WHITE '85 PONTIAC. TRAVELLING WITH A FIVE-MONTH-OLD BABY BOY. CONSIDERED DANGEROUS. HOLD FOR QUESTIONING. WANTED IN MARYLAND FOR KIDNAPPING.

Considered dangerous! What in the world had Lynne told the cops?

"Looks like snow. Get a morning sky like that out west and it means

FLIGHT

snow before night," the kid said, handing me change for the twenty. My fingers were trembling. "Cold, ain't it?" the kid grinned.

I nodded, stuffed the money into my pocket, and headed out. If I could get away in time, I kept telling myself, I'd be okay. They won't get me; I'd keep away from gas stations, main highways. I wasn't but five hours from the mountains of North Carolina. Once up on the Blue Ridge, I knew I'd be okay.

"Where are you heading?" the kid called after me. He had come to the office door.

"South," I said, backing away and smiling. I didn't want him to suddenly think I was behaving oddly.

"Keep out of the hills, then. Storm coming."

"I'll do that."

I was in the car and out of the station while he still stood inside the office door, watching me leave. The highway patrol bulletin hadn't meant anything to him.

I headed west out of Warrenton, towards Amissville and Sperryville where I knew I could get up on the Skyline Drive. It would be slower, but it would take me into North Carolina and keep me away from Route 81 into Bristol. Up on the Blue Ridge, I'd be less likely to be spotted by the cops.

In the seat, Timmy had fallen asleep. Still driving, I reached around and pulled the blanket up to his chin. He didn't move.

I kept glancing back at him as I drove. Now I wished I had left him strapped down next to me in the front seat so I could watch him. I couldn't look at him enough, couldn't get enough of him. All I had were the photos from his infancy. He had changed so much in two months. It was almost like a different child. But he was still mine, all mine.

On the long stretch of empty highway, I pressed down on the pedal and raced for the hills. The sun was up. I made out the outline of the ridge, the bank of snow clouds. The kid was right, I thought. There would be snow today. But that was okay. Better for me. The cops would have more to worry about than me if it snowed.

It began snowing when I went through Sperryville. Very light, blowing snow that whipped around the car. I kept on my headlights because even with dawn, it wasn't much brighter. I felt the wind buffeting the car and I slowed some as I climbed toward the Skyline Drive. The road was narrower and twisting as I climbed, and the rocking motion woke Timmy, frightening him again. He woke crying.

I pulled the car off onto the shoulder and stopped.

"Okay, sweetheart. Everything is okay."

He began to sob, rubbing his tiny fists into his eyes, then he fell back into the warmth of his blanket and kicked out in wild rage.

I reached over the back seat and lifted him into my lap. He was flailing at me with his small arms, banging his fists against my face and chest as he raged. Lynne had done this, I kept telling myself. If she had let Timmy have a relationship with his father, this would never have happened. He wouldn't be treating me like a stranger, a kidnapper.

I kept whispering to Timmy, holding him tight, and gradually, more from exhaustion than anything else, he calmed down, though he kept weeping. I set him on my lap and smiled at him. "All right, Timmy. You're all right." He leaned forward, as if to fill his vision and his whole world with my face.

He studied me a moment, tilted his head. It was Lynne's gesture, whenever she was being thoughtful. I suddenly thought: would I be always seeing my ex-wife in my son's face?

FLIGHT

Timmy turned his head away and stared out the front window, lost in the secret world of children. Then he grinned and raised his hand, as if to point.

I looked up myself at the thick, wet snow blowing across the road. Already there was a white film covering the road surface.

"Yes, snow, Timmy." I tried to sound pleased, but the snow, I saw at once, would make it tough going, especially up on the Blue Ridge. Well, I told myself, there was no turning back.

He kept pointing, but he couldn't quite point, his tiny fingers curled up on him and went astray. I found that I had to pull my attention from him. I wanted only to watch him, as if he were something totally unique, a creature from another planet.

"We have to go ahead, Timmy," I said, stirring myself, happy now that he was awake. I moved Timmy off my lap and strapped him into the seat. "Here, how 'bout a cookie?" I smiled, pleased to give him something.

I was happy to feed him. It was a treat, just being able to feed him. I reached into the bag and pulled out a cookie. His blue eyes sparkled as he grabbed for it. He could have a dirty face the rest of his life, as far as I was concerned.

I pulled the car back onto the access road and started up again toward the Skyline Drive. The car skidded at once on the new snow, fishtailing as I pressed on the gas. It was going to be a long trip and I was suddenly afraid. It wasn't the weather that I minded, but Timmy. How would he handle being strapped into the chair all day? I was afraid to let him loose in the back seat, where I couldn't reach him.

I had reached the mountain drive in twenty minutes. The weather was suddenly bright and clear. I had passed through the clouds, gone above the snow, as you do in a plane. It was pretty and bright, and I smiled at Timmy,

21

immensely happy to be with my son and on the road, all alone with him, after all this time.

"It's going to get better," I told him, "once you're older, and have things to say. Right?" I kept grinning.

He stared at me, his round pink face smeared with the chocolate.

I reached for the bag and fed him another. "You can have one every day of your life, how's that? We both will. Okay?" I laughed at my silliness. I wasn't making any sense, but it didn't matter. Timmy didn't understand what I was saying. I was just happy he wasn't crying. He had forgotten his mother, I decided, feeling better about that too. He had forgotten all about her. I pressed down on the accelerator. Yet he kept turning his head, trying to look around, as if he expected to see her in the back seat. Well, what could I expect? She had been with him every day of his life. He didn't know better.

And then he cried.

"Jesus Christ, Timmy!" I shouted and immediately felt like shit. Goddamn, I thought, why am I yelling at Timmy? It wasn't his fault. What did he know?

I kept glancing over at him, marveling that he was even alive, marveling that I had him with me, all alone. There we were inside the warm car, driving up into the Blue Ridge. I got out the bottle again and gave it to him, and this time, thank God, he took it, sucked hungrily though it was cold. I took a deep breath.

It was now quiet in the car. Timmy had the bottle in his tiny fists and I was helping him, steadying it. I could only hear the slapping of the windshield wipers and the sound of the heater blowing air against my legs, against Timmy's face. The world outside was silent and white. I had driven into more clouds and all there was to my world was the inside of the car. I felt safe and warm.

FLIGHT

I could see just the thin sliver of the dividing line, nothing else. I liked being lost inside this white world. I wished Timmy and I could live in it forever. I slowed. The snow was coming down heavier and I flipped up the speed of the wipers, let the rubber flip wildly back and forth across the wet glass. This was crazy, I told myself, driving on this mountain road. I grinned and whispered, "Crazy like a fox, right, Timmy?"

I glanced at my son. He had fallen asleep. The rubber nipple had slipped from his pink mouth, leaving a bubble of formula on his pursed lips. He slept like a toy doll, his tiny hands poised in the air, his eyes closed tight in a round, soft face.

The car skidded. I spun the wheel against the turning and brought it back under control, stalling it.

"Shit," I whispered, dropping my head against the steering wheel. I could feel my body give way, feel the tiredness of my bones and muscles. I hadn't slept all night, and now I couldn't stop, not until I reached North Carolina. I'd get a motel room then, someplace cheap and out of the way where they wouldn't ask a lot of questions about me and the baby.

I turned the engine over and touched the gas. The car skidded and went sideways on the steep incline. I gunned the engine and the wheels squealed, then caught on gravel, and the Pontiac jumped forward, fishtailing on the hillside. I kept the gas pedal against the floor, kept hunched forward in the seat, kept my hands squeezed on the wheel, and nursed the car forward, through the sheets of blinding snow, up and around the Skyline Drive turn.

We came out of the fog of snow clouds, higher on the ridge. I saw into a valley. There were houses in the distance and lighted windows. I dropped back into the seat and kept driving.

When I looked over again at Timmy he was awake and watching me.

23

"Hi, darling," I said, smiling, blowing him a kiss. He kept watching me, as if seeing me for the first time.

"We're going to make it now," I told him, feeling confident. This was the only way to escape, I told myself. Only a goddamn fool would be driving up on the ridge. I passed an exit with a road sign for Elkton, and another said that the Skyline Drive was closed for winter. I drove on, kept going up on the ridge. It was suddenly bright and shiny again. The clouds lay below me like endless pillows, stretching to the horizon.

"This will be a piece of cake," I told Timmy, grinning at him.

Timmy had closed his eyes.

"Sleep, sweetie," I whispered. "Please sleep."

He never needed sleep when he was first born. Some babies are like that, Lynne's doctor had told her. But that wasn't it. It was Lynne's fault that Timmy didn't get enough sleep. She was a bad mother that was all. I'm sorry now I never told her that. She was always the one after me, lecturing about how to do this, do that. She didn't even think I knew how to diaper the kid.

But now I knew her game. She was afraid I knew too much, more than her. I was the goddamn natural parent, not her. What she knew, she learned in books, or talking on the phone. She was always calling the pediatrician. She couldn't make a decision about Timmy until the doctor said okay. It cost me a fortune.

"No more, doctor, right, Timmy?" I glanced at my son. In the bright morning light above the clouds, his face glowed. He looked like an angel, one of those cherubs you see on Christmas cards.

When I looked out the front window again, I could see the storm clouds. They had come over the mountains beyond Shenandoah Park. The storm was rising out of the southwest and it wasn't the pillowy cloud below

FLIGHT

me in the valley. This one was massive and black, and ugly. It consumed the mountaintop, came tumbling over like it was the hand of God. I could see ahead to where the snowy Skyline Drive turned and disappeared into the enormous blackness. The cloud was moving fast, like a black racehorse, and bearing down on me. "Shit," I said out loud, and then, to Timmy, "It looks like trouble, right?" I was trying to pump myself up. Since leaving Lynne, since I started to live in the motel in Washington on New York Avenue, that's the way I was. Always jabbering to myself answering myself back, as if I were some sort of never-ending talk show.

There was something suddenly in Timmy's mouth. He had moved, and there it was. Not much. It had bubbled up like that trace of formula. But it wasn't formula. It felt sticky, and yellow, like a dab of paint, at the corner of his lips. It stood out against his soft pink face, his dark eyelashes.

My heart shot through the roof of my mouth. "Oh God, no!" I screamed, and forgot where I was, what I was doing, and reached for him. The car went into a great slow slide. I had Timmy in my hands, had him squeezed between my fingers, and I knew even as I was doing that, that I should be watching the road, getting the Pontiac parked. I looked again and saw the Drive, saw the menacing cloud approaching, and saw, too, that I was looking out the side window. The car was spinning, picking up speed. I grabbed at the wheel, with Timmy in my grasp, and then the little baby vomited into my face.

And he kept vomiting up this yellow shit. It kept coming from deep inside his little body, and I thought at once: he is going to die. He's going to die in my arms.

The car hit the guard rail and bounced off, then spun a half turn and hit the low rail a second time, and this time the weight and speed were enough to break through, and the car tumbled over onto itself.

25

It was all happening so slowly. I could have filmed it in my mind. I saw the car's movement, how the machine tumbled through the snowy embankment. The car had a life of its own; its own destiny.

I held onto the steering wheel with one hand, vainly tried to steer, to pull the machine under my control, but we were in space, floating off, disappearing into the white billowing clouds that spread across the wide valley.

"Timmy," I heard myself shouting, "Timmy, I love you."

I was cold and Timmy was silent. He lay against my chest and on top of me. We were squeezed together, trapped in the wreckage of the Pontiac. The windshield was broken. Snow fell onto my face. I could taste the water, taste my own blood. Or was it Timmy's blood?

"Timmy?" I whispered, struggling to move, to free myself. My son lay against me like a broken doll. "Timmy!" I shouted, trying to wake him, and then he did scream into my face, and I started to weep for joy at the sound of his voice. I would never again be angered by his crying, I promised myself.

I got my one hand free and reached up and had hold of the back seat. It was above us, and both of us were jammed beneath the dashboard. My head was caught between the brake and the accelerator.

Shit, I said. I was going to live now, I knew. I could feel my body hurting.

I could move, I realized, with great effort and great pain, but not while I had hold of Timmy. And there was no place to put the baby. The front seats had slammed down over us, like a makeshift tent. I raised one arm and pushed up against the cushiony seat, but the little effort left me dizzy, and I dropped my head back into the tight space between the pedals.

FLIGHT

Timmy had stopped crying. His eyes were open and he was watching me. We would die like this, I suddenly thought. He would die in my arms, watching me, waiting for his father to save him.

"We're going to be okay, Timmy, I promise," I told him, and tried to move the edge of his blanket up and across his face. Trapped as we were, we weren't protected from the heavy snow. Flakes landed on his face and clung to his cheek like cake icing. Why didn't the snow melt, I thought to myself, and then I whispered, "Help." My breath fogged in my face. I knew what was coming next. My body temperature would drop, I'd begin to shiver, and then at some point I'd simply drop off to sleep and never wake. Timmy would die first, I guessed. There was so little to him, and he'd freeze once he wet himself, once he cried himself into exhaustion.

Now he just stared at me. He had developed his mother's look, I saw for the first time. The same sort of quizzical gaze, as if he thought I was somehow putting him on. I had once thought it was Lynne's most endearing expression. I looked away from him, and shouted help, and when I did, Timmy cried, startled by my voice.

I reached up and managed to touch the car horn. I hit it once and the simple, clear blast of sound was loud inside my ears, but how far, I wondered, would the noise carry in the snowy woods? I kept hitting the horn until I could no longer hold up my arm, and then I slumped down further and hugged my son to my chest. He had fallen asleep, and I had the sudden, terrifying feeling that he would never wake up.

"Timmy! No!" I said shaking his tiny body.

He woke crying and I smothered his tiny face with kisses. Already, I could feel his body losing warmth. He would be shivering in a few minutes, crying from pain, and then he'd fall asleep and I wouldn't be able to save him.

27

I started swearing then, screaming into the fog and snow, and once more I fought with the jammed seat, until it exhausted me and I slumped down again, still trapped between the brake and the gas pedal.

I closed my eyes and started to pray, wild and disjointed words of prayer, as I begged for God's help. It wasn't my fault, I told God. I only wanted my little boy. He was mine, not just his mother's. She had taken him away from me, and it wasn't my fault. What had I done wrong? I was crying hysterically, sobbing into Timmy's blue blanket. I didn't even hear the old man. Perhaps the deep snow muffled his footsteps, I don't know, but when I looked up he was there, staring down through the broken front window, his beard and eyebrows thick with snow, his breath fogging in his face. But I could see his eyes, blue, bright, and sparkling, and he was smiling.

Thank God, I thought. Timmy has been saved, and the breath went out of me. I began crying, like a child.

"The baby," he said, and for a moment I didn't understand what he meant, but he reached down through the broken glass and seized Timmy. "Give me the child," he told me, and I did, realizing that Timmy was safe now, and so was I.

O

When I had time again to think and sort out what had happened, I was in the old man's cabin, wearing his clothes and with a blanket wrapped about me. I was sitting before the cast-iron stove and I had Timmy in my arms. He was changed and wrapped up, too, in a quilt, and I was telling the old man that he had saved our lives.

FLIGHT

He waved away my thanks and kept fiddling with the stove, making coffee for me, heating up a bottle of milk for Timmy.

"I heard the crash, you know, but wasn't sure," he said, and then he said something else, but I didn't catch all of it. He was an old man used to talking to himself, I guessed, and in the mountains of western Virginia the old timers spoke with their distinctive accent. I'd get used to it in time, I knew.

"Here now, feed the lad," he told me, shuffling over to me with the warm bottle of milk.

The old man shuffled off again, went back to the stove and poured two cups of coffee into tin mugs. I glanced around the cabin. It was nothing more than a small room, with a makeshift bed, made, I saw, of crude lumber, and a few pieces of handmade furniture. The table was pine, as was the clothes chest. There were no closets. He had his few pieces of clothes hanging from wood pegs on the wall and behind the door. There was real poverty here, I thought.

"You farm?" I asked the old man, raising my voice so he'd hear me, even if it was a small, tight room.

"I do a bit of everything," he said, returning from the stove with the cups of coffee and sitting down. He needed to pull over a wooden box and make use of that. I had the rocker, his chair. "A man my age, you learn to do what you can do." He sipped his hot coffee, smiled.

I liked his smile. Even with his full gray beard it managed to light up his face and give off warmth. For the first time since taking Timmy from his crib, I felt safe.

"Have you lived here long?" I asked, wanting to talk, needing to talk. I felt as if I had been pulled back from the edge of death, gained another life.

29

The old man nodded, staring into the red glow of the stove window. "A long time," he said, "some say too long." Then he glanced over at me, shifted just his bright blue eyes and asked, "Where were you all going with the little one?"

"South," I answered abruptly, immediately wary, and then to soften my reply, I added, "Home to his mother. We live in Georgia."

"Visiting relatives," I said next, still lying. It was getting so easy to live this fictional life. I now felt as if I had a whole new existence, that Timmy and I were creatures of our own, without history, and what lay ahead for us was just blank pages in our own book.

"Well, you better figure you'll spent a few days here," he said, nodding toward the window and the blowing snow. "It'll be two, three days before the county clears the Skyline. Come 'morrow we'll see about getting your vehicle out that ditch. I've got a tractor out back. Don't have no phone. Can't call the missus, I'm afraid."

"That's okay," I told him. I was thankful he didn't have a phone, nor a radio or television, not that I could see, anyway. It was better this way, the perfect hiding spot. Like hiding in the open. Again, I was silently thankful for my good luck.

"I think you and the little one should sleep in there," he said next, pulling himself up and motioning behind him.

I turned away from the stove and noticed, beside the hanging clothes, a small door, crudely cut into the side wall. There was, after all, an extra room.

"I don't want to put you out," I told the old man.

"No trouble. No trouble at all. Don't use the room myself. It was for the kid, when my wife was living."

30

FLIGHT

"Oh, you've had a family?" I said, pleased that we had something in common.

"Yes," he said, quietly, then added, as if for explanation, "once."

He went ahead of me, pushing open the door, flipping on lights, and showing me the extra room, built sometime after the cabin itself, I could see.

"It's a boy's room," I said, surprised by the small, neatly kept addition. There was a child's bed, made of brass, and made up with sheets and a quilt. The walls had a pinned-up poster of Superman, black-and-white photos of cowboy movie stars, and World War II posters of Eisenhower and MacArthur. On the shelves of a book case were model airplanes, Tinkertoys, dozens of tiny cars, and old-fashioned mechanical toys. It was a child's room from the forties.

"Your son's room?" I asked.

The old man nodded, and stepped aside. "Your baby will be fine here," he said, not looking into the room, and I realized that it pained him.

"Your son is dead?" I asked softly.

He shook his head, and this time, he did permit himself to glance inside, to look at the tiny bed, all the toys. There was a flash of tears in his eyes and he said simply, "His mother took him. It was back a ways." And then, catching himself from saying more, he showed me where there were towels, a basin. "I'll heat up some water. You'll want to wash him," he nodded to Timmy, who, like a forgotten angel, slept on in the cradle of my arm.

The old man had gone to the ditch and brought in what he could from the backseat of the car: my jacket, and the bag of baby stuff, the wipes, Desitin, and diapers. I lay Timmy gently on the bed, took off his blue stretchy as he slept, and changed his diapers. There was yellow shit in his diapers. It was sick, I thought. Something was wrong with him, but I couldn't focus on

31

it. I didn't want to know. I was afraid in my heart that I really couldn't take care of him. That I wasn't ready to be his real Dad, not any more.

When I had cleaned and changed Timmy, I arranged him in the bed so he couldn't roll off, then took the diaper back with me to the other room. The old man was sitting again by the stove fire, and had poured himself another cup of black coffee.

"Are you a drinking man?" he asked.

"Yes, I could use a drink."

"I have scotch whiskey, that's all."

"Scotch is perfect."

I threw away the dirty diaper and, accepting his drink, sat down with him by the stove, neither of us speaking for the moment. I was thinking of Lynne, wondering what she was doing, who she might be calling. The edge of my anger had gone, I realized, and I was feeling some guilt, like giant whitecap waves.

"You got yourself a fine boy, Nelson," the old man announced.

I sat forward, startled by him saying my name, and said at once, "You know who I am?"

"Heard it a while back, on the CB." He didn't look at me. He seemed embarrassed, knowing my identity. Then added, to make his point, "You're safe here with me."

"Where's your CB?" I wanted to know.

He reached out and flipped up the blanket that covered a small table and there, shiny and black, was a small CB, and as if to prove he had information on me, he flipped on the switch. Between bursts of static there were police calls and highway accident reports.

"Shit," I said.

"You're safe here," he said again, glancing at me, making his point.

FLIGHT

In the soft light of the stove, he didn't seem so much the grandfatherly type. I could see how well built he was under his flannel shirt, in his old trousers.

"What are you saying?"

"Nothing much. They say you took your kid. You're wanted in Maryland." Again he gestured toward the outside, the blowing snow. "They'll never find you here, not for a while, not with two feet of new snow," and then as he sipped the scotch, he added, "not if you want."

Old codgers like him are cagey, I knew. They didn't survive so long in the mountains of Virginia without knowing how to read a man.

"What do you want?" I finally asked.

"When my wife, she took my boy, I should have gone after her, you know, gotten him back, but I didn't. You know why?" He glanced my way, raising his thick eyebrows. The skin around his eyes was tight and wrinkled.

I didn't reply. I let him tell his own story, because he was a man who lived alone, and I could tell he liked to talk to himself.

"I didn't go for him because I wasn't right in the head, that's why. They kept taking me away, you know, over to Lynchburg. They had a place there for the likes of my kind."

"Your kind?" I could feel my fear. It started way off, in the tips of my fingers, in my toes, and was sweeping through me as I sat still there beside the old man, trapped as I felt now, inside his snowbound cabin.

"I was only a lad myself when I went to war, over there in Europe, the Second World War, it was." He shook his head. "I ain't been right since," he said, almost apologizing. And then he grinned.

His smile gave away the truth of the man. It was a loony smile, lopsided and warped, as if he had suffered electric shock, over there in Lynchburg, a few too many times.

"Jesus Christ," I swore out loud, and all my strength went out of me.

"And they killed him, too," the old man said, and then he giggled.

I realized now how he had held it together, kept himself under control for a few hours, until I was safely settled, locked up inside his isolated farmhouse.

"Hey," I said, talking fast, "what gives? You want some money, or what?" I leaned forward, as if to prove I wouldn't harm him, that I didn't want anything myself except for maybe a night's rest. In the morning I could be off. I'd walk to North Carolina if I had to.

"Arthur Lee was my boy's name. He and his mother, you know, they didn't have to run off like that, middle of the goddamn night, leaving me pissed in the head, sick and all. Oh, it ain't the boy's fault. He loved me, that one. The mother, though, she was one of those McGraffs, came from Scotland, and I swear to God there wasn't a good one among them. I buried two myself out back. Goddamn trespassers coming onto my land.

"And you!" He had his fist up and then he was pointing his finger at me. "You come driving out here in the middle of the winter, no one in his right mind would be up on Skyline Drive this time of year, storm coming and all." He nodded his head. "I know why you're coming. Can't fool me, even with that kid of yours. I know. I saw."

"What? You saw what?" I was still leaning forward, trying to catch what the old man was saying. He was speaking to himself now, rambling on, like another homeless crazy living on a bench in Union Station, downtown in Washington.

"Electrodes!" he said, shouting at me, and he pointed to his nose. "They put those electrodes in my nose over there in Lynchburg. I cut them, once I come home again." He raised his left hand and showed me two of his fingers that were curled up tight. "Electrodes did this, years ago."

FLIGHT

"Say, sir, I don't know anything about this," I whispered.

"Course you know. You work for the government, don't you?" He glared at me.

He had been through my wallet, I realized.

"I was a consultant, yes, but I didn't have anything to do with electrodes, or—"

"They put this electrode in my nose," he went on, "put it into me, all kinds of poor people to cause us pain, give us illness. You know what it did to Billy Wright?" He turned on me, and those blue eyes bulged in his bearded face. He looked like Santa Claus gone mad.

"Those electrodes just blew him apart. He was out there, this side of Slide Mountain, putting in his spring corn, and he just blew apart. Never did find all of him. Did it by radio. A plane was flying over. I saw it." He tore off the heavy rug that covered his CB. "You know why I keep it covered? It hears! It listens! They know." Then he tossed the rug over the box and sat back in the rocker. He was breathing fast now; he had frightened himself with his talk.

I would keep calm, I told myself. I would agree with him. I would do anything I had to until morning, until I had a chance to get away with Timmy.

"You may be right," I said calmly.

"You're damn right I am!" He shook his fist, stared fiercely ahead, and for a moment was locked up with his own demons.

Why was everything going wrong, I asked myself. I couldn't even kidnap my own kid. The storm. Now this. I should have stayed in the valley, taken my chances on the interstate.

"I know why you're here," he said at last. "I know why they sent you." He wasn't looking at me, but was instead watching the bedroom door.

"Why?" I asked, holding my breath. I knew I couldn't convince him otherwise, whatever he believed.

"You've come to get me, haven't you? Ain't enough that you killed my only friend, now you want me, don't you?" He kept watching the bedroom, looking into the dark room where Timmy was sound asleep.

I kept nodding, not fully comprehending.

"We got to get rid of him," he whispered, leaning closer.

"What?" I asked, still not understanding what he meant.

He jerked his head toward the little bedroom. "Him!" he said.

"Hey, what are you talking about?" I stood up and he was on his feet at once, moving faster than I would have imagined.

"He's sending radio signals back to Washington. They'll be here with their SWAT team. I've read about them."

I was sweating now, and felt the perspiration under my arms and down my chest.

"Hey, wait, old man! What are you talking about?"

"This!" He was pointing to his nose. "In '42 they put that in my nose. A tiny electrode. I didn't know it then. Over there in Lynchburg, they slipped it into my nose, beneath the skin, you see, and since then, every time they want, they throw a switch, or something, and it goes click, click-click and it tortures me. I get pains in my chest, my muscles jerk. I itch all over my body." He was shaking his head, and crying. "All of my life that's all I've had, pain and illness, because of this electrode. I went to see a doctor, and you know what he said?" The old man paused. He was staring up at me, his head cocked. I shook my head. "He said he couldn't remove it. Hear that? Couldn't remove it, and him a medical doctor!" The old man waved his arm, said with a long sigh, "They're all

36

in it together, all them medical doctors. What can I do?" He sat back into his rocker.

I sat down carefully on the small wooden box and said gently to the old man, "I'm not one of them. I mean, Timmy and I. You heard yourself. We're wanted by the police in Maryland."

"The only good people in this country are wanted by the police," he said finally.

I took a deep breath and glanced at the small bedroom. I had left the door open so I could see Timmy, but the room was dark. I couldn't even see the bed.

"That's all right," I said finally, not knowing what to say.

"I'll do it," the man responded, looking up, nodding.

"Do what?" I asked, but I knew what he meant.

"They took your own flesh and blood, just like they did with me."

I raised both hands, gestured for him to keep still. I was afraid I might have to hurt him if he went near Timmy.

"I'll prove it to you," he said, grinning.

"Prove it?"

He reached into his worn trousers and pulled out a Buck knife and snapped it open. "We'll cut the kid, see if he draws blood."

"Hey, are you crazy or something?" I yelled at him, backing off.

He kept waving the Buck knife. How in God's name did all of this happen to me, I kept thinking.

"He ain't human, that little one. I looked into his eyes." The old man was glaring at me, his eyes wild in his gray head. He kept coming, backing me into the corner. I suddenly realized I couldn't stop him. He was too crazy for me. "Okay," I said quickly. "We'll do it. I'll do it! I'll cut his finger, okay?"

I was panicky now, and sweating. I could feel the sweat on my tee shirt, between my legs. Jesus, I thought, had I pissed my pants?

He handed me the small bladed knife, nodding, motioned for me to go into the small room, to my sleeping baby, and he followed, still grinning and pleased with himself.

I knelt beside the bed. Timmy was turned on his side, hidden in the quilts. I could hear his soft breath, felt the warmth of his small body when I gently touched his smooth cheek.

The old man nudged me from behind.

It was going to be okay, I thought. I'd just nip his fingertip, draw a bubble of blood that was all. He would scream and wake, I know, but his finger would be fine; he'd heal within minutes.

I pulled his chubby fingers out from beneath the warm quilt. At once his fingers circled my thumb. I can't do this, I told myself.

"Hurry!" the old man shouted, poking me, "or give me that blade."

I reached out, took his tiny thumb in my fingers, pinched it, and then squeezing my eyes I laced the knife across the flesh.

"See! See!" the crazy hermit shouted in my face. I opened my eyes. Timmy's fingers had not bled. I could see a thin silver spring. It had popped through the fleshy skin. I squeezed Timmy's hand and another silver spring, like the insides of a delicate watch, came into sight. Behind me the old man kept shouting, hitting me in the shoulder.

I ripped off the tight blanket and pulled at his stretchy. He was crying now, hiccuping for breath. I grabbed him and lifted him, squeezing hard. I could feel the thin frame of machinery, and I squeezed all the metal and bolts, enraged. Timmy's doll's-blue-eyes bulged in the soft flesh. I watched the blue irises, wanting them to pop out. The eyes fell onto the bed, two round pieces of glass. Inside the empty sockets I could see the intricate wiring, all the tiny microchips.

"Goddamnit!" I shouted, screaming. "She tricked me!" Timmy was still with her.

I turned and heaved the worthless baby at the opposite wall, where its head bounced against the rough logs, then the body slid down to the floor, leaving a smear of wet blood.

Then I fled the room, ran for my coat and shoes. The old man came after me, hobbling on his bad leg, telling me to wait until morning, telling me to stay with him.

I wasn't listening. I wanted Lynne now. I wanted to get to her for stealing my kid. I opened the front door as I buttoned my jacket and felt the blast of cold and blowing snow.

"You're crazy!" the old man shouted after me.

I slammed the door behind me. I wasn't crazy. I just wanted my son.

I made it to the Skyline Drive, back to where my overturned car lay buried in the snow. I got a lift from the crew of a county snowplow, then reached 340 and at a truckstop hitched a ride back to Washington. It took over forty hours. When I reached the city, I took the Metro out to Rockville, getting off after dark, two days from when I had first come home and taken my son.

39

It had snowed in Rockville and my tracks were clear as I climbed over some backyard fences and came up behind my house. I stood shivering there in the cold, watching through the dark windows as my wife made dinner for Timmy.

They were both in the kitchen. Timmy was in the high chair and Lynne was talking to him, smiling, going back and forth between his chair and the stove. I could see the steam off the oven, almost feel the warmth and coziness of the scene. Mother and child.

Lynne had lost weight, I saw. After the baby she had been plump and I had got onto her about it, told her she looked like those fat women you see on the bus sometimes, the ones who can only fit into sweat suits, and feed themselves with hamburgers from McDonalds.

She didn't look bad, I thought. I got kind of a half erection, watching her. She wasn't wearing much, just her housecoat, no bra, and no panties, I knew. I slipped my tongue around my lips, wetting them.

It wasn't fair. Nothing was ever fair, not to men, not to me at least. I hadn't been warm in two days. My wet clothes had frozen on my body. My pant legs were stiff, my shoes and socks were soaked. I could feel water between my toes. She had done this to me, I thought. She had tricked me, driven me out into the snow like some homeless person.

I went over to the garage and took the extra key down from the ledge, unlocked the side door and slipped inside. It was warmer there, out of the wind, but I didn't need the warmth. I was too excited. I could feel my heart again, feel the rush of blood through my body. I grinned in the darkness at my own adrenaline.

The car took up all the space in the garage and I had to crawl over the lawnmower to reach the other side and the door to the breezeway that led to the house. Lynne always left it open, so I slipped inside, then ran across

FLIGHT

the breezeway. I didn't want her looking out the kitchen window, seeing me coming to get her.

When I opened the house door, I felt the warmth, smelled chicken cooking. She was making lemon chicken. She knew it was my favorite dinner.

It was dark in the entrance hallway. I could see Lynne's overcoat, and little Timmy's snowsuit, both hanging from the old-fashioned tree stand Lynne had found somewhere, at one of her goddamn garage sales. I slipped off my gloves and coat. I was shivering. I needed a drink, but I wasn't going to risk going into the living room, opening the cabinets. Besides, Lynne had gotten rid of the booze, ever since I started drinking.

"Honey? Is that you?" Her voice stunned me, knocked me back against the hallway mirror. I could see my hand in front of me, trembling with fear. I tried to make a fist, to imagine my fingers gripping her throat, ending her life. I could do it, I told myself. It would be easy once I got close to her and had hold of her neck. I'd give her a friendly kiss, a welcome-home kiss, and then I'd end her life, end all my misery, and take my son away.

Maybe I wouldn't leave the house, not with her gone, at least. Maybe I'd just get rid of her, bury her in the basement or somewhere, and stay there with Timmy. I grinned at myself in the dark mirror, excited by that sudden notion.

I put both hands in my pocket, felt the damp stickiness of the cloth.

"Aren't you going to come in and say hello to Timmy?" she asked next, still cheery, as if there was nothing at all wrong with the world, wrong between the two of us.

I shuffled around the hallway, leaving damp spots on the hardened floor. I moved through the shadows and toward the light of the kitchen doorway. Lynne was sitting at the kitchen table and feeding Timmy. I thought to myself: can I kill her with Timmy in the room? Would he remember?"

41

"Hi, darling," she glanced at me. "How was the job search?"

I slumped down across from her, keeping my hands hidden. They were trembling beneath the table, knocking against my knees. I nodded, saying nothing. If I spoke now, I knew I'd scream.

"Bert Lynch called, remember him? He and I worked together at HUD. He says that maybe you should check personnel at HUD. They're hiring." She glanced at me, still smiling.

"Okay," I whispered, nodding.

Lynne had turned her attention back to Timmy. She was cleaning off his face where he had spit up the apple sauce. I stared at him and he looked back, grinning. I smiled, happy for the first time in days.

"What did you do all day?"

"What?" I shouted back.

"Honey, there's no need to snap." Lynne glanced at me, frowning. "I just asked you a simple question: where were you all day, that's all."

"Out!"

"Yes, I know you were out!" She sighed.

I hated it when she sighed like that, as if I had done something irrevocably wrong.

"I was..." I stopped talking and stared across the room, trying to focus. I didn't know where I had been all day. I shook my head, trying to clear my mind.

"Honey, are you okay?" She looked at me, worried now. "Did you get everything at the store, the diapers?"

I nodded, then managed to say with great difficulty, "I got what we needed."

"Thanks, I'm sorry I forgot them today, but the interview went on longer than I thought. I think I'm going to get this job, honey, and then we won't

FLIGHT

have to worry about anything for awhile. And you'll find work, I know." She kept talking, glancing over as she cleaned up Timmy, took off his bib.

"I'll take him," I told her, avoiding her question.

"Oh, no, that's okay. He needs his bath. Why don't you start dinner, put on some potatoes?" She left the kitchen, never letting me close to my kid. When she passed me, I could smell her body. It almost made me throw up. I hated the smell of her vagina.

Timmy began to cry, once he was out of the kitchen. I could hear Lynne talking to him, cooing. All she cared about was him, not me, not any longer. I remembered when we used to make love, she'd coo like that to me, as if I were her only love, but not anymore.

My mind was jumping fast, popping ahead, making plans. I started to grin, just at the pleasure of knowing what I'd do next, later.

I glanced around the kitchen. It was brighter than I had remembered. There were more lights and they were burning me, like sun lamps. It felt as if I were down at the beach, sitting in the sun. I felt the sweat on my forehead, under my arms. I had too many clothes on, sweaters and shirts. I stripped down to my T-shirt and even then the heat of the kitchen lights burned my skin. Looking at my forearm, I could see that there were already bubbles of flesh, blisters under my skin.

I turned off all the lights, turned off the stove, and stood there in the fresh darkness of the house. When I felt cool again, I went over to the drawer and took out the knife, the thick heavy one that Lynne used to cut up chicken, and felt its weight. I loved this knife. I loved how heavy it was. Using it, I wouldn't even have to work up a sweat.

I went into our bedroom and stood behind the door and away from the light that spread out onto the carpeted floor. When I looked up, I was

43

standing in front of the full-length mirror. I could not see myself in the mirror. I could not see myself in the mirror, and I grinned.

"Honey, what are you doing?"

Lynne was beside me, speaking softly, as if I were just another child to attend to.

"And what are you doing with that soup spoon?" She was amused, and kept smiling quizzically at me.

I stared down at my hand. I had grabbed hold of the wooden ladle, not the black-handled knife.

"Honey, what's the matter?" She came closer to me, worried now. I couldn't stand to breathe. The reek of her genitals consumed the room. When I didn't answer, she said quickly, "I can't leave the baby," and dashed back to the bathroom. "Come with me!" she ordered.

I followed after her obediently, still staring at the wooden spoon. It was a mistake, that's all. In my haste I had grabbed the wrong instrument. I could still kill her, I thought next, spill her brains over the bathroom tile, let her blood drain in the tub. Then I'd clean out the basement freezer, throw away all the meat, and stuff her inside. I might have to cut her up some, but that wouldn't be much of a problem. I'd tell the neighbors she was out of town, traveling on business. She wouldn't be missed. She'd just be frozen stiff, that's all. I grinned at the thought.

"Aren't you going to shower?" Lynne asked next. She had her back to me and was drying off Timmy, wiping him with baby oil.

"Why?" I asked, surprised by the question.

Lynne turned around at me. "Honey, we're having dinner with the McCaffery's." Her voice had risen.

I didn't answer her. It was best not to answer her when she had an edge on her. I had learned my lesson well. I knew how to handle my wife.

44

FLIGHT

I went back into the living room and stood there for a moment, trying to decide what to do next. I had forgotten about the dinner with the McCaffery's. In fact, now that I thought about it, I didn't know who she was talking about. McCaffery who?

I was standing there for only a few minutes when the woman came back to me. She just wouldn't leave me alone.

"Honey, what are you doing? You've been standing in here for fifteen minutes. Why aren't you taking a shower? The sitter will be here in half an hour." She came around and stared at me, her eyes bulging again. I couldn't look at her eyes. "What's the matter? Are you okay?" she reached up and touched my face. "Honey, you're freezing." She sounded alarmed.

I wondered then who she was and why she was bothering me, asking me questions. I stepped away, not wanting this person to touch me.

"I'm going to telephone the doctor," she said with some urgency, "and we're not going out tonight. You're coming down with something, I know. Oh, dear God, and the baby will have it next."

She went off by herself into the kitchen. I could see her on the phone, talking to someone, and then she turned around and told me to look after the baby.

What baby? I wondered, turning slowly. I couldn't see a baby. I tried to speak, to tell this woman so, but my tongue felt thick in my mouth. It was gagging me and I stopped trying to speak and instead walked toward the bathroom. I needed to pee, I realized. That's all I wanted to do, just pee, and I was afraid that I'd do it in my pants, as I once did in school, years ago, far away.

In the bathroom I saw the baby. He was on the counter, sitting up in a little contraption. He had his arms up, waving or something, and grinning at me.

I told him not to look at me that way, but he kept grinning, even while I pissed, and I missed the toilet bowl and sprayed the seat, then the wall. I turned my body and sprayed the shower curtain. It sounded like rain hitting the plastic and I laughed, pleased with myself.

The baby started to giggle, laughing too, and I turned around and looked at him while I was still holding my pecker. I told him not to laugh at me, and he giggled again. When he smiled, his whole face lit up, like a clown. "I don't like you laughing at me," I told the baby, but then he giggled.

I zipped up my pants and went after him, grabbing his tight blue stretchy. "Don't laugh at me!" I shouted.

My voice startled him. His blue eyes bright in his face. Then his face twisted up and he turned red and screamed.

I picked him up with one hand and shook his fat little body, shouting at him to stop. His crying filled my mind. I couldn't think.

Out of the corner of my eye I saw the woman. She was suddenly in the doorway, blocking my way, her tiny face white and frightened. I liked that, seeing her so afraid.

"What are you doing, Nelson?" she yelled, reaching for the baby. I had held him up high, holding him at arm's length, like a fat football. When she dove for him I kneed her in the stomach and she gasped and tumbled over, falling forward through the shower curtain, and landed face-down in the tub.

I got away from her, ran into the living room, laughing at her, still holding the screaming baby. I told the little brat I'd smash his head if he didn't stop screaming, and I whirled around to face the woman who was after me, screaming out a name, telling me to give her the kid.

She dove for the baby and I swung him around, tucked him under my arm, as if he were a bag of potatoes. She slashed me with her nails, drawing blood.

FLIGHT

"Goddamnit," I yelled, and swung at her, hitting her face with my elbow, bashing her nose. I saw a flow of rich blood spread over her face.

She hit the floor, skidding on the hardwood, and when she got up again, she didn't come toward me, but ran into the bedroom, ran, I somehow knew, for the pistol that was in the top drawer of the dresser. I went after her, cutting through the other living room door, then vaulting the bed, with the baby tucked under my arm like I was some kind of football player.

She had her hand deep inside the drawer, reaching for the pistol. I kicked out and slammed it on her wrist, breaking her arm.

She screamed and screamed, hanging there, choking on her tears and sobs of pain. I let her suffer a little, let her feel the pain. Then I pulled open the drawer, let her drop to the bedroom floor, clutching her arm beneath her and bleeding from her nose and mouth.

I reached inside the top drawer with my one free hand, took out the heavy pistol, looked down at her, aimed, and blew a hole in the side of her head. She jerked like a snake.

When I went back into the living room, the old man was sitting there on the couch. He was grinning at the television, watching *Family Feud*. He glanced over at me and said, "What did you do with the woman?"

I shook my head, I couldn't remember right off, though I knew I had done something to her. I told him I had sent her to the store to buy a dress.

"Good!" He told me. "And what about it?"

I looked at my hand. I had forgotten that I had the kid in my hand. I had him around the neck and he hung there, dead as a chicken. I tossed him away, tossed him into an empty chair, where he bounced and then lay sprawled like a stuffed toy.

Then I sat down beside the old man, who asked me if I liked *Family Feud*. I shook my head, not knowing what to say.

He told me I wasn't going to get away, told me they'd follow me, the woman, too, because I had electrodes in my nose. He had seen them.

I reached up and tentatively felt the soft skin of my right nostril. He was right. I could feel the tiny microchip.

"What do I do?" I asked the man, trying to keep calm. It was important, I knew, to keep calm.

"You can't run away," he told me. "You thought about that, didn't you?"

I nodded, but I wasn't sure. I had a memory, but maybe it was a dream, of being on a cold dark Virginia highway, speeding south. Someone was with me, I think, or I was talking to myself. I like to talk to myself.

"They'll track you," the old man told me, nodding toward the television. "They know."

He kept nodding to the television, then reached forward and switched the channel. "Him!" he said. "He knows."

I saw Dan Rather watching me.

"See!" He pointed to the screen, to the small earplug in the anchor-man's ear. "He's listening to us. He knows. They all know." He glanced at me, grinning. It seemed to please him, showing the connection.

"Shit," I said, remembering the pistol, I reached up and blew a hole in Dan Rather's forehead. The screen hissed and blew up before us, and the both of us started laughing, seeing Dan Rather go black before our eyes. I hadn't thought about that before. I hadn't realized it would be so simple, getting rid of him, I mean.

We sat there for a while, just the two of us, and after midnight, when it started to get cold, I went into the bedroom and grabbed the quilt and pulled it over me. The woman was still there, sitting in a dark black spot of her own blood. I told her to go wash up, but she didn't respond.

When I came back into the living room, the old man was gone. I had half expected that. I was sorry now that I had put a bullet in Dan Rather's forehead. I missed him. I missed the kid and the woman, too. They'd been company at least.

I crawled up on the couch and fell asleep and when I woke it was daylight and the sun was in my eyes. I looked up and saw it had snowed overnight but now the sun was out and it was a bright day. A nice day. I saw my Pontiac in the driveway and I guessed the old man had done that, driven it up from Virginia, and then I remembered the electrodes he had told me about and I tentatively touched them. I felt oddly reassured that someone was monitoring me, looking after me, almost like, you know, an angel.

"Hello," I said, to whoever was listening.

I got up and went into the kitchen. The kid was still sprawled out crazy-legged on the chair, and I could see the woman's feet in the doorway of the bedroom.

I opened the fridge and took out some juice, some eggs, and made myself breakfast, standing up and eating it by the table. I wanted coffee but I was too tired to go to all the trouble of making it.

I was still standing when the phone rang. I think it was the phone. Maybe it was the electrodes, I couldn't tell. But when the phone rang, my teeth hurt.

When I answered the phone a woman said, happy and friendly like, "Nelson? Is that you Nelson, are you home again?"

I hung up the phone, but I was shaking so I couldn't take my hand off the receiver. Again my teeth began to buzz and I picked up the receiver.

"Nelson? Is Lynne there, Nelson?" Now the voice sounded worried.

"This is not Nelson," I answered coolly, "my name is Kellogg," I said, reading the name off the cereal box. Then I hung up the phone again.

It rang at once, buzzing my teeth, hurting my ears. I went back to the living room, found the pistol buried in the blankets and then realized I had no shirt on, no shoes. I got dressed fast, hurrying, for they would be here soon, come to find Nelson and Lynne, to find the people who lived here.

Dressed, I went to the door, and then I remembered my son. The image of his happy face came back to me, burned a hole in my heart, and I went back to him, back to where he had fallen asleep in the chair. I wrapped him up in a blanket, carried him easily with me out to the car.

Down the street I could see that the neighbors were up, and that a woman I seemed to know was hurrying toward the house, crossing the snowy street. She was wearing boots and her husband's heavy coat.

I think she was calling to me, but I got into the car, put the baby in the back seat, and jumped into the driver's seat.

She was hurrying now, running, calling a name. I could see the fog of her breath, see the fear in her eyes.

"Nelson!" she shouted. "Nelson, what is wrong?" I gunned the car, whipped it out into the cul de sac, and nearly clipped her legs as she jumped aside and then fell into the bank of snow.

"Did you see that, Timmy? Do you see that?" I shouted, as I gunned the engine and skidded away from the house, down the suburban street and onto the highway, free at last. "Free at last," I shouted.

My son slept. He slept without moving.

A CABIN IN THE WOODS

Michael remembered clearly the first piece of fungus: a thin, irregular patch twelve inches wide, grayish, like the color of candle grease, growing on the new pine wall of the bathroom. He reached up gingerly to touch it. The crust was lumpy and the edges serrated. He pulled the resinous flesh from the wood, like removing a scab, tossed the fungus into the waste can, and finished shaving.

He had come up from the city late the night before, driving the last few hours through the mountain roads in heavy fog and rain, and arriving at his new cabin in the woods well after midnight. It was his first trip to the lake that spring.

Michael had come home early in the week to work, bringing with him the galleys of his latest novel. He needed to spend several more days making corrections. It was the only task of writing that he really enjoyed, the final step when the book was still part of him. Once it appeared between covers, it belonged to others.

He was in no hurry to read the galleys. That could be done at leisure over the next few days, as Barbara wasn't arriving until Friday and their

51

guests weren't due until Saturday morning. It was a weekend that had been planned for several months to celebrate the completion of the new house.

So while shaving that first morning at the cabin, Michael found himself relaxed and smiling. He was pleased about the house. It was bigger and more attractive than even the blueprints had suggested.

It had been designed by a young architect from the nearby village, and built by local carpenters using lumber cut from the pine, oak, and walnut woods behind the lake. They had left the lumber roughhewed and unfinished.

The cabin was built into the side of the mountain, with a spectacular view of the lake. Only a few trees had been cut to accommodate the construction so from a distance, and through the trees, the building looked like a large boulder that had been unearthed and tumbled into the sun to dry.

"I want the ambiance to be *rustic*," Barbara explained to the architect. "A sense of the *wilderness*." She had whispered the words, as if to suggest the mysterious.

"Don't make it too austere," Michael instructed, "I don't want to feel like we're camping out. This is a cabin we want to escape from the city to; we want some conveniences, a place that can sleep eight or ten if need be." He remembered pacing the small office of the architect as he and his wife listed their requirements, banging his new boots on the wooden floor. Michael liked the authoritative sound, the suggestion to this kid that here was someone who knew what he wanted out of life.

"And cozy!" Barbara leaned forward to catch the architect's attention. She had a round, pretty face with saucer-sized blue eyes. She flirted with the young man to make her point. "And a stone fireplace the length of one wall. We may want to come up here with our friends during skiing season." She beamed.

The architect looked from one to the other but said nothing.

A CABIN IN THE WOODS

"He's not one of your great talkers, is he?" Barbara had remarked when they left the village.

"That's the way of these mountain people. They come cheap and they give you a full day's work. It's okay with me; I'd rather deal with locals than someone from the city."

Still, the cabin cost $10,000 more than Michael had expected. The price of supplies, he was told, had tripled. However, they had landscaped the lawn to the lake and put in a gravel drive to meet the county road. Michael said he wanted only to turn the key and find the place livable. "I'm no handyman," he had told the architect.

While the second home in the mountains was costly, Michael was no longer worried about money. When he had finished the new novel and submitted it to the publisher it was picked up immediately with an advance of $50,000, more than he had made on any of his other books. The next week it had sold to the movies for $200,000, and he was promised a percentage of the gross. Just before driving to the mountains, his agent had telephoned with the news that the paperback rights had gone for half a million.

"Everything I touch is turning to gold," Michael bragged to Barbara. "I told you I'd make it big."

What he did not tell Barbara was that this was his worst book, written only to make money. He had used all the clichés of plot and situation, and it had paid off.

O

He finished dressing and made plans for the day. The station wagon was still packed with bags of groceries. The night before he had been too tired after the drive to do more than build a fire and pour himself a drink. Carrying his drink, he had toured the empty rooms—his boots echoing on the oak floors—and admired the craftsmanship of the mountain carpenters. The cabin was sturdy and well built; the joints fit together like giant Lincoln Logs.

The three bedrooms of the house were upstairs in the back, and they were connected by an open walkway that overlooked the living room, which was the height and width of the front of the cabin. The facade was nearly all windows, long panels that reached from the floor to the roof.

One full wall was taken up by Barbara's stone fireplace, made from boulders quarried in the mountains and trucked to the lake site. The foundation was made from the same rocks. Barbara bragged to friends with newly acquired chauvinism, "All that's not from the mountains are the kitchen appliances and ourselves."

Michael moved the station wagon behind the house and unpacked the groceries, carrying the bundles in through the back door and stacking the bags on the butcher-block table. He filled the refrigerator first with perishables and several bottles of white wine he planned to enjoy in the evenings with his meals—his own special present to himself for the success of his newest book.

Packing the refrigerator gave Michael a sense of belonging, and with that simple chore he had taken possession of the place and the cabin began to feel like home.

He had carried the box of the remaining bottles of wine into the living room, knelt down behind the bar, and opened the cabinet doors. Inside, growing along the two empty, plain wooden shelves was gray fungus. It grew thick, and covering the whole interior of the cabinet; the discovery frightened Michael, like finding an abnormality.

"My God!" A shiver ran along his spine.

54

A CABIN IN THE WOODS

He easily pulled the fungus off the shelves and quickly filled several of the empty grocery bags with it. Then he scrubbed the hard pine boards with soap and water, and put away the bottles of wine.

It was the dampness of the house, he guessed, that had caused the growth, as it had stood empty and without heat since it the construction had been finished. He knew fungus grew rapidly in damp weather, but still the spread of the candle-gray patch was alarming.

He returned to the kitchen and apprehensively opened the knotty-pine cupboards over the counter. The insides were clean, with the smell of sawdust thick throughout them. He ran his hand across the shelves and picked up a few lingering shavings. Michael closed the door and sighed.

Barbara had given him a list of chores to do in the house before the weekend; the beds in the guest rooms should be made, the windows needed washing, and the whole house, from top to bottom, had to be swept. Also the living-room rug had arrived and was rolled up in the corner, waiting to be put down and vacuumed.

First, however, Michael decided to have breakfast. On Sundays in the city he always made breakfast, grand ones of Eggs Doremus, crepes, or Swedish pancakes with lingonberries. Lately Barbara had begun to invite friends over for Sunday brunch. His cooking had become well known among their friends and his editor had even suggested that he might write a cookbook about Sunday breakfasts.

Michael unpacked the skillet and, after turning on the front burner, melted a slice of butter into the pan. He took a bottle of white wine, one of the inexpensive California Chablis, uncorked it, and added a half-cup to the skillet. The butter and wine sizzled over the flame and the rich smell increased Michael's hunger.

He broke two eggs into the skillet, seasoned them with salt and pepper, and then searched the remaining shopping bags for cayenne. Barbara hadn't packed the spices so he'd have to do without it for now; he made a mental note to pick up cayenne and more spices when he drove to the village later that morning.

Michael moved easily around the kitchen, enjoying the ample space to maneuver that it provided. In their apartment in the city, only one of them could cook at a time but here they had put in two stoves and two sinks, and enough counter space for both to work at once.

Michael glanced at the eggs and saw that the whites were nearly firm. He found the toaster and plugged it in, noticing with satisfaction that the electrical outlets worked. That was one less problem to worry about. He dropped in two pieces of bread and then, going back to the bar, retrieved a bottle of vodka, opened a can of tomato juice, and made himself a Bloody Mary.

He was working quickly now, sure of the kitchen; he cut the flame under the skillet, crumbled Roquefort cheese and sprinkled it on the eggs, then buttered the toast and unpacked a dish and silverware. He smiled, pleased. He was going to enjoy cooking in this kitchen.

Perhaps, he thought, he should move full time to the mountains. He could write more, he knew, if he lived by the lake, away from the interruptions and distractions of the city. He fantasized a moment, and could see himself going down to the lake on cool, misty mornings; he could smell the pine trees and the water as he glided the fishing boat across the flat lake to bass fish before sunup. He could see the boat gracefully arching through the calm water as, behind it, a small wave rippled all the way back to the shore. He sipped the Bloody Mary and let the pleasant thought relax him.

A CABIN IN THE WOODS

Then he remembered the eggs, and he slipped them from the skillet onto the buttered toast and carried the plate and his drink out onto the oak deck. The deck was a dozen feet wide and built along the length of the east wall so as to catch the early morning sun. It was Barbara's idea to enjoy breakfasts on the deck.

The sun had cleared the mountains and now touched the house. It had dried the puddles of rainwater and warmed the deck so Michael was comfortable in shirt-sleeves.

They had not yet purchased deck furniture, so he perched himself on the wide banister and enjoyed the eggs. He could see the length of the front lawn from where he sat, and admired the way it sloped gracefully down to the shore and the new pier.

He had built the pier himself one weekend during the winter. He bought 300 feet of lumber in the village, hired two men from a construction firm, and driven with the crew out to the lake in four-wheel-drive jeeps. Along the shore they had found twelve sassafras trees that they cut and trimmed and pulled across the ice to Michael's property. They chopped holes in the thick ice and sledgehammered the poles into place to make the foundation, then cut two-by-eights into four-foot lengths and nailed them between the poles to make the pier.

Michael's hands had blistered and his back had ached for a week, but he was proud of his hard labor and of the pier which went forty feet into the water and could easily accommodate his two boats.

At first he could not see the pier because a late morning mist clung to the shore and rolled against the bank like a range of low clouds. But as he sat finishing the eggs and drink, the rising sun burned away the mist and the thin slice of pier jutting into the mountain lake came slowly into view like a strange gothic phenomenon.

"What the..."

Michael stood abruptly and his dish and drink tumbled off the railing. He peered down, confused to see that the whole length of the pier was covered with gray fungus. He looked around for more fungus, expecting to see it everywhere as he scanned the landscaped lawn and the pine trees which grew thick to the edge of his property. He spun around and ran the length of the oak deck, leaning over the railing to inspect the high rear wall of the cabin. He even glanced at the trash heap of construction materials left by the builders, but there was no sign of more mold.

Next he ran into the house and, taking the steps two at a time, raced to the second floor. He went into the bathroom and flipped on the light. No fungus grew on the pine wall. He turned immediately and ran downstairs, boots stomping on the wooden steps, and opened the cabinet doors below the bar. The bottles of wine and liquor were stacked just as he had arranged them.

Michael calmed down and gained control; he kept walking, however, through the house, opening closet doors and checking cabinets. He went again to the kitchen and looked through all the cupboards. He opened the basement door and peered into the dark downstairs. The basement had been left unfinished, but he still found no fungus.

When he was satisfied there was no fungus in the house, he left the cabin and walked across the lawn to the toolshed and found a shovel. He began where the pier touched the shore, scraping away the fungus and dumping the growth into the water, where it plopped and floated away. He shoveled quickly, the flat tenacious flesh of the fungus ripping easily off the wood. It was oddly exhilarating work and in a matter of minutes he had cleaned the length of the pier.

A CABIN IN THE WOODS

He stuck the shovel in the turf and went back to the house; he filled a mop bucket with detergent and hot water and returned to the pier to mop the planks. When he was finished, the pier sparkled in the morning sun.

Finally Michael locked the cabin, backed the station wagon out of the drive, and drove into the village.

The village consisted of a few streets clustered together where the interstate crossed the mountains. It had once prosperously grown up on both sides of a white river adjacent to railroad tracks, but now the tracks were defunct and the river polluted, the few buildings weather weary and old. The only new construction was the service station at the interstate, and a few drive-ins. When Barbara first saw the town, she wouldn't even let him stop.

But the hills and valleys beyond the place were spectacular and unspoiled, and when they found five acres of woods overlooking the lake they decided that in spite of the town, they'd buy.

"I looked down at the pier and the whole goddamn thing was covered with fungus. It's a gray color, like someone's puke," Michael said as he paced the architect's office. He had already told the young man about the fungus in the bathroom and beneath the bar and, without saying so, now implied it was the architect's fault.

"I'm not a biologist," said the young man carefully. He was unnerved by Michael, and the way he had barged into his office shouting about fungus. It had taken him several minutes to comprehend what the problem was.

"You're from these hills. You grew up here, right? You should know about fungus. What's all this mountain folklore we keep hearing about?" Michael quit pacing and sat down across from the architect, suddenly tired. The anxiety and anger over the fungus had worn him out. "That's a new house out there. I sunk $50,000 into it and you can't tell me why there's fungus growing on the bathroom walls? Goddamn it! What kind of wood did you use?"

"The lumber was green, true, but I told you we'd have problems. It was your idea to build the place with pine off your land despite our discussions about pine needing time to dry. Still..." The architect shook his head; he had never heard of such a thing and the growth of the fungus thoroughly confused him. But the man might be exaggerating, he thought as he glanced at Michael.

Michael was short and plump with a round, soft face, and brown eyes that were increasingly widening with alarm. He wore new Levi's pants and a jacket, and cowboy boots that gave him an extra inch of height. Around his neck, he had fastened a blue bandanna into an ascot. He looked, the architect thought, slightly ridiculous.

"Who can I talk to that knows about this fungus?" Michael asked. He had taken out another blue bandanna to wipe the sweat off his face which, in his exasperated state, now poured in thick rivelets.

"I guess maybe someone at the college..."

"And you don't think it's any of your concern? You stuck me for $10,000 over the original estimate and now that you've got your money, you don't give a damn."

"I told you before we started construction that we'd most likely get hit by inflation. We could have held the costs close to that first estimate if your wife hadn't wanted all the custom cabinets, those wardrobes, and items like bathroom fixtures from Italy..."

Michael waved away the architect's explanations, still mad at the kid for not solving the problem of the fungus. "Where's this college?" he asked.

A CABIN IN THE WOODS

"Brailey. It's across the mountain."

"How many miles?" Michael stood. He had his car keys out and was spinning them impatiently.

"Maybe thirty, but these are mountain roads so it will take an hour's drive. Why not telephone? You're welcome to use mine." He pushed the phone across the desk.

Michael fidgeted with his keys. He didn't want to let the architect do him any favors, but he also didn't want to spend the morning driving through the mountains.

"Okay. You might be right." He sat down again and, picking up the receiver, dialed information.

It took him several calls and the help of the college switchboard operator before he reached a Doctor Clyde Bessey, an associate professor at the state college. Dr. Bessey had a thin, raspy voice, as if someone had a hand held to his throat. He said he was a mycologist in the Department of Plant Pathology.

"Do you know anything about fungus?" Michael asked.

"Why, yes." The doctor spoke carefully, as if his words were under examination. "Mycology is the study of fungi."

"Then you're the person I want," Michael replied quickly. Then, without asking if the man had time, he described the events of the morning.

"*Peniophora gigantea*," Doctor Bessey replied.

"What?"

"The species of fungi you've described sounds like *Peniophora gigantean*, though it's more commonly called *Resin Fungus*. It's a rather dull-colored species that spreads out like a crust on the wood. You say the edges are serrated?"

"And it's lumpy..."

"Rightly so! *Peniophora gigantea*. Sometimes laymen mistake this species of crust fungi for a resinous secretion of the conifer."

"Does it grow like that? That fast?"

"No, what you've described is odd." He sounded thoughtful. "Fungi won't grow that extensively, unless, of course, a house has been abandoned, but even then, not that fast. We did have a damp winter and spring, still... you said the cabin was built with green lumber?"

"Yes, I'm afraid so." Michael glanced at the architect.

"Still..."

"Well, how in the hell do I stop it?" Michael was sharp, irritated at the laborious manner of the professor.

"I don't know exactly what to tell you. Your situation seems a bit unusual. Fungi doesn't normally grow as rapidly as you described. In laboratory conditions, we've had fungus cover the surface of a three-inch-wide culture dish in two days, but that's under ideal conditions, namely without competition from other fungi or bacteria. But, generally speaking, fungi do thrive better than any other organism on earth," he said with a flourish of pride.

"Doctor, I'm sure this is all just wonderful, but it doesn't help me, you see. I'm infested with the crap!"

"Yes, of course...If you don't mind, I'd like to drive over and take some cultures. I'll be able to tell more once I've had the opportunity to study some samples."

"You can have all you want."

"You've cleaned up the fungi, I presume..."

"With soap and water."

"Well, that should destroy any mycelium, but then we never can be sure. One germinating spore and the process begins again. Rather amazing, actually."

A CABIN IN THE WOODS

"Let's hope you're wrong. It's a $50,000 house."

"Oh, I'm sure there's no permanent problem, just a biological phenomenon. Fungi are harmless, really, when they're kept in control. Your home will suffer no lasting effects." He sounded confident.

"Maybe you're right." Michael was cautious. Still, Doctor Bessey had eased his mind and Michael hung up feeling better.

"Do you mind if I make another call?" he asked the architect. The young man gestured for Michael to go ahead. Actually he wasn't that bad, Michael thought, dialing Barbara back in the city.

"I'm sure it's nothing serious," Barbara said when Michael told her about the fungus. "The wet weather and all..." Her mind was obviously elsewhere, planning for the weekend, no doubt. "Did you have time to make the beds?"

"The whole pier was covered, like a tropical jungle. *Peniophora gigantea*... that's what the mycologist called it."

"The who?"

"Dr. Bessey. He studies fungi."

"Well, if it's that well known, then it can't be any problem...Have you had a chance to wash the windows? Perhaps I should come up earlier..."

"Don't worry about getting the cabin clean. I'll do that!" Michael snapped at her. He was upset that she hadn't responded, and fed up with her frustrating habit of not caring about a household problem unless it affected her directly. "I'll clean the windows, make the beds, and sweep the goddamn floors once I get rid of this fungus!"

"And the rugs..."

"And the rugs!"

"Michael dear, there's no need to be upset with me. I have nothing to do with your fungus."

"Yes dear, but you wanted the place built from our lumber, our *green* lumber."

"And you said it would make the place look more authentic."

"The lumber's green!"

"I don't see where that's my fault!"

"It might mean that we'll have to live with this goddamn fungus!" Michael knew he was being unreasonable, but he couldn't stop himself. He was mad at her for not taking the fungus seriously.

"I'm sure you will think of something." Barbara pampered him and then dismissed the whole issue. "You'll remember the windows...?" She sounded like a recording.

Before leaving the village, Michael went to the general store and shopped for the week. He did not want to leave the lake again for errands. He bought Windex, the spices Barbara had forgotten, a new mop, and a second broom. He also purchased two five-gallon cans of gas for the boats, a minnow box, a fishnet, a filet knife, and more tackle, including a box of lures that the store owner told him were good for mountain lakes. He would need all these items if he planned to do any serious fishing.

He realized that the impulse buying was only a compensation for the upsetting morning—now that he had the money, he tended to spend it quickly. It worked, and his good mood returned as he drove back to the cabin.

He would not clean the cabin that morning, he decided, nor would he make the beds. Instead, he'd take out the flat-bottomed boat and fish for bass in the small lagoon of the lake. He'd pan fry the catch that evening

A CABIN IN THE WOODS

for dinner along with some fresh vegetables, maybe asparagus or sliced cucumbers, and a bottle of the Pinot Noir.

Michael pictured himself on the deck frying the bass, a cloud of smoke from the coals drifting off into the trees, the late sun catching the glass of wine and tinting the pale yellow color like tarnished gold. He'd cover the fish a moment, stop to sip the wine, and look out over the lake as the trees, darkened on the other shore, became engulfed in a slow-forming mist. He'd get a thick ski sweater and put it on and when the darkness spread up the lawn to the house, he'd be the last object visible, moving on the deck like a lingering shadow.

As Michael turned the station wagon off the county road and onto his drive, the crunch of gravel under the wheels snapped him out of his daydream. He touched the accelerator and the big car spun over the loose stones. On that side of the property the trees grew thick and close and kept the house from view until Michael swung the car into the parking space and stopped. That's when he saw the fungus, growing widespread across the rock foundation like prehistoric ivy.

He ran from the car to the wall and grabbed the fungus. The mold tore away in large chunks as, with both hands, frantically, he kept ripping it away. Now it was wet and clammy, like the soft underbelly of a fish.

Michael left the fungus on the ground, left his new fishing tackle and other supplies in the car, and ran into the house. He pulled open the cabinet doors beneath the bar. The gray growth had spread again across the two shelves, thickly covering the wine and liquor like cobwebs.

In the bathroom upstairs the patch of mold was now the width of the wall. It stretched from floor to ceiling and had crept around the mirror, grown into the wash bowl, and smothered the toilet. He reached out and pulled a dozen inches away with his fingers. The waxy flesh of the fungus clung to his hand. Exhausted, Michael fell back against the bathroom door and wiped the sweat off his face with the sleeve of his jacket.

After a few minutes Michael realized how hot it was in the cabin. He took off his jacket and the blue bandanna ascot, then returned to the bathroom fungus. He filled five paper bags with fungus and dumped them into the trash heap behind the house. He went to the bar and removed the wine and liquor, and scraped the shelves clean again. He took the fungus to the trash pile and, going back to the car, got one of the cans of gas, poured it on the heap, and started a blaze.

The wet fungus produced a heavy fog and a nasty odor, like the burning of manure. Michael watched it burn with pleasure, but when he returned to the kitchen to put away the supplies, he found that the fungus had spread further and was growing extensively in all the cupboards and beneath the sink. It even lined the insides of the oven and grew up the back of the refrigerator.

Michael needed to stand on a kitchen chair to reach the fungus that grew at the rear of the cupboards, but he had now learned how to rip the mold away in large pieces, as if pulling off old, wet wallpaper. Still, it took him longer than that in the rest of the house because the fungus was more extensive, and nestled in all the corners of the custom-made cupboards.

He went outside and found the wheelbarrow and carted away the fungus, dumping it into the fire behind the house. The gray smoke billowed into the trees and the mountain air stank. He swept the kitchen clean and washed the cupboards, the bathroom, and the cabinets beneath the bar. It was late afternoon when he had the house finally in order; he went upstairs and flopped into bed, feeling as if he hadn't slept in weeks.

A CABIN IN THE WOODS

He woke after seven o'clock. It was still daylight, but the sun was low in the sky and the bedroom at the back of the cabin was made dark by the thick shade trees.

He had been deeply asleep and came awake slowly; it was several minutes before he remembered where he was and what had happened. When he did remember, he realized at the same time that the fungus would have now returned and was growing again in the bathroom, beneath the bar, and in all the cupboards of the kitchen.

He did not know, however, that the fungus had spread further and was growing along the green pine walls of the bedroom, had spread over the bare oak floors, and even started down the stairs as if it was an organic carpet. Michael sat up and swung his bare feet off the bed and onto the floor. His feet touched the lumpy wet fungus as if he had been swimming in the lake and had tried to stand on the mucky bottom. His toes dug into the slime.

He shoveled the fungus off the floor and threw it out the bedroom window. The shovel tore into the roughhewed floor and caught between the planks, and by the time he was done the floor was ruined. He took a rake from the shed and used it to pull the fungus off the walls, then cleaned the bathroom again and shoveled the fungus off the stairs. Repeatedly, he filled the wheelbarrow and dumped it outside where the fire burned steadily.

It took Michael three hours to clean the cabin and only when he was done, resting in the kitchen, sitting at the butcher-block table and drinking a bottle of beer, did he first see the fungus seeping out from under the cellar door. It grew rapidly before his eyes, twisting and turning, slipping across the tile floor like a snake. Michael grabbed the shovel and cut through the fungus at the door. The dismembered end continued across the tile with a life of its own.

He jerked open the cellar door to beat back the growth, but the gray fungus had filled the cellar and, with the door now opened, it smothered him in an avalanche of mold.

Now it was everywhere. The cupboards burst open and the fungus flopped out and onto the counter. A tide of it pushed aside the food and shoved cans to the floor.

In the living room it grew along the rock fireplace and tumbled down the stairs. It spread across the floor and came up between the cracks in the oak planks. It grew around the tables and chairs and covered all the furniture with a gray dustcover of mold. It oozed from the center of the rolled-up rug, like pus from a sore. There was fungus on the ceiling, crawling towards the peak of the cabin. It was under foot, and Michael skipped and slid as he ran from the house.

The fungus crawled along the rock foundation. It filled the deck and, under its weight, the wooden supports gave way as the deck crashed to the ground. The pier was covered again and the gray mold came off the wood and across the new lawn, ripping the sod as it raced towards Michael like a tide.

Michael got the other can of gas from the station wagon. He went inside the house and poured it through the living room, splashing it against the wooden stairs, the pine walls. He ran into the kitchen and threw a long, yellow spray at the cupboards, emptying the last of the can on the butcher-block table. When he dropped the can to the floor it sank into the thick fungus with a thud.

He was breathless, panting. His fingers shook and fumbled as he found matches, struck and tossed them at the gas-soaked mold. Flames roared up, eating away at the fungus as it caught hold of the pine and oak and walnut with a blaze. In the living room he tossed matches into the liquor cabinet and set fire to the bar. He lit up the stairs and the flames ran along the steps. He tore through the fungus covering the furniture and ignited the couch.

The fungus had grown deep and billowy and it felt as if Michael was trying to stand on top of a deflating parachute. He kept slipping and falling as the lumpy surface changed directions and expanded. The floor was a sea of mold and the front door was almost blocked from view as gray smoke began to choke him. He tumbled towards the door and fungus swelled under foot and knocked him aside.

Michael found the shovel and used it to rip through the layers of wet mold. He cut a path, like digging a trench, to the outside. He ran for the station wagon. The fungus had reached the parking space and was lapping at the wheels of the car.

Behind him the cabin blazed. Flames reached the shingled roof and leaped up the frame siding. The house burned like a bonfire as he spun the car around. The wheels slid over the slick mold like the car was caught on a field of ice, but he kept the station wagon on the gravel and tromped on the grass. The car fishtailed down the drive and onto the safety of the county road as Michael drove for his life.

"It's a total loss?" Barbara asked again, still confused by Michael's tale. Her blue saucer eyes looked puzzled.

Michael nodded. "In the rearview mirror I could see most of it in flames. I didn't have the courage to go back and check." He spoke with a new honesty and sense of awe.

"But to burn down our own home! Wasn't there some other way...?" She stared at Michael. It was unbelievable; he had arrived at the apartment after midnight, trembling and incoherent. She had wanted to call a doctor, but he raged and struck her when she said he needed help. She cowered in the corner of the couch, shaking and frightened, as he paced the room and told her about the fungus and the fire.

"I tried to keep cleaning it with soap and water, but it kept..." He began to cry deep, chest-rending sobs. As she went quickly to him and smothered him against her breasts, she could smell the smoke in his hair, the bitter aroma of wood that had smoldered in the rain.

"A smoke?" Barbara suggested. "It will calm you down." Her hands were trembling with excitement as she rolled them a joint; it was the first time in years that he had hit her, and the blow had both frightened and thrilled her. Her skin tingled.

They passed the joint back and forth as they sat huddled on the couch, like two lone survivors. Michael, again, and in great detail and thoroughness, told about the fungus, and why he had to burn the cabin.

"I know you were absolutely right," Barbara kept saying to reassure him, but in the back of her mind, growing like a cancer, was her doubt. To stop her own suspicious thoughts and his now insistent explanations, she interrupted, "Darling..." and reached to unbutton his shirt.

They did not make it to the bedroom. Michael slipped his hands inside her blouse, then he pulled her to the floor and took his revenge and defeat out on her. It was brief and violent and cathartic.

70

A CABIN IN THE WOODS

When they were finished, Michael held her tenderly, his arms wrapped around her, hugging her to him. He turned her head and kissed her closed eyelids. It was all right, she whispered. He was home and safe and she would take care of him.

Yes, Michael thought, everything was all right. He was home in the city and they would forget the mountains and the second home on the lake. He had his writing and he had her, and that was all that mattered. And then his lips touched the candle-gray fungus that grew in a thin, irregular patch more than twelve inches wide across her breasts like a bra.

CALL ME

It was not easy keeping in touch. There were so many demands, and hundreds of ways that my services were requested. The telephone and mail certainly, but also telegrams, meetings, and midnight visits. At all hours the doorbell rang and I asked through the keyhole: who are you and what do you want?

"My name is Michael. I'm a friend of Sherri's. She said to see you that perhaps you could help."

I disengaged the lock and opened the door. I have been robbed and mugged this way on more than one occasion, but what else could I do? I only wanted to help.

I had one wall of filing cabinets: steel, cardboard, makeshift files in boxes. They were all jammed with correspondence. I classified each message by name and address: VINICK, Richard L., 16th Street, N.W. I also cross referenced each name to subjects: *Lonely Hearts, Money, Travel, Pets*. I had 2,249 such categories.

At first, sitting at my desk constructed of plywood and milk cartons, I typed out the replies on my Olivetti Lettera 32. Much of the time it took me the majority of the morning, or longer if there were also phone calls and visitors at the door.

Then the letters and cards began to accumulate more quickly than I could manage them. I piled them up in my In Box, a giant galvanized trash can, and kept the excess in green Jiffy bags. I hired a part-time secretary. She was a recent graduate of a speedwriting secretarial school and could type ninety-five words a minute, as well as take dictation.

I dictated letters as she sat at my desk. She was a tiny girl from Rockville, Maryland. She wore her boyfriend's letter sweater on cold mornings and brought a lunch in a brown bag. Her voice was a whisper, the size of a small bird flying, and she sat with pencil poised, steno pad ready, while I paced my tiny Adams-Morgan apartment.

Gail was her name. She took the shorthand home and typed the letters there each evening, then delivered the finished copy the next day. While she made instant coffee, I re-read the letters and signed them individually. On a good day we could average twenty to twenty-five letters. My letters were long, three and four pages each. When dictating, I was expansive; I had a natural gift for it, and I tended to think in full paragraphs.

I handled the telephone calls well enough by myself. I operated three lines into the apartment and had a system for keeping callers on hold. My recorded voice said, "Hello, I'm busy now, but at the tone please state your name, telephone number, and your question."

I bought a telephone speaker so I could move about the apartment as I talked. It was necessary, since there were often questions of reference that I had to look up: What is the capital city of Chad? Where is Henry James' grave? Who won the 1925 Dempsey-Tunney fight?

CALL ME

My apartment was filled with dictionaries, directories, research reports, and government studies. I had a walk-in closet stacked with GPO documents. I had to move my clothes to the bathroom, and I hung my shirts and suits on the shower curtain bar.

The telephone rang, all night long it rang, and woke me from nightmares. I dreamed I was playing tennis and the base lines and net were crowded with people waving for my attention and shouting my name. I could hear the cries as the telephone rang like a screaming kettle.

"Hello?" The voice was distant and mumbled.

"Speak up, please, there's nothing to worry about." My voice, I was told, was like hot cocoa; it warmed the person immediately and seeped comfort into the soul.

"A friend of mine gave me your telephone number. She said you could help me. I hope you don't mind that I called so late."

Most of my telephone calls began that way. They came from out of the middle of the sad night, lonely and lost people dialing, telephoning from phone booths on the beltway. They had walked through the fog to the white booth glowing on the dark highway like a small, safe shrine. My name and phone number has been spread by thousands of grateful souls, scribbled on vacant walls. I had found it myself on the urinals in Union Station, and Gail whispered that she first saw it in the girl's locker room of her high school gym.

All night long the phone rang like an alarm until Washington went off to sleep. Then early again, before six a.m., a woman in tears screamed at me. "I want a divorce, goddamn it! I'm going crazy with this man. I want OUT!"

I did my best to calm, smooth, and comfort the anguished as I reassured, informed, and instructed. I preached and gospelized, encouraged and gave faith.

75

And then it was beyond me, this overwhelming research and volume of mail and telephone calls. I couldn't keep up as new kinds of questions began to arrive, questions of a biophysical nature that demanded a scientific background and more learning. I was not schooled in questions of psycho-pharmacology and utilitarianism, and I had no anthropological perspective, or any understanding of ethical issues.

It had all begun simply with a girl on the subway. We were sitting together, and she had asked, "How do I get to Gallery Place?" An easy question. One word would have done it or a simple shake of my head if I hadn't wanted to be bothered. But I live alone and have no friends, so I chose to engage her.

I had a Metro map and showed her the route; I am very good with directions and I take my time and speak slowly. The girl was a stranger to Washington, and she smiled with her brown eyes as I told her that she would need to change at Metro Center. She was a pretty girl with a fat face, and she thanked me profusely as she told me I was the first kind person she had met in the city. Washington was too big, she said, and we talked of her hometown of Pottsville, Pennsylvania.

"John O'Hara," I said.

She was impressed. "It is a little known fact," she answered, proud of her hometown and fascinated with my knowledge of subway systems and fiction writers.

"I collect information," I said. "It's a hobby."

We reached Metro Center, and I pressed my card into her hand before she departed.

CALL ME

I had thousands of such cards. They gave my name and address, my telephone number, and told people to call me any time of the day or night. For a time I travelled around the city on buses and left my card everywhere: at churches, near the poor boxes; in the lounges of Reagan Airport; on seats in subway cars. I left them wherever people gathered and waited.

"My girlfriend said she met you on the subway and that you were very helpful," another shy voice revealed to me one day. "I'm looking for work and was hoping..."

"Yes! Yes!" I bubbled into the phone. I was ready; I had the resources and the references, the *Post* want ads, and the *Dictionary of Occupations* from the Labor Department. I had names and addresses, and could write glowing resumes. And so it began.

She found work immediately, the very next day, in fact, and on her first interview she was hired as a Hot Shop waitress. She was gratified, and told her customers. Others telephoned and quickly it continued and multiplied and quadrupled. Then the visits started.

I had no office or reception room so they came day after day and sat on the stairs; I live on the fourth floor and the line stretched to the street.

The tenants of the building complained, but my visitors were polite. They took turns and sat only one on a step at a time to ensure that they did not block the stairs. They did not litter. Some listened to music while they waited, but they used earphones and never danced on the landings.

I had visiting hours two days a week and by appointment only, but I often ran overtime. We live in a world where it is difficult to keep a schedule, as life is not nine to five, and there was no way I could solve everyone's problems within an hour. I held their hands, and we shared a joint. I listened to them sing their songs. We talked and reminisced. People like to

77

talk; they are articulate and have something to say. They are not fools, and I paid attention to them and nodded reassuringly.

I became notorious in the neighborhood as the man with strangers at his doorway. No one had spoken to me before—they did not care about me—but now I was famous in both Adams-Morgan and throughout the city. I was written up in the Style Section of the *Washington Post*, and appeared on *Panorama*.

People mailed me money and told me to continue the good work. I opened a savings account and established a non-profit foundation. Publishers wrote and asked me to write my life story. I was invited to the White House and shook hands with the president's wife.

Then a woman called. She had a voice as lovely as that of a telephone operator. She praised me for my good work and offered to help; she was in touch with computers and networks of information and talked glowingly of retrieval systems and new kinds of technology.

Yes, I told her, I could see where my efforts were failing. Already I was months behind in my correspondence and I couldn't even manage to see everyone who came knocking at my door.

"We'll increase your effectiveness," she said. "Your productivity will jump!" She was sure and brilliant.

Their organization had form letters, she explained, that were as good as the original, and they had a device that could write my signature. They had 33 rpms in mono and stereo which would allow my calm voice to give advice and self-help on both tapes and records.

I could write books and have them translated into foreign languages. She asked if I had thought much about the Chinese? No, I confessed, I hadn't; I had been so busy. Yes, she understood, but now her organization would help. It all made good common sense, I had to agree.

CALL ME

My telephone calls were transferred first; the phone stopped ringing in the middle of the night and there was a strange, new quiet in the apartment. I enjoyed the silence and got my first full night of sleep in months.

A switchboard had been arranged with a tape of my voice and I talked to strangers as if I were there in person. Questions were asked, and the computers were activated as my voice gave data and advice. I could call the exchange and ask a question, listen to myself, and hear the confident answer. It was thrilling.

The stacks of mail disappeared from my door and the mailman began to talk to me once again. I had to let Gail go, but she understood. I tried to find her work and couldn't, but she telephoned my machine one morning and they found employment for her that very same day at a warehouse company off the beltway. I had never heard of the firm. "But it was your voice," she whispered. The wonder of it all.

I expanded my visiting hours, but no one needed the extra time. People telephoned from the phone booth downstairs and received immediate answers. They did not need to climb the four flights to talk with me.

Now I had time to think and reflect. I went for long, midday walks and attended the new movies in town. I visited the National Zoo and hung around DuPont Circle. I watched daytime quiz shows, and listened to all-news radio stations. I roamed the downtown streets and smiled at tourists at the mall. I waited every day for the mailman, but he had only third-class mail and letters stamped Addressee Unknown.

Then last month after midnight my telephone rang suddenly. It was the first call I had received in five months, and I grabbed the receiver. It was the wrong number; a man wanted to talk to Sara. I said I didn't know her but I would help him find her number. I hurried for the directory, but he hung up before I could reply. The silence in the apartment trembled my hands.

Call me.

CATHOLIC GUILT

He drove west across the flat farmlands of Illinois where the cornfields stretched to the horizon. He followed the sun on back roads and rural highways until he reached Joliet and picked up Old 66, going south on that historic, narrow, two-lane route.

What the fuck, why not? he asked himself.

It would be his last time in the state, his last time going home. He would do it his way, driving through one godforsaken town after another, places not even recognized by GPS.

It had been decades since he had last been back home. He was the child who had escaped, but, of course, he hadn't really. There was no escape from the family, the farm, the town, the parish and priest, from all that had been done to him and his little brother.

He pressed the accelerator. Who would last longer, he wondered, the Honda or himself? He eased his foot off the gas and slowed. There was no rush. No one was waiting. He would begin his crusade at home, he had decided; it was only poetic justice.

As if to reassure himself of his cause, he glanced over at the bulky file folder he'd placed on the passenger seat. It contained all the clips and emails he had collected through the years. They weighed on him like a guilty conscience.

Nevertheless, he tried, even in his rage, to take some pleasure in the landscape, the calmness of cornfields, row after row of stately yellowing stalks, smooth expansive green fields of second-cut alfalfa, acres of pastureland dotted with milking cows: Holstein, Guernsey, Brown Swiss, and Jersey.

It was a Thomas Hart Benton landscape of a warm summer day, picture-perfect and pastoral. He passed a red barn on a rise, enveloped in pines and cottonwoods, separated from the farmhouse by an apple orchard in midsummer bloom. There were white sheets drying on lines in the August sunshine and children playing with a golden retriever on a front lawn that sloped to the road and a rural mailbox.

A stranger, he thought, a woman traveling down from Chicago, might point and exclaim to her husband, "Oh, look, honey! How lovely!"

Angrily, he squeezed the steering wheel with both hands and again pressed hard on the accelerator. He had been gone twenty years from the flat Illinois land, yet outside the car's windows it was like yesterday. He remembered in heartbreaking ways how he had cared for his brother after their mother's sudden death. And how he had failed to protect him.

He grimaced and shouted, "Fuck you!" into the enclosed space of the car. The sound of his voice, booming in the car's interior, stunned him. He had been crossing the country in silence, letting himself wallow in his wrath, feeding off his sickness, the history of his life, all his failings. But now he had a calling, a way to redeem himself.

A highway sign flashed in his peripheral vision: Prairieland, Pop. 5,168.

CATHOLIC GUILT

O

He tapped the brakes, bringing the Honda back to the speed limit, recalling how the town's cops camped at the last bend to catch drivers speeding on the empty highway, slapping strangers with tickets to pay for the officers' Christmas presents, holiday parties, beer money.

Ahead of him, stretched across the flat horizon like a mutilation, was the town. Schultz's twin grain elevators still guarded the entrance to two blocks of low red-brick stores and old wood-framed offices, the bank and police station, Grace's Diner, Hank's Hardware, Carnegie's library.

Driving slowly, he worked his way along Main Street. He could have been seventeen again, cruising with Billy Hanlon in Billy's Chevy, looking for the guys, looking for girls, looking for trouble, looking for anything that would break up the loneliness of his life.

The town was still in the nineteen fifties. Here and there was a new sign, a strange name on an old office window, a recent film on the marquee of the Towne Theatre. The price of gas at Murphy's service station was $2.58. He had paid twenty-five cents a gallon when he was a teenager, filling his pickup with the few dollars he earned from serving as an altar boy at Saturday weddings and old folks' funerals. His first paying job, working for God.

With relief and regret he saw that nothing had really changed. He drove slowly past the Town Hall and the grassy mall, with its ancient cannon recognizing the Civil War dead. He passed the Lutheran church, freshly painted. The Lutherans had always kept up their church, he remembered. They were the wealthy ones, not the Catholic immigrants—Irish, Polish, now Mexican.

He passed Prairieland High School. The Fighting Prairie Dogs. A billboard schedule of the coming fall football games.

He kept driving, knowing where he was going, and why.

O

A block farther, he turned onto Dasson Street and, looking up the rise, saw Saint Patrick's for the first time in a quarter century. The church and the hill both looked smaller. Tall poplars now shaded the buildings, sheltered the empty tarmac parking lot. The red brick church was circular, resembling a wedding cake more than a house of God. Beyond it was an elementary school, also red brick, but closed and abandoned now. The archdiocese had declared that this rural corner of Illinois no longer had enough Catholics to support a school.

He turned into the empty lot and stopped the car, parked haphazardly across the white stripes, and stared at the church, wondering if its doors were still routinely left unlocked. Father O'Shea had always said proudly that Saint Patrick's was open twenty-four hours a day for any parishioner wanting to make a visit.

But he didn't want to make a visit. He touched the gas pedal and drove slowly across the parking lot. Then he followed a new asphalt drive that curved around the confection of the building and he stopped the car at the front of the small rectory.

Father O'Shea wasn't one of those pastors who spent the collection money on himself, he thought, giving the old man some credit. Opening the car door, he stepped out, being careful of his unfamiliar, rented clothes. That morning, at the motel in Indiana, he had put on the black, long-sleeved,

84

ankle-length, hoodless Semi Jesuit Cassock he had found online. To Father O'Shea, he'd look like a fellow clergyman come to call.

Reaching into the back seat, he picked up the brown bag and opened it, glancing inside to check on the pliers and his father's old Ruger revolver that had been sent to him by the realtor when the farm was sold. It was all he'd asked for, all he'd wanted from his past. He slipped the heavy pistol in his pocket in case it became necessary to use it and slammed the door, locking the car.

Everything he owned was in the back seat. When he was a kid, no one would have stolen from a car parked in front of a rectory. Now, no one respected religion or the religious. And he knew why.

Behind Saint Patrick's, tucked away like a pastoral secret, was the parish graveyard, several dozen headstones in a flat patch beside the rectory. With a familiarity that surprised him, he crossed the yard to the cemetery and went through the gates to his grave. The memory of his brother's death, the email he had received from Mickey explaining what he was doing and why, and then vividly recalling the black-and-white police photo of Mickey's crumpled body at the kitchen table, blood soaking the tablecloth, arm draped over the sides, his fingers still caught in the trigger of his father's Ruger—all burned like a brand in his brain.

He dropped to his knees beside the grave, blessed himself, and said again and again the prayer the nuns had taught him: "O Virgin of virgins, my Mother, to thee do I come; before thee I stand, sinful and sorrowful."

Leaning forward he kissed Michael's name carved like a command-ment into the marble slab. Under the summer sun, the headstone was as warm as his little brother's face when he kissed him goodnight and tucked him in.

O

It had been his plan to reach Saint Patrick's in the waning hours of daylight. No housekeeper would be working; no parishioners would be knocking on the door. His only worry was that the pastor would not be home, that he'd have gone out for an early dinner with one of the farm families. He dearly loved home cooking, the priest had always reminded his congregation from the altar, and he would be pleased to come by at dinnertime to bless their homes with prayers and holy water. "Anything for a free meal," he'd joshed.

The memory of that long-ago joke drove a sharp wedge of fury into his heart. He quickly rang the bell, listening as the chime echoed through the empty house. As was fitting for a dying parish, Father O'Shea lived alone, with no younger curates needed to help out.

In the glass panels that framed the door, he caught an image of himself. He did look like a priest, he thought, with his tall body robed in clerical black. He did not, he thought, look his age. Here was the way he saw himself: strong and muscular, a man who had taken care of himself. Someone God would want to do His work on earth.

He had been blessed with thick black hair that was now salt and pepper but still full and strong. A face hardened by work and weather, shaped by his teenage years spent farming the land, plowing fields, mowing hay.

From deep inside the rectory, he heard the old man call out. Looking through a glass panel, he saw O'Shea shuffling down the length of the uncarpeted hallway. He had woken the priest from his Sunday afternoon nap.

CATHOLIC GUILT

He glanced quickly over his shoulder, swept his cold eyes across the parking lot, the church, the school, making sure there was no stray witness to spot him on this quiet summer afternoon.

The door opened, and there was Father James O'Shea.

He stood bent over, blinking, dazed by the sunlight. His blue short-sleeve shirt and worn khakis hung on his skinny frame. His sockless feet were pushed into slippers.

The pastor pulled himself up, smiled, pleased by the unexpected sight of another priest.

"Father O'Shea, you're still with us." He smiled nicely, as if they were friends.

The priest stared at him, his cloudy blue eyes watery and empty, his face frozen in puzzlement.

"I'm Mickey Nolan's brother. Dennis."

The old man flinched and fumbled for the doorknob.

With his right arm, Dennis reached out and blocked the priest's attempt to close the door.

Smiling, whispering, he let his calm words cut into the old man's memory. "Don't you want to invite me in as you did my little brother? Don't you remember how you told us in religion class that you were doing God's work? Were you doing God's work with Mickey, too, Father?"

"Leave me alone!" O'Shea demanded. "I don't know what you're talking about." This time, he got the door halfway closed before Nolan gave him a shove. The priest stumbled on the throw rug in the entrance hallway, but he reached out and grabbed the pastor before he could fall on the hardwood floor.

"Don't die on me now, O'Shea. I'm not finished with you."

"What do you want? Get out! I'm calling the police."

"I've come to pay you back, you motherfucker."

"Leave me be. I'm an old man."

The pastor hunched over, cringing away from Nolan.

He grabbed the trembling old priest with one hand and kicked the door closed. Then he smiled, safely inside the rectory and alone with O'Shea.

He pushed O'Shea again, sending him flying into a high, deep-cushioned wooden chair that he seemed to remember had once been on the altar of the church. The pastor curled up in the deep red velvet cushion.

"What do you want?" Father O'Shea cried out again.

"I've come home to see that you pay for your sins. We all have to pay, don't we, Father? Isn't that what you taught us in religion class? Or did you think you were doing God's will when you told me to go out and enjoy myself, that you'd take care of Mickey—and then jammed your prick up his eight-year-old ass?"

In his rage and regret he whacked the old man on the side of the head. The skull was soft under his blow, and he was suddenly fearful he might have killed the priest before he had a chance to do what he wanted to do.

He hit the priest again, this time with the palm of his left hand and Father O'Shea's head popped back, blood squirting from his mouth.

Reaching out, he grabbed the priest by the front of his shirt, lifted him off the velvet cushion, and dragged him across the hardwood floor into the dining room. Blood was on his hand and the black sleeve of his rented cassock. He could hear the priest gasping for air.

With a jerk, Nolan lifted up the priest and tossed him onto the bare, polished dining table. He grabbed the priest's trousers and pulled them down along with his underwear, exposing the skinny man's shrunken scrotum and shriveled penis. The priest struggled to sit up. Nolan hit him again, this time on the forehead, knocking him back.

Swearing at the priest's resistance, he fumbled inside the brown bag and pulled out the pliers, the nine-inch burdizzo emasculatone, just like the one he once used on the farm and seized the loose sac of the priest's scrotum.

Trapping the cord of the left testicle in the burdizzo's jaws, just as he had done to hundreds of calves and goats, he swiftly clamped the pliers shut and heard the crisp, crunching sound as the device crushed the cord. Father O'Shea screamed as if struck by the wrath of God.

Opening the jaws of the pliers, he grabbed the old man's other testicle, crushing the spermatic cords with one squeeze. When he pulled the burdizzo off the priest's scrotum, all he saw were two small white grooves and a spot of blood on the skin of the old man's sac. These were the only signs of his castration.

Dropping the pliers into the paper bag, he took one last long look at the howling priest curled up on the dining table. Father O'Shea was cupping his genitals as if they were the Holy Chalice.

"Ite Missa est," Michael whispered, reciting the pastor's closing words of Latin at the end of Sunday Mass. Then he walked out of the rectory as if he had just been on a pastoral visit.

O

Inside the Honda he took a moment to steady himself. Then deliberately, slowly, now full of confidence, he typed into the keyboard of his iPhone where he was going next, southwest into Iowa and the town of Gatesburg, Saint Mary Margaret's, the parish of Father Martin Dwyer.

Fishing through his fat, overstuffed file, he found the only published account in the *Chicago Tribune* of how Dwyer had been accused by a teenage schoolgirl in Lake Forest. The charge had been dismissed due to lack of evidence, though a month later, Dennis knew, the diocese had quietly removed the priest from teaching at the Lake Forest school and sent him to a parish in Gatesburg.

That parish was less than two hundred miles from Prairieland. He could spend the night at a nearby motel, Dennis decided, so as to be at the rectory before dawn. Wearing his Jesuit garb, Dwyer would let him into the rectory, and there Dennis would do his job.

He would then take Father Dwyer into the church itself, Dennis decided, and leave the castrated priest on the altar for the old ladies to find him when they arrived early, as they always did, for six o'clock Mass.

SNOW MAN

When Marc entered the clasroom, "peace corps go home" had already Been written on the blackboard. It was neatly done, and that eliminated all but two of the Ethiopian students.

They were watching him now, but he only laughed. Stepping up to the board, he erased the words, deliberately sending a spray of dust into the room. The girls near the windows waved their arms to keep the dust away, and Kelemwork stood and opened one of the windows.

Nothing was said.

Marc arranged his books on the teacher's desk, making sure he looked busy and important in front of the students. The second bell rang and he looked up at the class. A few faces turned away. They were unsure of what he'd do, and that made him feel better. Still, he had to take a couple of deep breaths to stop the wave of his own fear.

"You're unhappy about the quiz," he began, speaking slowly. Even though the students were in their third year of secondary school, they still had a hard time understanding English. He spoke slowly, too, because it

91

helped to calm his nerves. "All right! I'm unhappy, too! A teacher must set standards. You understand, don't you?"

He wondered how much they did understand. He crossed the front of the room, pacing slowly. No one was watching him.

"What do you want from me?" he shouted. "All hundreds? What good will that do you? Huh? How far will you get? Into fourth year? So what?" He kept shouting. He couldn't stop himself. His thin voice bounced off the concrete walls.

Still the class sat unmoved. A few glanced in his direction, their brown eyes sweeping past his eyes. In the rear of the classroom Tekele raised his hand and stood.

"We want you to be fair, Mr. Marc."

"Am I not fair?"

Tekele hesitated.

"Go ahead, Tekele, speak up." Marc lowered his voice.

"You are difficult."

"Oh, I'm difficult. First I am unfair, now I am difficult."

Tekele did not respond. He looked out the window, and then sat down.

The room remained silent. Marc stared at each one, letting the quiet intensify. He could feel it swell up and fill his eardrums.

"All right," he told them. "We will have another test."

They stirred immediately, whispering fiercely in Amharic. Marc opened the folder on his desk and, taking out the mimeographed sheets, began to pass them out, setting each one face-down on a desk, telling them not to start until they were told. When he came back to the front of the room he announced, "You have thirty minutes. Begin."

No one moved.

SNOW MAN

He walked slowly among the rows, down one, then the next, and when he reached the far left rear corner of the room, he said, "If you do not begin, I will fail everyone. You will all get zeros."

Still they did not move.

He went again to the front of the room, letting them have plenty of time.

"All right!" he said again, pausing. If only one of them would weaken, look at the quiz, he would have them. "That's all!" he announced. "You all get zeros. No credit for the quiz, and I am counting it as an official test." He gathered his books into his arms and left the classroom.

As the door closed, the room ignited. Desks slammed. Students shouted. Marc turned from the noise and went along the second floor corridor to the faculty room. Helen was there grading papers. She glanced at her watch when Marc entered and smiled, asking, "Did you let your class go?"

He shook his head.

"What, then?" She watched as he went to the counter and made himself a cup of tea.

"They won't take my quiz."

She waited for his explanation.

"I left them in the room."

"Marc!"

"They wrote 'Peace Corps Go Home' on the blackboard."

"My, they're out to get you." She smiled, sipping her tea and watching him over the rim of the cup. She had a small round face, much like a smile button, and short blonde hair.

Marc wanted to slap her.

He heard footsteps on the stairs, voices talking in Amharic, and then silence as the class walked by the open door of the faculty room. The students were headed for the basketball court.

"What are you going to do?" Helen asked, trying to be nice.

"Nothing."

"Aren't you going to talk to Ato Asfaw?"

"Why should I? He said discipline was our problem."

Helen put down her cup. "Marc, you're making a mistake."

"You're the one who thinks it's so goddamn funny."

"Okay! I'm sorry I made light of your tragedy." She began again to correct her students' papers.

Marc sat with her, waiting for something to happen. The faculty room was hot with the dry, hot early morning air of the African winter. Through the open windows, Marc could feel the hot winds coming off the Ogaden Desert. He was from Michigan and that very morning he had heard on the shortwave radio that the American Midwest was currently being hit with a blizzard. He tried to remember snow, tried to remember the wet feel of it under his mittens when he was only ten and walking home from where the school bus dropped him off at the edge of the highway.

He was still sitting staring out at the desert when the school guard came and said in Amharic that the headmaster wanted to see him. Walking to the office, Marc glanced again at the arid lowlands and thought of snow blowing against his face. It made him feel immensely better.

"Mr. Marc," Ato Asfaw said, "why are 3B on the playground?" The small, slight headmaster was standing behind his desk.

"I left them in class. They refused to take my test." Marc sat down and made himself comfortable. He knew his casualness upset the

SNOW MAN

headmaster—it was an affront to the Ethiopian culture—but in the two years he had been in Ethiopia, he had learned what offended Ethiopians and took joy in annoying them.

"But you gave them a quiz last week." The headmaster sat down behind his enormous desk, nearly disappearing from sight. With his high, pronounced forehead and the finely sculptured face of an Amharia, he looked like the Emperor Haile Selassie.

"Yes, I gave them a quiz last week. They did poorly, so I decided to give them another one."

Asfaw nodded, hesitated a moment, then said, "3B has other complaints. They say you are not fair. They say you call them monkeys, tell them they are stupid."

"They're lying."

"They say you left the classroom; is this true?"

"They refused to take my quiz."

"Perhaps you may give them another chance."

"Why?"

"Because they are children, Mr. Marc, and you are their teacher." He spoke quickly, showing his impatience.

His desk was covered with papers typed in Amharic script, stacks of thin sheets fastened together with small straight pins. How could he help a country that couldn't even afford paperclips, Marc wondered.

"I don't see them as children," he told the headmaster. "Some of those 'boys' are older than I am. They know what they're doing. They wrote 'Peace Corps Go Home' on the blackboard." Marc stopped talking. He knew it sounded like a stupid complaint—Helen was right—yet he wouldn't back down in front of the Ethiopian. Americans never back down, he reminded himself.

"You have been difficult with them," the headmaster went on, still speaking softly, as if discussing Marc's sins. "They are not American students; you are being unjust, treating them as such." He stood again, as if to gain more authority.

"I am not treating them as American students, or any other kind of student, except Ethiopians," Marc answered back. He crossed his legs, knowing it was another sign of disrespect.

"Mr. Marc, your classes in Peace Corps training taught you Ethiopian customs. Am I correct?"

Marc nodded, watching Ato Asfaw, waiting for the catch.

"You learned that we have our own ways. Your teaching methods are, what do you call it, 'culture shock'." He smiled.

Marc shrugged. They had all been told about culture shock, how everything in the new country would disorient them. But he had weathered "culture shock" on his own, he reminded himself, and said to the headmaster, "This country has a history of school strikes, am I right?"

"Not a history, no. There have been some strikes, but never over anything as trivial as this, this quiz!" His voice rose as he finished the sentence.

"Well, what are you going to do?" Marc asked. He hooked his arm over the back of the chair.

Asfaw picked up a sheet of paper off his desk.

From where he sat, Marc saw that the paper was full of handwritten Amharic notes.

"There are many complaints on this paper," the headmaster said. "The students are sending a copy to the Ministry of Education in Addis Ababa." He looked over at Marc, enjoying the moment. He had the brown saucer eyes, just like all Ethiopians; Marc thought Ethiopian eyes made women look timid and lovely, and made men look weak.

SNOW MAN

"These complaints are lies. You know that!" Marc stood. "I want an apology before consenting to teach that class again." He turned and walked out of the headmaster's office without being dismissed. It made him feel great, as if he were the protagonist of his own life story.

O

The students in 3B were still on strike at the end of the week, and Marc did his best to keep out of their sight. He stayed in the faculty room when not teaching other classes, spending his time reading old copies of *Time* magazine. None of the teachers, including the other Peace Corps volunteers, ever mentioned the strike. The volunteers stationed at the school were the Olivers, a married couple from Florida, who lived out near the school, and Helen Valentino, who had an apartment next to Marc's place.

The town was called Diredawa and it was built at the edge of the Ogaden. There was an old section which was all Ethiopian, mostly Somalis and Afars; the newer quarter is where the French had lived when they built the railway from Djibouti across the desert and up the escarpment to Addis Ababa in the Ethiopian highlands.

Marc never saw his students in town, and had no idea where they even lived. Unlike the other volunteers, he had never been asked to any of their homes for Injera and Wat. He now thought about this fact as he killed time in the faculty lounge awaiting the end of the period for his class who was on strike.

He did see the students from his class on campus, though, saw them as they passed along the open hallways, going to and coming from class to class. They watched him with their brown eyes and said nothing, did not even take a sudden breath, as was the Ethiopian custom when making a silent note of recognition.

He thought of them as brown rabbits, like the ones he hunted every fall back home on the farm. He liked to get close to the small animals, to see quivering brown bodies burrowing into the snow, and then he'd cock his .22 and fire quickly, catching the fleeing whitetail in mid-hop and splattering blood on the fresh whiteness.

Marc raised his hand and aimed his forefinger at his students lounging in the shade of trees beyond the makeshift basketball courts. He silently popped each one of them off with his make-believe pistol.

"Singh has had classes with 3B for the last week," Helen told him. "I just found out."

It was the second week of the strike when she came over to his apartment with the news. He was dressed in an Arab skirt and sitting on his bed chewing the Ethiopian drug chat. The chat gave him a low-grade high and a slight headache, but it was the only drug he could get at the edge of the desert.

"That bastard," Marc said.

"Singh is telling the students that they can't trust the Peace Corps volunteers. He's telling them we're not real teachers."

"That bastard," Marc said again.

"What are you going to do about it?" she demanded.

Marc shrugged. The chat had made him sleepy.

"We're all in trouble because of you," Helen told him. She was pacing the bedroom, moving in and out of the sunlight that was filtering through the metal shutters. The only way to keep the apartment cool was to lower the shutters during the long hot days.

"It's my class," he told her, grinning.

They had been lovers in training at UCLA, and during their first few months in Diredawa.

"Yes, but we're all Peace Corps!"

"Screw the Peace Corps."

"Marc, be serious!" She was in tears and held herself in an effort to try to keep from crying.

"I am serious. I don't give a damn."

"I'm calling Morgan in Addis. I'm getting him down here," she shouted back.

Marc wanted to pull away the mosquito netting from around his mattress and ask her climb into bed with him, but he didn't have the nerve.

"I don't want him here. I'll handle this," he told Helen.

"You just said you're not going to do anything. Look at you! Sitting here all day chewing chat!" She waved dismissively.

"Want some?" he asked, grinning through the thick netting.

Helen left him in his apartment. The chat had made him too listless to keep arguing, to go running after her, or to pull her into his bed and make love to her. Besides, he knew she would call Morgan. She was always trying to run his life.

Marc went to the airport to meet the Peace Corps director. It might have been more dramatic to let Brent Morgan find him, to track him down in one of the bars, to see him come in perspiring from the heat with his suit crumpled, his tie loosened. But then Helen would have had first chance at him, and Marc didn't want that.

The new airport terminal was under construction and there was no official place to wait for the planes. Marc parked the Peace Corps jeep in the shade of palm trees and watched the western horizon for the first glimpse of the afternoon flight from Addis.

He himself had first arrived in Diredawa via the day train. They had been in Ethiopia for two weeks, and all the volunteers were leaving Addis Ababa for their assignments. They were the only ones traveling by train.

The long rains had recently finished, and they could see the clouds rolling away from the city, leaving a very pure blue on the horizon. It was still chilly, but not the same piercing cold they had felt when they first arrived in the country. No one had told them that Ethiopia, or Africa, could be so cold. But they were going now, everyone said, to a beautiful climate, to warm country, to what Africa was really like.

It had been their first trip out of the city. They did not know anyone, and everything was new and strange. They sat together on metal benches and watched the plains stretch away towards the mountains as they dropped rapidly into the Great Rift Valley.

The land, after the long rains, was green and bright with yellow Meskal flowers. On the hillsides were mushroom-shaped tukul huts that sat as thick brown spots on the green hillside among the yellow flowers. There were few trees and they were tall, straight eucalyptus, which grew in tight bunches near the tukul compounds.

In the cold of early morning, Marc and the others saw Ethiopians going off to church. They moved in single file across the low hills towards the Coptic

SNOW MAN

Church that was set in a distant grove of eucalyptus. A few Ethiopians rode small, short-legged horses and mules, all brightly harnessed, and everyone on the soft hills wore the same white shammas dress and white jodhpurs.

Marc had never been so happy in his life.

Now, sitting in the shade, he saw the Ethiopian Airlines plane come into sight and, spotting it, he realized his eyes were blurry and that he was crying.

Marc wondered why he was crying, but quickly disregarded the tears; more and more often lately he was finding himself experiencing waves of unexplained emotion.

The Peace Corps director was the first off the plane. His coat and tie were already off and his collar was open. From the hatch of the small craft he waved, then bounded down the ramp, swinging his thick brown brief-case from one hand to the other. He came over to where Marc sat in the front seat of the open jeep.

Marc reached forward and turned over the engine.

"Tenastelign," Brent said, jumping into the front seat.

"Iski. Indemin aderu," Marc answered in Amharic as he spun the vehicle out of the dirt lot.

Brent grabbed the overhead frame as the small jeep swayed.

"Where do you want to go?" Marc shouted, glancing at the Peace Corps director.

"School...?"

Marc nodded, and turned the jeep abruptly in the direction of the secondary school.

Brent kept trying to make conversation, shouting to Marc over the roar of the engine, asking about the others, telling Marc news from Addis. Marc kept quiet.

He was being an asshole, he knew, but he couldn't help himself. He wanted Brent to have a hard time. It was crazy, but he couldn't stop.

When they reached the school, a few students were standing in the shade of the building, leaning up against the whitewashed wall and holding hands, as Ethiopian men did. Brent straightened his tie and put on his coat as they went to the headmaster's office.

Asfaw stood when they entered the office, and he came around his desk to shake hands with them both, gesturing for them to sit. Brent began to talk at once in his quick, nervous way, telling the school director why he had come to Diredawa, explaining that the Ministry of Education, as well as the Peace Corps, was concerned about the situation with Marc's class.

Asfaw listened hard, frowned, nodded, and agreed with everything, just as Marc had known he would. He nodded to Brent's vague generalizations about the headmaster supporting the faculty, and the ministry supporting both.

Marc wondered if Brent really believed all this bullshit.

"Of course, Mr. Marc has not been very strict with his pupils," Asfaw finally said, not responding to what Brent had said.

"Well, perhaps," Brent answered, gesturing with both hands as if he were trying to fashion some meaning of the situation from the hot desert breeze. "But that really isn't the question. I mean, in the larger sense." He pulled himself forward on the chair, straining to make himself clear. Suddenly he stopped when he noticed the film of confusion cross Asfaw's brown eyes, and asked, as if in defeat, "What do you think is the solution?"

"Mr. Marc is not very patient with our people. They are not used to his ways."

SNOW MAN

"There are certain universal ways of good behavior," Marc interrupted, raising his voice. "They deliberately did not take my test. That's an insult! And you! They know you're too afraid to do anything."

"All right! All right!" Brent spoke quickly, halting Marc.

Asfaw nodded, then began. "If you do not mind, Mr. Brent Morgan, I would like to say something." He waited for approval and, when Brent nodded, gestured with both hands.

"We have a strike in our school. Now this is something not unknown in our country; we have had many strikes. I even participated in strikes when I was a student. I only say this because I do not want Mr. Marc to feel that he is being subjected to prejudice by his students. We must not say 'Why do the students strike?' but rather 'How we can bring them back to school?'

"For you, Mr. Brent, you have said education is very important for Ethiopia. We must not allow ourselves to be so hindered by these petty problems, but look instead towards the larger issues. Do you not agree? Is this not what you have said?" Asfaw glanced at both of them, his face as alert as a startled rabbit's.

"Why, yes," Brent answered hesitantly. "We can certainly agree on that, but let's not dismiss some basic educational principles."

"And what is this?"

"That a teacher commands a position of authority within the community, and that the students respect this authority," the Peace Corps director answered quickly.

"A teacher, according to what I was told when I studied at Ohio University, achieves respect by proving to his students that he deserves it."

"Yes, this is very true, but that is difficult to achieve when your students know the teacher is alone in his authority," Morgan answered.

"Or when they would rather have merely a passing grade than an education," Marc butted in.

Asfaw smiled at Marc and said softly, like a caring parent, "To be truly honest, Mr. Marc, you, too, were probably concerned mostly with point averages, I believe the term is, when you were in school."

"Let us try," Brent began slowly, "to look at this issue again." He maintained a smile, adding, "We have been missing the main point. The strike must cease. The students must return to school. Now, what avenues are open to us?"

"But I have already made my decision!" Asfaw seemed surprised. He looked from face to face, his brown eyes widening.

"Certainly, but do you really think Marc should return to class without an apology from the students?"

"Oh, an apology is such a deceiving thing. Yes, perhaps in America, it is important, but you must remember that this is Ethiopia. We have our own ways, don't we, Mr. Marc?" The headmaster smiled, and then shrugged, as if it were all beyond his power.

"And in Ethiopia the mark of a clever man is his ability to outwit another person," Brent answered. "You must realize that if Marc returns to his classroom without an apology, or some form of disciplinary action taken against the students, he will be ineffective as a teacher."

The small headmaster leaned forward, putting his elbows on the desk. "I will first lecture the class, and tell them such a demonstration will not be tolerated. And Mr. Marc, if he wishes, can have them write an essay, which I will also see is done."

"And what happens the next time I give a test?"

"I should think, Mr. Marc, that as a clever person, you will review your teaching methods. I think you are aware of the fact that none of the other teachers, including those provided by the Peace Corps, are having difficulty with their classes."

"I have to maintain authority in my class."

"I think Marc is correct. We must be united on this point, take a firmer position," Brent added, making a fist with one hand.

"How might you handle it?" Asfaw asked Marc.

"Give them some manual work."

"They cannot do coolie work! They are students!"

"That's the point! They don't deserve to be students. A little taste of hard labor will prove my point. They won't mouth off again."

"It could be symbolic, I should think," Brent suggested. "You could arrange a clean-up of the compound, perhaps. It would be very instructive, really."

"Nothing less than three days. The first day it will be all a joke, but for the next two they'll work up a little sweat!" Marc smiled in anticipation.

"You are asking very much." Asfaw shook his head. "It is against their culture to work with their hands."

"I'm asking only enough to let me return to that classroom with the respect due to a teacher."

Brent kept glancing at Marc, who in turn, kept avoiding Morgan's eyes. He liked pushing the headmaster up against the wall.

"If you have them do at least three days of work around the school," Marc finally said, surrendering to the pressure of the moment, "I'll forget about the apology and go back to teaching."

Brent glanced quickly at Asfaw.

The headmaster hesitated.

He was thinking of what all this meant, Marc knew. He wasn't going to be outwitted by this *ferenji*.

"It is not completely satisfactory," the headmaster responded slowly, "but the students are not learning. I must put aside my personal feelings for the betterment of education in Ethiopia. I will call the boys together and explain the requirements." He smiled.

Brent slapped the knees of his lightweight suit and stood. He was beaming with relief even before he reached across the headmaster's desk and shook the small man's hand.

Marc drove back into town after he dropped Brent at the airport. He drove past the Ras Hotel where they went to swim, and where they ate lunch and dinner on Sunday, which was the cook's day off. He turned at the next block and went by the open-air theater, then slowly drove along the street which led to their apartments and the piazza.

The street was heavily shaded from trees and the houses with big compounds, which were built up to the sidewalks. It was one of the few towns in Ethiopia which resembled a city, with geometric streets, sidewalks, and traffic signs. But the bush was present. Somalis walked their camels along the side streets, herded small flocks of sheep and goats between the cars and up to the hills. Behind the taming influences of the foreign houses was Africa. Marc felt as if it were beating against his temples.

The apartment the Peace Corps had rented was not the type Marc had imagined he'd be living in. He'd had visions of mud huts, of seamy little villages along the Nile. But Diredawa was a small town with pavement, sidewalks, warm evenings filled with the smell of bougainvillea bushes, and bars with outside tables. It was, in all reality, a little French town tucked away in the African desert.

He parked the jeep in front of the apartment building, then walked over to Helen's apartment and, going onto the porch, knocked on the door. When

SNOW MAN

she didn't answer, he walked in and went into her bedroom, whispering her name. When she still didn't answer, he sat on the edge of her bed and watched her enjoying the nap she always took after her last afternoon classes.

She continued to sleep, breathing smoothly, her arms stretched out at her sides. He could see she was naked under the white cotton sheet, and he observed her in silence for a while before leaning forward and kissing her softly on the cheek. She stirred and blinked her eyes.

"What time is it?" she asked, waking and pulling the sheet closer.

"After three. Morgan's gone. I took him to the afternoon plane."

"Why didn't you wake me?" She turned onto her side.

"I didn't know you wanted to see him."

She shook her head, pressing her lips together.

"You want to have dinner?" he asked, ignoring her anger.

"I can't, I'm going out."

Marc watched her for a moment, and then said, "Do you want me to ask with whom?"

"I have a date with Tedesse. We're going to the movies."

"When did this start?" He kept his eyes on her.

"Nothing has started." She shifted again on the bed, sensing her own nakedness under the sheet.

"What about us?" he asked weakly, wanting her to feel his pain.

"Marc, I have no idea what our relationship is, not from one moment to the next." She was staring at him. "Sometimes, you're great. You can't do enough for me. The next day, you know, you barely say hello. What do you expect?" Her eyes glistened.

"The school's bugging me, that's all. You know that. Can't you understand, for Christ's sake?"

"There's nothing wrong with the school," she answered. "You've created half the problems yourself." She had pulled herself up and was now wide awake.

"And you top it off by dating some Ethiopian!"

"Marc, quit all this self-pity. It's very unattractive."

"I wanted to go to the movies."

"Then go!"

"Sure, and have you there with Tedesse?"

"Do what you want." She turned her face toward the whitewashed bedroom wall. "Now please leave. I want to get some sleep."

"Are you in love with him?"

"I don't want to talk about it."

"I need to know."

"Marc, don't badger me."

He slammed the apartment door as he left and a Somali knife on the living room wall fell down with a crash.

The students began to move rock on Monday. Marc walked out to the field behind the school and watched them work. It was malicious of him, he knew, but he enjoyed it.

He stood on a mound overlooking the work area and even though he did not speak, he knew they were aware of him. He saw them glancing at him, whispering among themselves.

They continued to work and after a few minutes, he turned and started back toward the school. It was almost two o'clock, time for his afternoon classes.

Just then the first stone flew over his head. Marc didn't react to it; in fact he wasn't even sure where it came from. Then the second one clipped

SNOW MAN

his shoulder, and the next hit him squarely in the back. He wheeled about, ducked one that had been aimed directly at his head, and started back toward the students.

There were no obvious attackers, and he saw no upraised arms—everyone was working as docilely as before. He stopped and cursed them, but no one looked his way or offered satisfying smirks on their brown faces.

He stayed away from the work site for the next two days, but watched them from the second floor corridor; he made sure they saw him, standing there, grinning, while they sweated under the hot sun.

On Thursday morning class was returned to his oversight. He decided to begin teaching immediately, rather than to dawdle on their punishment or the rock tossing. He planned to teach just as Mr. Singh, the Indian, did, with no class discussion, nothing but note taking. He would fill the blackboard and let them copy down the facts. No more following questions where they led, no more trying to make his classroom exciting and interesting; he didn't care if they learned anything more than what they could memorize.

He rode his bike out to school early, getting there before the students or the other teachers, and went upstairs to the faculty room to wait for the first bell.

A few of the teachers said hello as they arrived, but when Helen arrived on her bike shortly after seven, she asked what was wrong with their students.

Marc didn't know what she was talking about, so followed Helen to the front windows and watched the compound.

The students were too quiet, she told him. Something was wrong.

Marc stepped onto the breezeway and looked up at the three stories of classrooms. The railings were crowded. The students stood quietly, waiting and watching. A few, mostly girls from the lower grades, were playing on the basketball court, but all the others in the compound were clustered in small groups of three or four. There was a little talking, but only in whispers. Gradually they all turned and noticed Marc; they watched him without expression, their soft brown eyes telling him nothing.

He stepped back into the faculty room.

The sports master, an Ethiopian, had just come in. He scanned the teachers until he spotted Marc, and came directly to him.

He had once played football for the country's national team and had a small, well-built body. Around his neck a whistle dangled from a cord. The man was sweating.

"We're having a strike," he told Marc. "Asfaw has sent for the army."

As he spoke, two Land Rovers swung into the compound and a half-dozen soldiers tumbled out. The students' reaction was immediate. The passive, quiet assembly rose up clamoring. Those students on the three tiers of the breezeway began to beat the iron railing. Girls began the strange high shrills they usually saved for funerals. And then rocks began to fly.

The windows of the Land Rovers were broken first. An officer was caught halfway between the school and the Rovers; he hesitated, not sure whether to keep going, or to rejoin his men.

And then the barrage escalated. From all sides, from everywhere, came the stones and rocks. One solider was hit hard, faltered, and grabbed his buddy. From the second floor faculty room, Marc could see the blood on the man's face.

The officer ran back to the Land Rover and grabbed his Uzi. Spinning around, he opened fired on the students, spraying them with a quick burst of bullets. The small bodies of boys and girls bounced backwards and smashed up against the whitewashed walls of the school.

SNOW MAN

Time **magazine was** sold at a barber shop near the apartment. The barber saved Marc a copy when it came in on the Friday plane and he picked it up on Saturday, the day after the shooting at school, to read in the Ras Makonnen Bar. There were soldiers in the piazza, loitering in the big square facing the bar.

Occasionally a jeep would careen through the open square, its tires squealing. There were no students in the piazza, but periodically Marc heard gunfire coming from across the gully. He wondered if it had to do with the students. Were they catching more of them, chasing them down in the dark alley of the Moslem section? He smiled, thinking that this might be happening while he enjoyed a peaceful breakfast.

He ordered orange juice, pastry, and opened *Time*, flipping rapidly through the pages for articles about the Midwest.

There had been another ice storm in Chicago, he read, that had closed down O'Hare Airport, and caused a forty-five-car pile-up on I-94. Marc read the article twice, lingering over familiar names and the details of the storm.

He kept smiling, thinking of home, wishing he were there for the storm. He imagined what his Michigan town might have looked like, buried deep in ice and snow. He could feel the sharp pain of the wind on his cheeks, feel the biting cold. He looked up and stared through the thick, bright, lush bougainvillea bushes.

There were tears in his eyes, cold tears on his face, but he didn't know that he was crying.

He wiped his face with the small, waxy paper napkin, and looked out at the bright square; the loitering soldiers had found shade beneath several false banana trees and had abandoned their rifles, leaving them propped against the base of a tree. He wondered why the soldiers weren't cold.

He thought again of the killings at the school, how the officer with the Uzi had killed eight in the first burst of gunfire.

Helen had begun to scream. She was holding her ears, trying not to hear the students' cries, but still she couldn't look away from the slaughter.

He couldn't, either. Several of his students, long, lanky kids, jumped and jerked when they were hit. The bullets tossed them around, made them hop and dance, before slamming the children back against the whitewashed walls of the school where they splattered like eggs, breaking bright red yolks.

Helen wouldn't stop screaming, even after silence fell in the school yard, after the officer stopped firing, after the students who were still alive scattered.

She was standing at the windows, screaming. Marc couldn't go to her; he couldn't figure out how to walk. Mr. Singh finally seized her, pulled her away from the window as the headmaster began yelling in Amharic at the soldiers.

Marc walked out the door then, and down the stairs. He walked straight by the soldiers as if what had happened meant nothing to him. He walked away from the school, went across the open brush land to the dry gully river, which he knew he could follow into town. From the river bed, he heard the sounds of an ambulance coming out from the French hospital.

He walked to his apartment and locked himself inside, then crawled into bed and slept through the heat of the day. Helen came to get him after dark. She had told him martial law had been proclaimed and that she and the Olivers were leaving, going up to Addis Ababa on the night train. It was no longer safe in town, she told him. But he wouldn't leave, he told her, he wouldn't let the students drive him out of Diredawa.

Now Marc stood and walked out of the cafe bar and into the piazza. It was empty except for the soldiers. He wondered where everyone had gone, why no one was on the streets. He was lonely, knowing that he was the only Peace Corps volunteer in Diredawa, and perhaps the only white man left in town.

But it wasn't true. There were French doctors at the hospital, missionaries from the Sudan Interior Mission, and French workers with the railway. Tourists. Yes, the desert town was full of white people.

Still he hurried, cut across the open square, going home, back to this apartment where, behind locked doors, he'd be safe until the Peace Corps staff came to get him. They wouldn't leave him alone, he knew. This was a mistake, he thought at the same moment as he crossed the empty street. He shouldn't have left his apartment and taken a chance on the streets. There might be students around.

He broke into a run.

Just then a rock hit him on the side of the head and bounced off like a misplayed golf shot. He stumbled forward, but knew he was okay. It had only been a rock. They couldn't kill him with rocks; he was too tough, too much of an American. These were just people in some godawful backward third world country, half starving to death every few years.

He pulled his hand away from the side of his face and saw that his fingers were bright with blood.

"Shit!" he said, thinking of the mess that would surely stain his clothes and the fact that he hated the smell of blood. He stumbled forward, finding his feet, knowing he had to keep running. They couldn't catch him in the middle of the street.

A half-dozen soldiers were still loitering by the entrance of the movie theater, less than a dozen yards from him. He waved to get their attention and shouted out in Amharic as another rock hit him in the mouth.

He tumbled over onto his back and rolled in the dirt, coughing up pieces of his teeth and globs of blood and spit. Marc raised his hand and tried to shout at the soldiers. Why weren't they helping him?

He crawled forward in the direction of his apartment, thinking only that if he could get to the gate and behind the iron fence, he would be safe.

He coughed up more blood and in his tears and pain knew he had to run, that they might swarm out of the streets, or from wherever they were hiding deep in the palm-lined street, and seize him, take him back into the Old City, where it was another tribal law that would deal with him. An eye for an eye.

He got to his feet and ran.

There were more rocks, coming from the right and left, showering him, bashing his head and knocking him over once more. He fell forward, into the gutter, and smashed his head against the concrete.

He knew that if he stopped he would be dead. His only hope was to reach the iron gates. Gebra, his *zebagna*, would keep out the crowd of students.

Why weren't the soldiers helping him? They hadn't hesitated to shoot when they were pelted; why couldn't they protect him?

He burst through the metal compound gate, startling Gebra. Marc shouted at him to bolt the compound door, as it was the guard's job to protect him now.

He ran up the stairs to the second floor apartment and slammed the back door, locking it behind him. Running from room to room, he pulled the wide cords that dropped the heavy old metal shutters, blocking out the sunlight and sealing the apartment in a shadowy dark.

SNOW MAN

He fell in a corner, sweating from fear and exhaustion. Then he reached up and touched his forehead, felt for the rock bruise. When he took away his hand, he couldn't see his bloody fingers in the darkened room.

His hands were shaking. And he was freezing. He crept across the floor, going toward the bed, keeping himself below the windows, afraid the students might figure out which ones were his. The shutters were metal, but he couldn't be too careful, he told himself.

His whole body was trembling. It was funny, he thought. How could he be so cold in the middle of Africa? At the edge of the desert?

He thought of when he was in school, waiting beside the road for the school bus and standing in the freezing cold. He shivered, and crawled under the mosquito netting, covering himself with the sheets. He would be okay soon, once he was warm. Why didn't he have a blanket? he wondered.

He watched the slanting sunlight filter through the metal window shades and stir the dust off the desert. It lit the room with shafts that looked like prison bars. He felt his face and wondered why there was no blood. He waited for the rocks to begin again. He thought about waking in the warmth and comfort of his farmhouse in Michigan, where he knew everyone and everything, where he was safe, and no one was different. He shivered, freezing from the cold. He opened his eyes again and saw that it had begun to snow in Africa. The flakes falling through the sunlight filtered into the room.

He would be all right, he knew. He understood cold weather and deep snow. Ethiopians knew nothing of snow. He smiled, thinking: let them try to shovel snow! They'd need him. Snow was part of his heritage. He would teach the students how to make a snow man, he thought with a grin, and realized that everything was going to be okay. He was in the Peace Corps, and he had a job to do.

THE CRAZY CHINAMAN

Afterwards Pete wished they had never said anything to him, but of course by then it was too late. They had been pitching pennies at the base of the water tower when he came up, and Joe, the bigger of the two, looked around and said,

"Hi, Chinaman! Why aren't you smiling?"

Pete, the other kid, who was skinnier than the first caddy and smaller, laughed. It was a big joke among the kids.

"Why do you always call me a Chinaman?" the man asked. "I am a Filipino. Before the war, my family members were important people."

As he spoke, his small body trembled. He was in his late twenties, but the exact year was hard to determine, for his face was boyishly soft looking and the color of copper.

The two boys stared at him and then the older one said, laughing, "Well, if you're such a big shot in the Philippines why don't you go home, 'cause you ain't nobody here."

The caddy was right. The Filipino wasn't anyone. He worked at the club too, during the summer months when he was out of college, in the kitchen at night cleaning the dishes and stoves.

The boys had seen him many times, just as they did today, walking alone in the late afternoon. He was always dressed in white, and always walked slowly with his hands stuck in his back pockets, his face passive and his eyes down.

As the caddies kept pitching, the Filipino came over and stood for a moment, watching. Then he said to Joe, "What have I done to hurt you?"

The boy kept pitching and answered without looking at the man.

"You ain't done nothing. What are you asking a screwy question like that for?"

"Because you, more than any caddy, want to hurt me."

"You're crazy," Joe said. He had lost four successive times while lagging and, turning to the Filipino, added, "Come on, Chinaman, leave me alone. You're bringing me bad luck."

"I am not Chinese. I am a Filipino. Now you tell me why you dislike me."

"Okay, Chinaman; I'll tell you. My old man was getting your job, see, but the manager said, 'No we got to save it for our little Filipino.' Now my old man ain't got no fuckin' job 'count of you."

The Filipino was silent for a moment. He stood still, his body leaning forward, staring at the ground, his hands still stuck in his back pockets. Then he said, "That is the reason?"

"Why don't you stay in your own fuckin' country?"

The Filipino did not reply, but he kept looking at the young boy. His face stayed passive. His eyes, which were small and dark, blurred briefly with tears. Then he said to the caddy, almost apologetically, "You tell your father

118

he can take my job. I am finished with it." He turned away from the caddies and walked toward the main road of the country club.

The caddies did not say anything until he was out of hearing range.

"Hey, Joe," the smaller boy asked, "what's the matter with him?"

"How in the fuck should I know? That Chinaman is crazy anyway. Come on, pitch!"

The Filipino walked all the way down to the main road, then turned and came back, and began to climb the water tower. It was only then that the two caddies again paid attention to him.

"Hey Chinaman, whatcha doing?" Joe asked. He had stopped lagging to watch the Filipino. The man did not answer, but kept climbing, one rung at a time.

Down below, the smaller caddy asked, "What's he gonna do, Joe?"

"How the fuck should I know?" Then to the Filipino he shouted, "Hey, Chinaman, you're going to kill yourself."

"I betcha he's gonna jump, Joe. I betcha!"

"Shut the shit up, will ya? He ain't gonna jump. Come on, pitch."

"No, I wanta see." The boy moved back from the base of the tower for a better view.

The Filipino had reached the top leg and pulled himself through the small hole in the platform that surrounded the white water tank. He stood up and looked over the rail of the hundred-foot-high tower.

The caddies noticed the sharp contrast his dark face and hands made against his white clothes and the white tank. It was when he began to walk slowly around the tank, looking out into the distance, that Joe said, "I told you he was just lookin' around. Come on, let's go home."

"I ain't goin' anywhere, Joe, until I see if he's gonna jump."

"What difference is it of yours if some crazy Chinaman jumps? He ain't your friend."

"He'll kill himself."

"What the fuck do you care?"

The Filipino had come back around to their side of the tower and was standing directly above them.

"Hey Chinaman!" Joe yelled to him. "What are you gonna do—jump?"

The Filipino did not answer. He was leaning against the railing, his face turned upward. Everything was white, the clouds, the tank, his clothes. His tanned face and hands were the only dark splotches in the picture. Slowly he swung his left leg, then his right leg, over the railing so that both caddies could see his legs dangling over the side.

"I told you, Joe; I told you he'd jump!" Pete was yelling, not looking away from the figure perched on the high rail. "It's your damn fault, Joe; it's your goddam fault."

"It ain't my fuckin' fault!"

"You called him a Chinaman."

"So did you, so did everyone. Don't go blaming me, man."

"Yeah, but you started it. Come on, we got to get somebody."

"Hold it; we ain't gettin' no help," Joe answered. "That's what the fuckin' Chinaman wants. As soon as we leave he'll come down. We'll get fired if we bring everyone running down here and the Chinaman is alive. That fucker!"

"You think so, Joe?"

Joe did not answer, but called out to the Filipino, "All right, Chinaman, jump. I'll catch you. Come on. What's the matter, Chinaman, you scared?" He held out his arms.

THE CRAZY CHINAMAN

It was then, while Joe was holding out his arms, that the figure pushed itself off, and the black and part of the white were ripped from the picture, falling gracefully, slowly, arms and legs outstretched.

For a moment both caddies were stunned, then Pete jumped away and ran. It was Joe who couldn't move. His hands outstretched, he kept waiting for the falling white figure. Then, at the last moment, he turned away, frightened to look, as the body hit the ground, bounced up again higher than him, and hit a second time, jerked once, then lay still.

Pete was screaming: "I told you he'd jump! I told you!"

Joe stared at the body, at the way the blood pumped from the Filipino's gaping mouth, and then he ran to the man, yelling at him, "Why did you jump? Why did you jump, you crazy Chinaman?"

WINTER MORNING

It was the first Saturday after his eighth birthday. He was leaning over the top section of the cow barn door, shooting his new pump-gun at tin cans in the barnyard, and watching the sun clear the rows of corn stubs on the horizon, when the first cry of the cow came down to him on the morning breeze.

At first he was not sure of the sound; there was no other noise except the occasional shuffling of animals in their stalls and the clatter of the milking machine as his father moved it from cow to cow. But then the cry came again, low and bleating, each utterance complete and final, shattering the silence. He turned to his father, who had heard the cry and paused, waiting for the repetition of the sound.

"Its old man Fisher's cow," he said, anticipating the question. "She must be calving."

The boy looked out over the half door in the direction of the cries. He could see the dark roof of Fischer's barn over the tops of the corn stubs. He watched the rooftop as if waiting for a sign, and listened closely to the cries. He stood that way until his father was finished his work.

They took the milk cans over to the milk house. The wind was stronger now; it blew down on the boy, cutting his thin face, bringing tears to his eyes.

"She really seems in trouble," this father said, coming out of the milk house and looking in the direction of Fisher's farm. "Maybe we'll drive up there a little later. What do you think, boy?" He rubbed his hand roughly, playfully, across the top of his son's head, and walked past him toward the house.

The boy watched his father walk slowly up the hill. Then, cradling the pump-gun in his arms, he turned and headed toward the small creek behind the barn. It wasn't much of a creek, just a dried-up hollow that cut across the lower section of their land. Most of the year it was dry, but in April, when the snow melted and the spring rains started, it caught and carried off the water that washed down the hill. Now, in November, it was filled with matted leaves and driftwood.

The boy moved up the creek to a clump of tall pines that grew along the bank. He could see sparrows clustered in the branches, looking, from his distance, like tiny brown balls of cotton. Then he began to shoot. At first he couldn't hit any; they flew off in crazy circles as the pellets whizzed past them. He was just growing tired of the game when a pellet caught a bird, sent it tumbling through the bare branches onto the creek bank, among the dry leaves.

Holding his gun majestically, glorying in his kill, the boy walked over to it. The bird flipped convulsively as its life drained out into the leaves. Then it lay still, panting, blood trickling down its beak. It stretched its ruffled neck once, gasped for air, and died. The boy was nauseated at the sight. Straightening up, he glanced around quickly to see if anyone had been watching. With his left foot he kicked leaves up over the bird; then he turned and walked swiftly up the hollow back to the barn.

His father was waiting at the barn door and the boy wondered if he knew.

"I'm going up to see Fisher's cow," his father said. "If you want to come, put your gun inside. I'll wait for you in the truck."

The boy ran to the house and put his gun on the floor just inside the back door. Then he went down to the chicken coop, where the truck was parked, and climbed up beside his father.

Fisher's farm was two miles away, a group of wooden buildings isolated in the center of flat corn land. When his father turned the truck off the highway and up the dirt road, the boy could see the cars and trucks of other farmers parked in the yard between the house and the barn.

His dad parked the truck and, climbing out, walked across to the farmers grouped around the barn door. The boy hurried after, grabbing his father by the trouser pocket.

The farmers turned to look as the two approached, and clearing apart, let them pass inside the circle. The cow was a big brown Swiss. She stood secure in a stanchion, her four legs loosely restrained with rope. The boy could see Bill Jerkin's oldest son, Clifford, standing directly behind the cow. A second later he realized that Clifford's hand and arm were stuck up inside the animal.

"Do you feel anything?" a small, stout man asked.

The boy suddenly felt sick and he clutched his stomach, breathing deeply to ward off the squeamish feeling.

"Can you feel the head?" the stout man asked. His face was huge, with heavy rolls of skin disappearing into his collar. He looked from the cow to the farmers who formed the circle. "My hands are just too damn big," he said, almost apologizing, "I can't get in there."

"Old Clifford's doing all right, Doc," one of the men said. "But then, he's had lots of practice." The men laughed, and the one who had made the joke grinned happily with tobacco-stained teeth.

"Well, it ain't never felt like this before," Clifford answered, picking the cigarette from between his lips. They laughed again and the boy glanced curiously at their faces, then at his father, who was staring at the cow.

"What's the matter with her Doc?" his father asked.

"It's the calf, Mr. Warren; he's setting wrong. She can't drop him."

The cow cried out again, pulling at the ropes, and swung her head around to look at Clifford. Her eyes were brown and wild, and the boy thought he could see the hurt in them. She cried out again, extending her neck in the stanchion, pushing the pain out as far as she could.

"Where's Fisher?" his father asked.

"He's up at the house," the vet answered. "He doesn't want me to do anything, Mr. Warren. When he called me over this morning he said I couldn't touch her; he just wanted me to tell him what the matter was. Maybe you might go talk with him and see if he'll let me work on her. She'll die, otherwise." He watched the boy's father through small, sad eyes.

"Maybe Fisher is scared you'll do the same thing to the cow as that doctor did to his wife," one of the farmers said. "He ain't never got over that."

"Well, I'll go talk to him anyway, Doc. Maybe I can reason with him."

WINTER MORNING

His father dropped a hand gently on the boy's shoulder and directed him to follow. They walked silently up the hill toward the barren farmhouse that stood frozen against the November winds. The boy listened closely to the sound of their feet on the hard ground, and when they stepped up onto the porch, the hollow noise their shoes made. His dad knocked on the broken screen door and stood back, patiently waiting for it to open.

The boy drew his coat tighter around him and faced away from the wind. It was colder now. The sun had slid behind snow clouds and as he looked back across the yard he saw the shadow descend on the cow and men. It came first across the corn fields, then the trees and the yard, engulfing them, and then ran up the side of the barn and out of sight.

The door of the house opened slightly and his father spoke swiftly to the dark face that appeared in the small opening.

"Morning, Sadie. I'd like to see Mr. Fisher, if he isn't busy."

The door opened slowly, cautiously, and his father pulled back the broken screen door and stepped into the house.

It was dark in the room and the boy caught the strong animal odors. As his eyes adjusted to the darkness, he noticed they were in the kitchen and it had been a black woman who had opened the door.

"The old man is in the front room," she said, walking away from them. Her voice flowed like music and the boy was startled by the sound of it. He had never heard a woman's face sound so lovely.

A chicken flew up from the floor and landed on the table. It walked confidently across piles of dirty dishes until the woman grabbed a broom and slapped the bird off the table.

"Place full of damn animals," she muttered, kicking at a small dog lying under the sink. She turned around and looked at the boy and his father. "I told you he's in the front room." She tried to snap out the words, but they came through her thick lips mellowed and lyrical.

"Thanks, Sadie," his dad answered, nodding and smiling. "We'll be out of your way in a minute."

Taking the boy's hand, his father started down the long dark hall toward the front room.

Unlike the kitchen, the front room was large and well lighted by two windows which looked out on the barn. There were a few pieces of furniture scattered around. In the center of the room sat Fisher, in an old rocking chair. He was a small man with a tiny head resting uncertainly on a long neck. The blue working overalls hung loosely on his body.

"Morning, Mr. Fisher," his father said as they entered.

Fisher glanced up curiously and studied them; then he motioned toward two chairs.

"Morning, Warren," he said, after they had settled themselves. His voice was brittle and birdlike. They were quiet again. The boy, sitting close to his father, watched the old man's hollow cheeks move in and out slowly, like a shrunken bellows.

"How about a drink?" Fisher asked his dad, rocking back and forth as he spoke.

"Oh, no, sir," his father answered, waving off the suggestion.

Fisher nodded, then tilted his head back and shouted.

"Sadie...Sadie...come here." He settled back into the rocker. "That damn woman," he muttered. "Ain't worth the money I give her."

Heavy footsteps came shuffling down the hall and the bulky form of Sadie appeared in the doorway.

"What the hell you want?"

WINTER MORNING

"Bring me the bottle, the good stuff, and some cups." He straightened up a little in the chair and glared at her. "And hurry up about it."

She stood regarding him with flashing eyes, then, turning, she said softly, as if only to reassure herself, "I ain't no nigger slave."

"The vet wants to know about the cow, Mr. Fisher," his father said, after the woman had left.

"The vet knows what I want done," Fisher answered back. "I ain't going to be telling him all day."

"What's that?"

"Nothing." He snapped the word out.

"She'll die. Have you heard her out there?" His dad's voice rose as he pointed toward the barn.

Fisher pulled himself painfully from the chair and walked to the window.

"That cow has been giving me nothing but trouble since I got her. Now she's got a calf stuck up inside her all wrong. Well, let her die; let her die." He turned around and looked at the boy and his father. "Look at them," he said, spitting out the words and pointing toward the barn. "All of them out there waiting to violate that goddamn cow. Well, let them wait till they freeze up like corn stubs; they won't touch her." He walked slowly back from the window and sank exhaustedly into the rocker.

Sadie came back into the room carrying the bottle and two cups.

"Do you want one for the boy?" she asked.

"No," Fisher answered quickly. "He'll have enough time for that without my encouragement."

The woman handed his father the cup, filled it half way, then walked over to the old man. Holding the cup herself, she filled it full and gave it to him.

"You're going to lose both the cow and calf," his father said again to Fisher, "if you don't let the vet..."

"That fat old slop," the farmer said. "Him and his dirty hands. I'd rather have her die than let him at her." He pulled himself up in the chair. "She wouldn't die anyway," he added with conviction.

"All right; I'll tell the vet." His dad stood up and set the cup of whiskey down on the chair.

"I'll tell him myself," Fischer interjected, starting to rise.

"No, you ain't," Sadie called from the hallway entrance. "You ain't leaving that chair." She pointed at him to remain seated.

"I'll do what I damn please," he shouted back, his weak voice betraying him.

"I ain't having you go out there and die of cold. As long as I'm working here, trying to keep you alive, you'll listen to me." She stood big and motionless in the entryway.

Fisher watched her for a moment.

"Is this the way you'll beat me...waiting till I'm too crippled to fight back? After all these years of living off me. I should have thrown you out with that son of yours long ago." He looked at the boy and his father. "Take pity on someone and they'll stay around long enough to humiliate you for it. Remember that, boy! Don't take pity on any of the sons of bitches." He sat quiet then, his small hands grabbing the arms of the rocker in desperate determination.

The boy and his father followed the woman down the hall and back into the kitchen. When his father went to open the door the woman spoke.

"You mustn't mind the old man; he ain't feeling well."

His father nodded and said he understood, then opened the door. It was still cold and the cry of the cow hit the boy again.

WINTER MORNING

They walked down to the group of men in silence and when they reached him his father slackened off his pace and stopped.

"Fisher said to leave the cow alone," his father told them, raising his voice so they could all hear. "He said he doesn't want the cow violated."

"She'll die," the vet stated flatly, and the boy noticed the corners of his small eyes sparkle with tears.

"The old man's crazy," Clifford butted in. He had his arm out of the cow and the boy could see traces of dried blood up on his elbow, where he had missed while cleaning himself. "Let's go ahead and turn the calf around."

"No," the vet answered, turning slowly and gathering his equipment. "We'll leave her alone. It's Fisher's cow."

"Come on, son." His father touched the boy's head. "There isn't anything we can do here."

The boy followed his father up to the truck, looking back only once at the cow. She was standing quietly in the stanchion, her belly swollen, let alone to die.

When they reached home the boy left his father and ran across the yard to the barn where he picked up a shovel. Then he walked down to the hollow. He had forgotten exactly where the bird was buried and it took a few minutes of shifting leaves carefully before he found it again. He dug a hole, then lifted the still bird with the shovel and dropped it in. He refilled the hole with earth and covered the spot over with leaves. He wanted to do it thoroughly, completely, so that tomorrow he would not know where the hole was located.

When he had finished he ran back to the barn and replaced the shovel, wiping off the dirt so there would be no trace of digging. He suddenly felt very relieved, and sighing deeply, he started to walk back up to the house. It was then that he noticed the cow had stopped crying. The sound had been there in the wind, strong and constant as it had been since he first heard it, and now it had stopped. He glanced around, looked back at the horizon as if for a sign, an explanation of all the things he didn't understand, but there was only silence and the cold November wind.

He stepped slowly up onto the back porch of his house as the sun broke through the clouds. It was high in the sky now, and brighter than it had been that morning. He wished, standing alone on the porch and remembering the morning, that he had not begun the day.

A GAME IN THE SUN

Betsy was not allowed to play croquet with her husband and the Reverend, so she sat in the shade of the trees at the top of the mound. The mound overlooked a lush African rainforest, which grew thick and dense to the edges of the mission compound. The view was compelling and frightening to Betsy. The close, steamy jungle made her feel insignificant, and as she half listened to Mrs. Shaw's chatter, she watched the bush as if it were alive.

The Reverend and Mrs. Shaw had started their mission twenty years before. Landscaping woods near a village of mud and cattle-dung huts, they cut into the underbrush, leaving only the ancient acacias and gum trees for shade, and planting lawns and gardens. The African laborers had instructions to keep the lawns neatly trimmed during the rainy season, well-watered the remainder of the year.

The Shaws had been the only white people in the district until Betsy and her husband arrived with the Peace Corps to teach in the government school in the fall of 1970. It was their second year in-country, and as Betsy had calculated that morning, she had only eighteen more Sundays left in Africa.

"You really won't know Africa for ten years. It takes that long to get a feel of the land," the Reverend had said when he first dropped by to say hello and welcome them to the village. He had crowded himself into their doll-like house, held on to his farmer's straw hat, and looked with alarm about the inadequate place. "The Peace Corps is not giving you much cooperation, are they?" He shook his head, frowning over the lack of facilities.

He was a big, fleshy man, dressed in worn jeans, a tight-fitting plaid shirt, and heavy-duty boots. His face was burned from the long self-appointed days in the African sun. Only his forehead, protected by the straw hat, was chalky. His eyes were tiny and squinted against the sun. Dark lines clustered at their corners. The rest of his face was soft and slightly moist. He kept a white handkerchief folded in the palm of his hand and continually wiped the running sweat off his red cheeks, as if he were polishing them.

"Look, kids, I want ya to come to our place anytime. Anytime. Come tomorrow for lunch, a game of croquet." He glanced again about the house. "You're going to need all the comforts of home you can get. But with the help of God...with the help of Our Lord."

O

Before the game, the Shaws' houseboys, barefoot and in starched white uniforms, moved like tropical birds among them, serving iced tea. The two men talked about the week, the news from the school and mission, while Mrs. Shaw took Betsy through the gardens, the beds of exotic flowers that grew in the heat and humidity, brilliant and thick, and mapped out in the clearing of the African jungle like a formal English garden.

A GAME IN THE SUN

Mrs. Shaw wore gloves and with a horticulturist's eye clipped flowers and presented them to Betsy. The older woman was concerned about the Peace Corps couple living in the village, in a mud-and-dung house, among the Africans. The flowers were to pretty up Betsy's life, she told her.

Mrs. Shaw lay her scissors on the lawn table and pulled off her gloves, then she rubbed baby lotion thoroughly into her hands. The scent was stronger than the flowers and reminded Betsy of the home where she'd grown up.

"I learned years ago that baby lotion was the answer. Just ordinary baby lotion keeps me just fine," Mrs. Shaw smiled. "This weather is so cruel on people, women especially."

Unlike her husband, Mrs. Shaw looked as if she had never been in the sun. Her skin was milky under the protection of a wide-brimmed bonnet, and deep in its shadows her eyes flashed like a cornered animal's. "After a while you learn these little hints. It takes time, of course, but with the help of God." Her voice bore inward like a drill.

Betsy was no longer listening. She had closed her eyes and was leaning back in the lawn chair, resting. She knew she must not begin to cry in front of these people. She must not be vulnerable. There were, after all, only eighteen Sundays left. She had gone that morning into the bedroom, to the homemade calendar behind the door, and crossed off another day. Briefly she had felt lighthearted, but that exhilaration had slipped away in the hot room, in the heat of the day. Betsy sighed and then, unexpectedly, shivered, and began to cry.

"Are you all right, dear?" Mrs. Shaw reached over. Betsy could feel the damp fingers, the baby lotion sticky on her own arm.

"Yes. It's nothing. I'm fine." She gathered herself together, managed a thin smile, blinked away a rush of tears, and said quickly, shading her eyes and looking over the lawns, "Are they finished?"

"You've been remembering your quinine, haven't you, dear?"

"Oh, of course. It's nothing really, Mrs. Shaw. We'll be into the rainy season soon. Maybe I'm feeling the first chills. You know how cold it suddenly seems?" She talked rapidly to keep herself from screaming.

"Yes, perhaps even in the hot sun one can feel chilled." And Mrs. Shaw let the subject slip away, as if it were an error.

On the lawns before them the game was drawing to a close. The Reverend was ahead as always, banging his mallet against the wooden ball, moving quickly from one wicket to the next, looking awkward, too huge for the lawn game.

"I've gotcha, Jesse. I've gotcha again." His voice was buoyant.

Betsy's husband, behind him, struggling, hit the ball. It bounced erratically across the grass. Thin and undernourished by comparison, Jesse followed Reverend Shaw. He had lost weight in Africa and now his trousers were baggy. He laughed at his miscalculations, amused by his inability. Betsy watched him with eyes bled of color, gray and watery, studied him with detachment, as if watching a stranger. Who was this person she married, she wondered?

The game was over. They came to her through the heat, haze, and sun, their bodies shimmery. Maybe she *was* sick, she thought. Tentatively she touched herself, felt the clammy skin of her forearm. Her fingers were cold, and around her the lawns and gardens were airless.

"Had enough for one day, boys?" Mrs. Shaw chirped. "I'll have lunch ready in minutes." She clapped once, like a single piano note, and the houseboys stepped from the shadows and carried food to them on the lawn.

"How's the little lady?" the Reverend asked and spread himself on the lounge chair beside Betsy. "You're lookin' peaked, dear."

A GAME IN THE SUN

"I was just saying so myself, Walter. Betsy doesn't look at all well. Don't you agree, Jesse?"

They wouldn't let her alone. All of them gauged her with worried looks. Her husband stared. His mouth flopped open. He touched her and she jerked away, furious at his inability to win at croquet, to do anything right with his life. How could she have not known he was so incompetent?

"Betsy, why don't you lie down a while, until the day cools?" Mrs. Shaw was at her side.

Betsy had to get away from these people. She did not know them. And these lawns, the enclosing rain forest, had not happened to her. She would go somewhere cool, somewhere out of the heat. She could hardly breathe. Why won't it rain? The smell of baby lotion again and the touch of the woman's warm flesh.

She let herself be guided from the hot gardens into the house, where curtains were drawn and there was a bit of air. The bedclothes were soft silk, not the coarse linen from the village. They let her sleep.

The rains began the next day. Standing at the windows of the third form, Betsy watched puddles form on the dry football field. She reached out the window, and the cool water soaked her arm. She smiled for the first time in weeks.

That afternoon Betsy was going to tell Jesse she wanted a divorce, but he had come home after school—wet and muddy into the tiny house—said something silly about her hair, something she knew was meant to cheer her up, and she had gone to the bedroom, slammed the door, and cried herself to sleep.

Their marriage was her mistake. She had done it in a rush in the weeks after commencement to keep Jesse from being drafted, from keeping herself from having to go back home after school without a job, without a future, and nothing more in her life to cling onto than a college degree. It was her idea, too, to join the Peace Corps, to leave the country, to escape her life, to hide away in Africa. It was all her own fault. She should have realized that when she couldn't even find the country they were being sent to on a map of Africa.

It was raining again when she woke. The rain pounded on the tin roof, deafeningly. She jerked the sheets around her without getting up, and slept. When she woke again, it was dark; Jesse had lit the lamp and made her soup.

"You'll feel better after this." Jesse held up the cup as if it were a present. She took the soup without speaking, without looking at him. The cup in her fingers was as warm as a small bird, and she kept both hands tight around the porcelain, afraid to let it go.

Jesse kept talking, incessantly, as if afraid of the silence between them. He had met the Reverend in the village, and the Shaws had asked about her, wanted to know if Betsy would like to move into the mission for a few days, until she felt better.

"I feel better."

"Yeah, sure. I told the Reverend you were okay. I told him it was just the heat, you know, Sunday." Jesse sat tentatively on the edge of her bed.

They had requested a double bed from the Peace Corps early in their tour, but it had never come, and now she was grateful. If she could only be alone. That was the problem: she couldn't get away.

"I want to sleep." She handed back the cup, careful that their fingers did not touch.

"Again?"

138

A GAME IN THE SUN

She did not respond. She pulled the sheets up around her and turned away, dismissing him with silence. This time, however, she did not sleep; she only watched the dark room, the dung walls, whitewashed with lime. Jesse left her, taking with him the shaky yellow lamplight. Betsy could hear him in the other room, trying to be quiet, moving carefully. She sobbed into the sheets, buried her face in the soft pillow.

Betsy did not go to school the rest of the week. Every morning, after Jesse left for school, she would wrap herself in a robe and, wearing boots, slip and slide through the mud to the outhouse and throw up whatever little she had eaten into the deep, smelly pit. And then, trembling, she'd sit there among the cobwebs and the stink of the tin outhouse until her strength came back and she could make it again back through the slush to the mud house and her bedroom.

Betsy woke from another faulty daytime sleep and found the Reverend and Mrs. Shaw standing tensely at the foot of her bed, filling the room like massive furniture. Mrs. Shaw held aloft a flaming bouquet of flowers. The room was drunkenly disheveled, drawers left open, clothes scattered. It had a close, stale smell, the smell of unwashed bodies.

"My dear, my dear!" Mrs. Shaw rushed through the mess to Betsy, felt her temperature, and began fussing with the linen.

"I'm fine, I'm fine. It's just the weather, that's all. I'm feeling better every day." Betsy slipped a smile on and off her face.

The Reverend, with one hand mopping the sweat from his red cheeks, said from the end of the bed, as if calling from a great distance, "We want to see you Sunday. Gotta get you in a game."

Betsy did not respond. She let Mrs. Shaw wipe the perspiration from her face and neck.

"Walter, you go ahead. I'll stay a while with Betsy." She smiled down at her patient, then began with busy efficient hands to tidy the covers and make Betsy presentable.

When Betsy woke again, Mrs. Shaw was gone, the room straightened, and Jesse was home from classes, moving about in the other room. He seemed to bang into everything. Why was he so inept? How had she not known that about him? He appeared cautiously in the narrow doorway.

"Bring me the calendar," she said, though her weak voice lacked authority. Jesse was happy to help; he hurried to find her Magic Marker and homemade poster board.

She took the calendar without thanking him, though he waited for the words, hoped to hear a bit of kindness. She couldn't say thanks, couldn't give him a civil remark. Why didn't he take control, take care of her? She slashed black lines through the dates while he stood beside her bed like one of Mrs. Shaw's houseboys.

"I want you to beat the Reverend at croquet," she said, finishing with the calendar.

"Beat the Reverend?" Jesse frowned, moved to look at her face. "But I can't beat him!" His voice touched the edge of alarm.

"You never try. That's your problem." She tossed the calendar aside and kept her eyes locked on a small patch of wall where a chunk of dung had swollen and the whitewash had peeled away, like a scab. "If you had tried, we wouldn't need to be in the Peace Corps. You could have gotten out of Vietnam another way."

"It's not a question of trying!" Jesse stuck his small hands into the pockets of his baggy trousers and began to pace. "And it was your idea, remember."

A GAME IN THE SUN

"I'm sick of going out there, week after week, talking to that old woman, watching you get beaten."

"It's a game, Betsy, for God's sake!" He moved to the end of the bed to catch her eye, but she kept turning her face away. "You know he likes to win. Croquet is his big deal—the way he takes care of those lawns, sets the wickets."

"You could beat him just once, that's all. No! You're such a damn weak sister." The sentence spilled out, uncontrolled. She watched him hunch up against the words. "Him and his dumb wife, God! How have I stood all of you?" Tears stopped her, and she clamped both hands across her mouth to keep from screaming.

Jesse's arms went uncertainly around her. He smelled of sweat and the local soap. She did not like his odors. He washed casually, one bath a week. It was too much trouble to haul and heat water to take a sponge bath in the metal tub in the kitchen. There lingered about him a rancid odor, reminiscent, she suddenly realized, of the young sweaty boys in her classes.

"Get away." She pushed him. "Why don't you wash?"

He left, slamming the door. Later, before falling asleep for the hundredth time that day, she heard him heating and pouring water in the washtub.

○

Betsy stared across the lawns and watched the bougainvillea bushes growing wild at the edge of the dense jungle. They were beautiful blue flowers and she took some comfort in how they edge the lawn and kept the real Africa jungle at bay.

The minister's wife returned from pruning flowers in her garden and set the shears down and then wrapped a shawl about Betsy's shoulders, as if to make her more comfortable in the lawn chair.

The woman kept talking and her voice rang in Betsy's ears like a siren. She was full of chatty news from the church congregation, stories of conversions to Christ. Betsy turned her head slowly in the direction of the woman's voice, and Mrs. Shaw's face slid out of focus.

Betsy was cold and clammy, and the wool shawl felt damp on her shoulders. There was again the oily smell of baby lotion, mixed with the scent of carnations and roses. A gift of flowers, wet with rain, lay abandoned on the table. There were seventeen Sundays left, and Betsy knew she could not make it.

Bright-colored balls shot over the lawns, trailing sprays of water, and the two men followed from wicket to wicket, halting, swinging fiercely, then hurrying to catch up. Reverend Shaw was ahead, banging the painted balls, calling out, poking fun at Jesse's fumbling.

Mrs. Shaw leaned over the flowers and whispered, "Dear, are you with child?"

Betsy could feel her breakfast of eggs, toast, and weak tea catch in her throat. Mrs. Shaw pressed forward. "You're showing all the signs. I told the Reverend. I said, 'Betsy is with child.' I know. I have an uncanny knack for such things." Her eyes flashed.

Betsy touched her abdomen, sensed something growing inside like fungus. The Peace Corps had not sent the pills. Days and weeks had passed. She'd kept away from him, begged to be left alone while he panted like a stray dog. It was she who woke one humid night in the single bed, stripped herself naked in the heat, and, padding around the house to the refrigerator,

A GAME IN THE SUN

drank a glass of cold water that cooled her like rain. She touched the tip of her breast with her wet fingers and shivered. Then she went to Jesse's bed, pulled away the sheet, and woke him with her hands and mouth.

"I've gotcha now, Jesse!" Reverend Shaw smashed the ball against the final pole, then turned to her husband, still among the pattern of hoops. The Reverend wiped his cheeks with his handkerchief and, laughing, took off his straw hat. He waved to her. "I got them, Betsy. I got him again! In ten years maybe, in ten years."

She came running wildly down the soft slope, her face flaming with rage. They dropped the mallets, glanced at each other as if there was some mistake, raised their hands, but she had reached them with the shears.

SOCIAL CHANGE

The news of the transfer came on the third day of the month. She was not surprised. Transfers always came two years and three days following assignment. After eleven years with MAMMO, they were as much a part of her life as a new Companion.

What was a surprise were the co-ordinates. She read the numbers: W7564387TZ, then reached for her device and imputed the sequence. On the purple screen flashed the data.

TITLE: DIRECTOR-PROGRAM & SYSTEMS
LOCATION: CENTRAL DIVISION-OMAHA-
LIVE IN COMPANIONS
MALE (26)–DEPENDENT –FEMALE (AGE 5)
 • TWO VEHICLES
 • LAWNSHOUSE +5 RATING
 • 14 HOURS WORK WEEK
 • TWENTY WEEKS LEAVE
CONGRATUATIONS

The position of director surprised and thrilled her and she felt a moment of sheer joy. It had been months since she let loose with any personal emotions. She was trained to be professional, to be calm in such situations. Now, of course, was no time to be careless. The Company would be watching her reaction. She shut her eyes and concentrated on breathing, skills she had learned from yoga. She pulled her tall, thin, elegant body under control. She whispered her mantra.

This transfer was a Plus-11 promotion and she quickly calculated that she was now 2.3 years ahead of her age-group. It meant in simple terms that she'd be a Super-Set of the Company before the age of thirty-six. She smiled, thrilled by the career advancement, proud of herself, and then just as quickly she thought of Companion Dave, their boys, and she felt a brief ping of nostalgia and sorrow.

It was not time, she knew, to experience pangs of conscience, or ruminate on the challenges of change. She quickly returned to work, blocking from her thoughts any wistfulness of her comfortable life with her Companion and his boys.

Into her monitor she typed her acceptance. That was a formality. Failure to accept a transfer-promotion was an act of history, a legacy of the twentieth-first century. Next she flashed David a note, a standard ZYR3 message, saying she'd be home late for dinner. He would know why and she did not have to explain.

She'd have to spend some time at her work situation saying goodbyes. Oddly, MAMMO liked that "human" touch with their employees. There would be no farewell party. With everyone transferring on rotation such affairs were redundant, and besides, within six months she'd be working again with some from this office. At least those who had been promoted, transferred and not terminated.

SOCIAL CHANGE

Dave, she knew, had already been informed. He, too, had received a Notification of Adjustment and by the time she reached the Residential Zone, switching the vehicle off Guideway, and manually driving the last short blocks to their home for sentimental reasons, he was in the Conversation Zone with her drink and favorite *hor d'oeuvres*. Dave was, in every sense of the word, a very good Companion.

When she stepped into the house, she saw his forlorn look. It was one of her worst qualities, her compassion for others. Her intense likes and dislikes had, she knew, already blocked her passage to promotions in the past.

Dave, too, couldn't handle social change. His one serious fault was his inability to accommodate.

"You heard?" she asked, needed to break the tension of the moment. She kissed him softly on his cheek.

"The text came an hour ago." He gestured to the device in his right hand, then he fleetingly touched her arm as she moved past him to pick up her drink from the serving table and settle into the mock sofa. It was the only piece of furniture that wasn't standard, that hadn't been provided by the Company. "Just to be 'unique'," Dave had suggested when they were assigned together; he had bought it off an antique web site.

She couldn't have cared less about the furniture. The house meant little to her. She had lived in a half a dozen similar ones, including the one where she had grown up in Florida. Now, of course, she was moving on. A Lawnshouse was a different status, a different rank.

She would take a few mementos with her. Her citations and awards, certainly. The snapshot of her standing on the moon. The photograph on the moon she'd put in her new office cube. After all, not many people from MAMMO had been there.

"When do you leave?" Dave asked. His voice was edgy, she noticed immediately, but he was keeping control of himself. Perhaps he had already taken his medicine. Reaching out, she touched him, traced her fingers lightly along the length of his arm. He was deeply tanned from the Texas sun, having spent the last eight months working on the new crop plantation.

It was a terrible job, and she knew without even asking that his next Company assignment would be even more of a hardship.

"Tonight," she answered, "after dinner. After the boys are asleep. It is better that way," she knew from experience. It was children who had the hardest time adjusting to change.

"Have you heard who's coming?" she asked casually, knowing, of course, that he had.

"Someone from Detroit. You were in Detroit once, right?"

"Yes, I went there from Trenton. What's her name? I might know what she's fond of, sexually. You could please her on her first night." She smiled.

Dave returned her smile. She would miss that smile, she thought. Wry and witty, showing a hidden personality, a certain sophistication that he knew to keep under wraps.

"June Smith, of all things." And then they both laughed.

"First April, now June. Give her a nickname, like you did with me."

"I always do," he whispered.

"But not mine," she added quickly, suddenly experiencing another tinge of nostalgia.

"Never! There's only one Spider in the world, in my world at least." Now he looked directly at her and there were tears blurring his eyes.

SOCIAL CHANGE

"Why, Spider? I never asked." She kept talking, not wanting Dave to turn maudlin or to beg her to stay until the next day so they might have one more night together.

"Oh, I don't know. It was the way you looked, I guessed, when you first walked into this place. You were so thin, all legs. My Companion before you was kinda chubby. She took pills for her weight. The damn place was full of pills. We didn't get along, really. I know I should not be telling you this. I trust they're not listening at the moment. Oh, hell, I don't give a damn if they are. April, I love you." He looked directly at her and his eyes had welled up again and he ducked his head and quickly took a drink.

She was briefly concerned, worried that he might lose control. It wasn't uncommon among male companions during Transfers. It was one of those situations where the Company had done a poor job in restraining the human emotions.

"What about you? How do you feel?" he asked next, pulling back and holding his head up. "What about me, the boys? Will you miss us at all?"

She was edgy and tense now. She had gone through a similar situation once before when she was just a young trainee. She was the man's last Companion and he had taken it badly, knowing she was his farewell gift from the Company.

"Of course you're upset," she began, using the protocol all females were taught. "It's only natural you feel this way," she continued, avoiding directly answering his question. "When your new Companion arrives, you'll be caught up in all that excitement. As for myself...until I'm settled in Omaha... naturally I'll think of you and the boys."

If she had been younger, less experienced, she would have lied, taking into account his emotions and romanticism, but that in the long run always made it much more difficult to say goodbye.

Dave nodded, as if understanding and agreeing, but he didn't. He had hoped for something more, she knew, a few kind words, something to remember her by.

"I was hoping you wouldn't be leaving too soon," he finally said, accepting what she was carefully trying to tell him.

"It's the only sensible way, Dave. We both know that. When is June arriving?"

Dave shrugged. "A week perhaps. She's scheduled for annual leave so she's doing that first. She only has three weeks...she's Level Six."

April did not pick up on that information. They both understood what Level Six meant. Dave, too, was in transition. It would be someone from Level Six, then Level Seven. Like her, he was programmed though life. Five years more and the boys would be on their own, and then Dave would himself reach Level Twelve and be assigned his first MAMMO Trainee.

"Are you taking anything with you?" Dave asked next.

"A few transfilms, that's all. I've learned it is best to leave empty handed."

"This one?" he nodded to a blow-up of the boys and them, taken when she had first arrived. They had taken a weekend jaunt to Nepal, just to get to know each other. In the cloud photo, all four of them were smiling happily.

"You shouldn't keep it on the mantle, Dave. It might make the transition awkward for June."

"Doesn't it matter if the transition will be difficult on me?"

"Control yourself, Dave. This isn't the way to respond. We're not teenagers."

"It's a lousy system, that's all. I don't care what MAX MIND rules. Do we all have to forget we're human? We can't turn on and off feelings like they were devices."

"There are pills, Dave. I'll give you an injection before I leave. In the morning you won't remember my name. It will be easier that way."

SOCIAL CHANGE

"I don't want to forget you," he whispered.

For a moment they were both silent, staring like lovers into the depths of each other's eyes, and then he whispered, "What if you refuse the transfer? Stay with me."

April slowly shook her head. She sighed and stated flatly, "I'd be given twenty-six hours to reconsider. That's all MAMMO allows. I'd have to meet the Emergency Board and then we would have to leave, go to Brazil. That's where Rejects are assigned today. The Sudan is too crowded.

"I'd be given some sort of low level clerical position in Records and Statistics. You would work most likely in the jungle, manual labor. We'd be forgotten, naturally, and live the rest of our lives in the jungle. The boys, of course, wouldn't be allowed to go with us. They are not expendable."

"Would you consider doing..." He stared at her, his eyes once again moist with tears.

Although she didn't like admitting it to herself, there was something special about Dave, and she felt wonderful when he did touch her. She let herself fantasize for a moment. She thought of how nice it might be to leave her job, to settle far away in one of the Frontier Campuses in Brazil, to be isolated from others and have no real responsibilities, to have a long life together, to grow old together. What a strange, old-fashioned idea.

She had read On-Line about couples staying together, but she had never met any. No one was allowed in a Frontier Campus. She realized, even as she fantasized, that it would never work.

Life might be wonderful for a while, beautiful and calm and idyllic, then they'd grow to hate each other in their isolation, hate being cut off from progress, hate being discarded and passed over. A long life with one

Companion never works for normal humans. She shook her head and then asked quickly, to change the topic.

"Is it time for dinner?"

Now she wanted to push time forward, to hurry though these last domestic chores and be on her way to Omaha and her new Companion and life.

She didn't say goodbye to the boys, only kissed them goodnight after they were asleep. She gave them both injections. In the morning neither one would miss or remember her. In a week's time, when she arrived, they'd greet their new mother as if she had been with them all their young lives.

"You're sure you don't want a Terminal injection?" she asked Dave as they walked to the new vehicle assigned to her. "I won't mind..."

"No! Please leave me something."

April kept quiet. Later, she knew, Dave would take some sort of tranquilizer to calm himself, but he wouldn't allow an injection to forget her. That was his way. He didn't have the good common sense to get over the past.

"When do you reach Omaha?" he asked, trying to make conversation, and trying, too, she knew, to keep her from leaving by asking questions.

"By ten. I've already set my vehicle on storage and sent it back to Exit Port, but if you want it."

"I don't want it...June will have her own transport."

"You're entitled to one, Dave. It's part of the arrangement. Besides, you'll need it for the boys. Life goes on, David," she added forcefully, driving home her final point, trying in these last moments to have him act responsibly.

SOCIAL CHANGE

"I don't give a damn. With you gone, I wouldn't be able to stand the sight of your car."

And with that, impulsively, he took her forcefully into his embrace.

She allowed herself to be held. She let herself be comforted. She let herself be briefly dependent on him. He had been a good Companion. It could have been a lot worse, these last two years. And why argue over a silly vehicle? Why argue in the last moments they would be together? She would never see him again. The Company was very good at keeping that from happening.

She left him on the small patch of artificial green grass in front of the house. He was crying. Two years and three days before she had found him in a similar state. It had taken her two weeks of careful attention before he accepted her as his new Companion. It was no wonder he was unable to advance at MAMMO.

April didn't bother to wave goodbye. She knew Transfers were often videoed and she did not want to endure a Company consoling session once she reached Omaha. It was best to appear on camera calm and confident and in full control. Instead April fed the vehicle the GPS directions she had been sent by the Company, sighed, and sat back in the deep, soft seat. It was only then that she looked again at the Transfer printout of her new situation and speculated about her future.

April knew that her new Companion would be younger than Dave, and that his child would be younger than the boys she left behind. That was standard Company protocol.

She thought next that perhaps with the new Companion she should have her own offspring. It wasn't against policy, not for someone with her rank and position. She wondered next why she had never thought before of having her own child. Perhaps it was true what the manuals said: women do have biological clocks.

She studied the printout information and made the simple wish that her new Companion was compatible. Two years and three days was a long time with the wrong sort. She had been lucky. There wasn't one of her six Companions that was truly regrettable. Still, algorithms did fail from time to time and people did have subtle changes from one assignment to the next. It was impossible for programs to always be accurate, even in this day-and-age.

April did not, however, let herself worry. It was too happy a day for that. She made herself a drink, using the car bar and took out two pills, one to keep up her spirits and another to wipe out her recent past. Then she counted her blessings.

The new man would be better looking and younger. New Companions always were for those on the star-track at MAMMO. And now she was a Director.

She speculated, if everything worked out smoothly, she'd have two more Companions before reaching a VP level and being transferred to New York. Then she'd receive someone truly young, seventeen or eighteen, and a virgin.

April smiled, thinking of the Company's hiring slogan: MAMMO Saves Virgins for their Vice Presidents.

And with that, April toasted herself and her bright future with the Company, and downed her two pills.

OBSCENE PHONE CALLS

"You're a sonovabitch!" It was a woman's voice, strong and wide awake.

"Hello?" Steve yawned and glanced at his SONY Digimatic glowing in the dark. It was already past midnight.

"You're a bastard!" She spoke again with authority. "I've been up half the night and you're not going to sleep at my expense."

"Hey, what's this?" Steve whispered back. Beside him, the woman stirred.

"Why are you whispering? Got some woman with you?" Her voice was quick and sharp.

"Say, listen, sweetheart, you've got the wrong guy..."

"You really are something else!"

"It's the middle of the goddamn night, and you've got the wrong number, sister."

"Your name is Steve Mirachi and you live in an apartment on Hillyer Place above Dupont Circle, and this evening at Discount Records you spent ten minutes eyeballing me and I just wanted you to know I think you're a goddamn sonavabitch!" She slammed the receiver in his ear.

155

"Bitch!" Steve swore and then, shaking his head, replaced the headpiece.

"What's that?" the woman mumbled.

"I have no idea. A wrong number, I guess." He slid down next to the sleeping woman.

He remembered watching several women in the record store, but he always watched girls, and now no particular face or body came to mind. Whoever it was must have followed him home, seen where he lived. Weird! The thought made him nervous.

He had gone out again later in the evening, around the corner to Childe Harold, and there he had met Wendy. He glanced at the girl burrowed in bed beside him. Or was her name Tiby? He couldn't remember, and he fell asleep trying to recall her first name.

The next morning he was up early and out of the apartment before the girl woke. He disliked awkward morning goodbyes and he left her a note next to the Taster's Choice:

I'm off; Saturday shopping day!

Leave a phone number, okay?

We'll get together...

Love ya,

Steve

Steve had been transferred by his company to Washington D.C., that spring and when he wasn't on the road selling his line of leather goods, he spent his Saturday mornings in Georgetown, wandering from shop to shop, watching the women. Then he'd go to Clyde's for a Bloody Mary and omelet, and stand by the bar so he could see the door.

OBSCENE PHONE CALLS

He had never seen so many women who were tall and thin and braless. Breathtakingly beautiful women! They'd come through the door, toss their long hair into place with a flip of their heads while scanning the room with wide, dark eyes. They never missed a thing, or a man. He could see their eyes register when they spotted him.

On Saturday mornings he always dressed well. The clothes alone attracted their attention on this particular Saturday. He was wearing a bold flower design shirt and had left the four top buttons open to show his chest and, in the patch of thick black chest hair, an imitation Roman coin dangling on a gold chain.

Steve was built like an offensive lineman, with short legs, a thickly trunk, and no neck whatsoever. His square head appeared as if it had been driven down between his shoulders with a sledge.

It was a head with surprisingly small features. The nose, lips, and ears were tiny and delicate, almost feminine. His eyes were gray, the color of soot, and set too close together. He had lots of hair that he let grow, but it was fine hair and wouldn't hold its shape, even with conditioner.

Steve spent at least two hours every Saturday at Clyde's, watching and meeting women. It was an odd Saturday when he didn't come home with a new name and telephone number. Steve was on a first name basis with all the bartenders at Clyde's. He was also known at Mr. Smith, up Wisconsin at the Third Edition, and at most of the bars on M Street. For a newcomer in town, he thought with some pride, he had gotten around, become known.

"You've been a pig with a friend of mine." She phoned again a week later, and again it was after midnight.

"Who are you?" Steve whispered. The girl beside him began to stir.

"Don't you respect women?"

He strained to recognize the voice.

"You only make a woman once or twice, is that the average?"

"Go screw yourself!" Steve slammed down the phone, and it rang again immediately.

"Who's it?" the woman in bed mumbled.

"Some goddamn nut case..." The phone kept ringing. Steve swore again and, climbing out of bed, took the receiver off the hook. He wrapped a towel around the headpiece, as if he were smothering a small animal, and put the telephone in a dresser drawer. The next morning, he told himself, he would have his number changed and left unlisted.

Nevertheless, for several weeks afterwards whenever he brought a woman home with him, he'd take the phone off the receiver and place it in a drawer, out of sight and earshot. He also found himself searching for the caller. He listened carefully to all the women he met on the job and after work in the local bars. He made lists of the women he had slept with since moving to the District, and eliminated those he knew wouldn't call.

Still, he wasn't certain, and he became less sure of himself around women. At Bixby's where he always stopped after work, he found himself drinking alone, like some married guy from out of town. And for a while, he even stopped hustling in the bars.

"You're doing lots better, Stevie," she said, telephoning two weeks later.

"How did you get this number?" he demanded.

"Friends. Women stick together, Stevie, haven't you heard? I just called to congratulate you." She sounded friendly.

"Thanks."

"I passed you at the bar in Bixby's and you even kept your hands to yourself, didn't make one smartass remark."

"I probably didn't see you."

"You saw me."

"Are you going to tell me your name? Let me take you out on a date." He was nervous, asking her this.

"Oh, Stevie, com' on!"

"Why not? We're probably neighbors." He pressed like a teenager.

"You're not my type."

"Bitch!"

She slammed the phone in his ear.

Steve sneaked about town on dates for the next few weeks just like he had done as a kid, looking for a place to park. He rented motel rooms in Virginia when he had to, or stayed overnight at the place of the woman he'd found that night. He was convinced the caller lived on Hillyer and he spent hours watching through closed blinds the houses across the street. He checked all the names on the mailboxes and then telephoned each one. He listened to the way they said hello. Nothing turned up.

A month later, the first time he did bring someone home, she called as he came into his apartment.

"I'm having this call traced," he told her.

"Let me speak to the woman."

"You're crazy, did you know that?"

"And you're a pig. Let me talk to her!"

"I'm alone."

"She's got shoulder length, blonde hair, five-six, wearing a knit blue shirt, carrying a sling purse with a gold chain strap. And she's about eighteen, I'd guess. When did you start hanging around sock-hops, Stevie?"

"You live across the street, right? One of those brownstones." He stretched the cord and peered through the front window. She was there, he knew. Somewhere in the dark houses across the quiet street, she was watching him. It gave him the creeps.

"Quit staring out the window. I'm not outside. I don't live across the street."

"How do you know I'm looking?"

"You're the type. You don't have much imagination. Now, come on, Stevie, let me talk to the woman. Or are you afraid?"

Steve muffled the receiver with his palm and explained to his date. "It's some crazy chick that keeps calling me. She wants to talk to you."

"Oh, no!" The teenager backed away.

"It's okay, I'm here." He smiled his little boy smile to show she had nothing to fear, and coaxed her towards the phone.

She took the receiver cautiously and, keeping it at bay, whispered hello. She was a cute peaches 'n cream high school graduate from Virginia that Steve had met that night at The Greenery. Steve wasn't sure, but he thought her name was Shirley.

Shirley listened attentively to his caller and Steve had a moment's panic. He had an urge to pull the telephone from her, but he didn't want to seem nervous. Instead, he went into the kitchen to mix drinks, and when he returned, the girl was replacing the phone as if she had just heard bad news.

"I'd like to leave," she whispered.

OBSCENE PHONE CALLS

"For Christ's sake...what did that dyke say?"

"She's not...that way."

"Like hell! That's the reason she's after me. I know about that stuff." He kept talking rapidly, afraid to let the girl talk.

"Would you please call a taxi?" she finally managed to say.

"You can't pull that crap on me! I have a right to know what she said."

"It doesn't concern you."

"It's my damn telephone!" He began to stride around the apartment, pacing to its walls, then spinning around and striking off for the other side of the room. "Goddamn dyke!" he mumbled as he finished off his drink. To the girl, he said, "If you want to leave, leave, but find your own taxi!"

She left without a word and when Steve heard the door close behind him, he spun around and gave the finger to the empty room.

O

He now couldn't find a date in all of Washington D. C. The word, he knew, had spread about him. That woman had done it to him. At night when he wandered up and down M Street, women looked away. It was done subtly; their eyes swept across his face when he walked into a bar, registered him, and then kept moving. No one seemed to even see him, and it was as if he wasn't there any longer.

He went home early after work, turned on the tube or worked with his weights. Then before ten o'clock, he took a cold shower and dropped into bed. He let the radio play all night to keep him company.

At work when he made his calls, none of the saleswomen noticed him. And there were women in those stores that he had taken home, who had cried for him in the night, and whimpered against his chest. Now they let him pass. His swaggering attitude crumbled. He no longer winked at strangers, checked out women's legs. He began to hedge with work, phone for orders, and never leave his desk. He took days off to sit by the window of his apartment and watch the street like an abandoned pet who had been left home alone.

"Are you sorry?" She telephoned again, early one evening.

"I haven't done anything. I'm no worse than the next guy. You're being unfair."

"Have you been fair to us? The women you've taken home?" Her voice had a curl to it.

"They came out of their own free will, yet I'm the one being punished. No one in Washington will date me, and you started this!"

"It's not my fault you can't date. Washington's a small town. Word gets around."

"You owe me at least one meeting, you know, after all of this." Steve began to pace. "I'm not giving you a line. How 'bout a drink some night? We'll meet at Bixby's...you like that place, apparently."

She was silent and Steve let her take her time deciding. With women like this, he knew he had to be cool.

"I'm not sure."

"One drink. A half hour. I'd like to ask you a few questions, to hear your rap, okay? Maybe you've got a point."

"No drinks."

"Okay. Lunch?"

"No. I'll meet you at five o'clock in Dupont Circle."

"Fine! How will I know you?"

"Don't worry, I'll find you." And she hung up.

OBSCENE PHONE CALLS

Steve would have rather met her at the Dupont Circle Hotel. A nice, cool and dark afternoon lounge where there were private booths, well-dressed people, the feeling of leather under his fingers. He appreciated quality, and operated best in such places. But Dupont Circle! The park was full of young people and the homeless who cluttered the grass like litter.

He sat away from the center fountain, picked a spot in the shade apart from the crowd. He had come ten minutes early to give himself time to be settled and positioned. Steve had taken time dressing. He wanted to look good for this woman.

He had dressed conservatively and wore a navy blazer, a striped tie, a white shirt, and summer linen slacks. It would impress her, he knew. Also he had a couple days of an early summer tan, and his weight was down. Just thinking about the fine impression he'd make made him feel great.

He'd be boyish with her, he decided. He'd keep the conversation general, and not push her for a date. Only a name and a phone number. She was going to be someone special. Anyway, he thought, it was about time he dropped all those salesgirls and secretaries. A guy with his position, the whole District as his territory, he could do a lot better, he knew.

"Hi!" A woman spoke to him.

Steve glanced along the bench at the young girl that had been sitting there. He looked over at her defensively, expecting trouble. She smiled. She was wearing a short dress, sandals. Her blonde hair was long and loose. She wasn't bad looking, with big brown eyes and a bright smile. She looked, however, to be about sixteen.

"Your questions?" She tossed her hair away from her face and stared regally at him. Her eyes tightened and her wide mouth sealed up like a long white envelope.

"You?" He began to perspire.

She nodded.

"Well...ah...I was...I guess I was expecting someone else." He shifted around, clapped his hands together as if gripping a football, and thought: she made the whole story up. She was some kind of sex freak. He had never in his life tried to pick up a kid. "Okay, sister, you're not what I had in mind. Forget I arranged this, okay? We don't have anything to say to each other."

"You poor bastard."

"Why don't you stay with your gang?" He waved toward the grass.

"What's the matter? You don't hustle young girls?"

"I wouldn't touch you with rubber gloves. No street traffic for me." He wiped his face with a handkerchief, looked away.

"I bet you're something in bed." She kept a smile on her face like an insult.

"Better than anything you've had, sister." He sat up straight.

"I'm not going to call you again," she said calmly. "I had this notion I might be able to reach you, but you're such a pathetic person. Oh, you'll get women to date you, Steve. Silly women who don't know better. But you have nothing to offer a real woman."

"Hey, bitch, you don't know me."

"Stevie, you boys are all alike." And with that she left him alone on the bench.

OBSCENE PHONE CALLS

He retreated to the cool, dark bar of Dupont Circle where he bought the only other guy at the bar—a furniture salesman from North Carolina—a round of drinks. Steve told him about the girl, about his phone calls, and meeting her in the park, but the salesman didn't see the joke. Well, Steve summed up, you had to have been there.

He stood back from the bar, shook his head and grinned, "Goddamn bitch!"

He'd get another apartment, he decided. He'd move out of the District. He'd live somewhere over in Virginia or Maryland, maybe Vienna. He'd live out where normal people lived, and get away from the crazies in the city.

Several months later, just before he moved out of the District, not to Vienna but instead to Gaithersburg, he saw her again. Steve's boss was in town and he had taken him to the Hay-Adams for lunch. It was the kind of restaurant Steve liked to be seen in. People in position and with money, he knew, ate there, and sitting among them made him feel special.

He saw her when she was leaving the restaurant. She was passing tables and causing a stir. All around the room businessmen looked up and smiled at her. She moved gracefully and quickly through the tables, her long blonde hair styled and swept away from her face. She was wearing makeup, but not enough to draw attention away from her brilliant, bright eyes and her perfect white skin.

She was wearing a pinstripe trouser skirt, long sleeve shirt, weskit, and blazer. In one hand she carried a thin leather attaché case. Steve realized as he watched her that she was the most beautiful woman in the city.

She saw him. Her large brown eyes held him briefly in focus and then she looked away and continued past him. He didn't exist at all.

THE ECOLOGY OF REPTILES

From the air it appeared that all the vegetation had been scraped together into a thicket behind the village, stretching a few thousand yards down to the edge of the Baro River at the western edge of Ethiopia. A dozen women were washing clothes among the rocks, and children were playing on the shoreline, throwing pebbles at a crocodile that cruised beyond their range.

Four foreign relief workers had camped at the river for the weekend, and one of them, an Englishman, Roger Sample, was telling the others about crocodiles, lecturing on the ecology of reptiles.

Roger was tall and thin and had deceiving looks. From certain angles, and in certain lights, his profile was strikingly handsome, but full faced, his features were in disproportion. His nose was too small, his lips too thick, and his eyes set too close together, as if at birth his face had been pinched.

Roger's wife, Hetty, who was from Nice, had left the group for a smooth patch of sand. She was very unlike her husband. She was small and stout, with no startling features, no figure whatsoever. Nevertheless, she was sensual and in some ways resembled Simone Signoret.

The trip had been planned by Mark Mayer, an American CARE employee, and his lover, Paula Lance, a missionary nurse. Mark had sent his houseboy to deliver the invitation to Hetty and Roger, inviting them to a "beach party in the Horn of Africa."

Mark, who had been sitting with Roger in the noonday sun, now stood and walked up the patch of hot sand to join Hetty in the shade of the acacia trees.

His recent years in Africa had been hard on Mark, leaving him pale and underweight. Hetty, watching him approach, was swept with a wave of compassion, seeing his gauntness, and wanted to gather him in her arms and hold him close, to comfort him like a child. But instead she looked away, out at the muddy Baro River.

After a moment she realized she had been watching a crocodile as it slipped through the mucky water, drifting a hundred yards, then, with a violent slap, turning to go upstream. It was the first crocodile she had ever seen.

"Have you decided?" Mark asked.

"Yes. I'm leaving Roger." The hot day flashed before Hetty's eyes like camera flashes.

"Good."

She reached out to touch Mark, but he moved, leaving her to make an empty gesture.

On the first Saturday afternoon they had made love, Mark whispered to Hetty that he loved her. His words angered her. She turned away, noticing his new digital watch and the time—3:09—then looked across the room and out the window. She could see a bit of the sky. It was a brilliant March day, with a breeze tossing the white curtains and cooling the Ras Hotel room. Roger had flown up to Lalibela that morning to inspect a UNICEF resettlement camp, and she was glad he had good weather. She could picture him tramping along in the sun, pushing ahead of the others, speaking loudly in Amharic in his crude Cockney accent. She began to cry.

Paula Lance was also American with the Seventh Day Adventist Mission Hospital. She was a nurse assigned to their mission hospital in a village several hours north of Addis Ababa on the Gondar Road. She had never been out of the United States until she flew to Africa, and all of it—the harsh living, the primitive conditions, the famine and wholesale poverty—had stunned her, so that even now, nine months after arriving, she was afraid to go anywhere by herself.

She had met Mark Mayer four months after she arrived in Addis Ababa, at the ambassador's Fourth of July party. She was walking toward the hospital's Land Rover, where the driver had tucked a small pistol under the seat in case they were attacked on the road. She hoped she was drunk enough to kill herself. Instead, Mark had found her weeping on the path of the grounds and taken her down in the bushes behind the tennis court and she had eagerly given him a blow job. That saved her life, she told him afterward.

Now, obediently, Paula listened to Roger talk about crocodiles and how they were territorial flesh eaters, though she had stopped paying attention to what he was telling her and was thinking only that she wouldn't be able to wash her hair later in the Baro River.

Paula had not been in the country long enough to have the harsh life and high plateau climate wear her down, and she could obtain enough cosmetics at the American commissary and the little Italian beauty salons near the Ethiopian Hotel. She saw glimpses of the countryside, of the hot desert and the lowlands of the escarpment, only on weekend trips out of her village with Mark.

Now she had only one wish. She wanted to be away from Africa and she knew she would leave Mark if it meant she could go home to Virginia.

O

Hetty, squinting into the sun, saw that her husband had been abandoned in the heat. Paula, too, had come up the shore and moved into the shade and stretched out on her sleeping bag, but away from where Mark had fallen asleep beside Hetty. Paula had not said anything to her, Hetty noticed, when she came to the shade of the acacia and saw Mark there, beside her.

It was quiet on the bank of the Baro. Hetty panned the shoreline and stopped again to look at Roger. He sat with his back to her, scooping sand with one hand, aimlessly, like a bored child. She put her book aside and stood, being careful not to wake Mark.

"The croc is gone?" Hetty asked, walking down to her husband and shading her eyes to search the surface of the river.

"He's been gone for hours, if it matters to you." Roger kept up with the sand.

"Don't be a son of a bitch, Roger."

THE ECOLOGY OF REPTILES

"Why the fuck not?"

"You'll get sunstroke staying out in the sun," she advised.

"As if you give a shit."

"You didn't have to come."

"And let that bloody Yank bang the both of you all weekend?"

Hetty's feet turning in the sand crunched in his ears, and then receded. He strained to follow the sound, like listening for an echo, until all he heard was the rush of water, birds shrieking in the trees, and the muffled sounds of the jungle racing to the edge of the bank.

The trees across the narrow stretch of water seemed to teeter. The thick branches pulsed before his eyes like his own heartbeat; palm leaves spread themselves a hundred yards, then shivered and expanded. In his ears, the sound of the river grew and gushed. He heard Tississat Falls a thousand miles to the northeast, and standing he turned toward the two tents, pockets of darkness in the blaze. He tried to raise his arm in a faulty gesture, then tumbled face-first, teeth biting into the coarse sand. His body twisted like a crippled bird's, but before he fell, his stomach retched an early-morning breakfast of bacon and hard rolls, coffee and melon, onto his face and shirt.

O

When they reached him, sand bugs had already converged on his vomit.

"Put him on the cot and take off his shirt," Hetty instructed. As the director of surgery at Boru Meda Hospital she instantaneously took control of her husband's condition. She was always her best when giving directions and order. "Paula, get that canteen and douse his forehead with water." She stared at Mark for a moment. A wedge of fear was caught in his eyes as if he had seen something frightening and there was vomit on his face. Hetty looked away, ashamed for him.

"We should have warned him about the sun," Paula commented weakly, feeling the need to show sympathy.

"He's been in Africa long enough," Hetty answered, peeling off his shirt. "It's his own fault." She felt suddenly very tired of having to care for her husband, and snapping at Paula, told her to fetch more canteens of water. She wanted the woman away from her so that she could deal with her husband alone.

Paula, startled by Hetty's anger, went for the water. Paula also wanted to suggest that they go into the village for help. The airline clerk spoke some English, she knew, and Mark had told her there was a white missionary at the leprosarium across the Baro, but she was afraid to suggest anything to Hetty who was always telling her what to do. The truth was, Paula never really knew what to do in Africa, and was always secretly grateful when others gave her orders.

On the way to get the canteens in the Land Rover, she slipped into the tent to find her cigarettes and would have liked to hide there a while, but the heavy canvas was airless and she had to step outside again to breathe.

Her slight body and heavy breasts were hidden in sloppy clothes: a pair of Mark's jeans cut off above her knees and his old work shirt that she had tied in a knot at the waist because she thought it made her look something like Marilyn Monroe. She loved to wear Mark's clothes. It made her think she really belonged to him. Her hair had lost most of its color since she had come to Africa, but she was afraid to let any of the hairdressers touch it.

THE ECOLOGY OF REPTILES

Now it had returned to its natural dirty brown, a color she had not seen since she was in junior high. Back in Virginia she took pleasure in doing her hair and putting on her makeup in the morning. Now she couldn't bear to look at herself in a mirror.

Roger had come around. His hand reached for his forehead, and he moaned, complaining of a headache. Hetty was kneeling by the cot, mopping his face slowly and efficiently, as if he were just another patient recovering from surgery.

Paula looked away. She finished one cigarette and lit another from the butt. She was suddenly worried that she hadn't brought enough cigarettes for the weekend. Maybe they'd go home early, now that Roger was sick. That gave her hope, and then she remembered she was told to get the canteen and went rushing to where they had parked the Land Rover, hating Hetty for being so competent, but still thankful that she had something to do.

O

"What's eating you?" Hetty asked. She had followed Mark when he took his cup of tea and walked away from the tents.

"Feeling crowded, that's all."

"You know, you have a unique ability to make me feel like shit."

He set the cup on a rock and felt in the pockets of his bush jacket for his cigarettes, letting the remark wither away.

"Can't you be nice? Can't any one of you be nice?" A gush of tears swelled to her throat, and she swallowed quickly to keep from crying.

"What do you want, for Chrissake?" He turned on her.

173

"I'd like you to talk to me. Roger gets stupidly sick and you walk off, leaving me to help him. And then Paula...!" Hetty could hear the whine in her voice and she stopped speaking. It angered her when she lost control of her emotions. She spun away from Mark and walked off.

There was always an edge of coolness about Mark, like early-morning frost. It was as though he woke angry with the world.

She hadn't realized this at first. He had been witty and entertaining when they met, and such a change from the other Americans in Ethiopia. She lingered over a cappuccino with him, sharing stories of where they had done relief work in the world, and excited by the chance meeting at the Ras Makonnen Bar. A day later, while she was pulling her VW onto Menelik II Avenue, he stopped her. He waved from his Land Rover and, pointing toward the Hilton, asked if she had time for a drink.

O

"Where's my wife?" Roger demanded, sitting up in the cot.

"Would you like some water?' Paula offered up the canteen at once, nervous about being alone with him.

"Where is she?" Roger was enjoying the sound of his demands. It made him feel better.

"She's gone for a walk," Mark shouted from the shoreline.

Roger lay back on the cot, not responding to Mark. He knew his wife was sleeping with the American. She had come home after meeting Sample and insisted that he be invited for dinner, then, a week later, she met him again in Addis, and there was more talk about the "witty American." He knew for sure then but when he pressed his wife about inviting Mark for dinner, she made excuses. Now that she was sleeping with the man she did not want the two of them together with her in the same room.

O

"I shouldn't have come camping," Paula was saying to Hetty. "It's not my kind of thing." She smiled apologetically. They were sitting two hundred yards downriver from the campsite.

"Oh, Paula, it's not so..."

"I'm uncomfortable, you know, all over. I feel dirty. And my hair!"

"In another hour it will be cooler. We can go swimming. I saw a lagoon earlier. Just us girls." Hetty smiled, trying to be encouraging. In twenty minutes the sun would be down. There would be no lingering sunset that close to the equator, and Paula, she knew, would be happier with the cooler evening and something to eat.

"I'm not going swimming! There's a crocodile. I saw it."

"They're territorial. It'll never leave that stretch of the river."

Paula's throat tightened, listened to Hetty's little speech. She always had them ready, like mini sermons, but before she could say more, Paula asked in a rush of words, "Are you sleeping with Mark?"

"Paula! What a thing..."

"Everyone says so."

"That doesn't give you...Do I pry into your life?"

"Yes, you do!" Paula turned to stare at Hetty. Her eyes were red and puffy from the weather and her rage. "You're always interfering, telling me what to do."

"Paula, you're upset. I've only tried to be..."

"Who asked you?"

Hetty stared back at Paula, and, without saying more, she stood. It was time to organize dinner. She forced herself to plan. These people were not dependable, she thought again. She had to do everything herself.

Roger, alone in the shade, watched his wife prepare dinner. She ran their home that way, relentless in her organizing. It had been a dark, unattractive house when they arrived two years earlier in Ethiopia, but she had needed only weeks to make it like their suburban London home. She had it whitewashed, made curtains and pillows, put down Dessie rugs, hired the help and trained them. She even planted a flower garden and several yards of vegetables.

Roger watched with fright and fascination. She made a portrait of the place for Ethiopians to see and marvel at, for the other relief workers to envy. Still he hated the house and what she had done with it. It reminded him of London.

After dinner he would often go back to his office in the resettlement camp where books and papers were piled on the floor, in a disarray that Hetty would never have tolerated. He loved his own squalor. It made him feel comfortable.

Hetty insisted Mark get the same room at the Ras Hotel: a corner room with windows that overlooked the garden and interior courtyard. The third-floor room also caught the soft afternoon light and the breeze from Mount Entoto. She would check in early, leaving him drinking in the bar. She wanted to be alone and take a bath, to fill the tub and pour in bubble soap she had bought in Athens, on the way to Africa. It was French and expensive, and she loved the scent. She'd slide deep into the water and listen to the noise of the capital. She felt as if she were away from the famine and poverty of Africa. She felt safe, as if she were home again as a child in Nice and listening to the Mediterranean from her bedroom window.

Hetty showered, washed and set her hair, and, sitting naked on the bed, did her nails and dried them quickly, wandering about the room barefoot on the hardwood, waving her arms. She combed her hair out next, then stripped the blanket off the bed and slipped between the sheets. Mark would find her sleeping when he came into the room. It was the way she wanted him to discover her.

O

Hetty had stopped sleeping with her husband, less than five years after they had married hastily in Uganda where they had met working for UNICEF. It was just after she discovered she was pregnant, a pregnancy that resulted in a miscarriage only weeks following a brief honeymoon at Victoria Falls. It was a marriage—her first and his second—that she realized within weeks was wrong.

One morning she set up a bed in the extra room and put up curtains and bright furnishings. Nothing was said between them, but both welcomed her decision. They no longer had to worry about each other. When she went off on Saturday morning to Addis Ababa, he'd bring the maid into his room.

They'd get drunk, and the girl—giggling and encouraged by Roger—would dress up in Hetty's underwear and prance half naked around the house.

○

"Mark, what do you feel for me?" Hetty woke him in the hotel room with her question.

"I'm very fond of you. You know that."

"Never mind." She turned away, ashamed of her question, and of his answer, and watched the windows until it was light enough for her to get out of bed and take another bath before Sunday breakfast.

○

Every other weekend Hetty made a shopping list and boarded the bus in the dark dawn. Roger would not give her his Land Rover, saying it might be needed for his work as director of the Boru Meda Hopital, so she squeezed onto the local bus with the peasants, their chickens and goats tied up beneath the seats. The bus was full of rancid smells, human and animal odors, and she would always get sick before she reached Addis.

Hetty always planned on doing the shopping quickly and returning home, telling herself she would not go to the bar and let herself be used by Mark. But she would go anyway, half dreading that Mark was waiting for her.

He was always waiting, drinking the local beer and reading his mail. She was jealous of his mail. Her letters were shared with Roger. Even her mother wrote them both, "Dear Hetty & Roger." All their friends knew them as a couple. She knew no one by herself, except for Mark.

178

THE ECOLOGY OF REPTILES

Mark read his mail in silence, then folded the thin airmail stationery back into the light blue envelopes and put it away. Only then, when he had ordered another beer, would he turn his attention to her.

O

Late on Sunday afternoons, after he had made love to Hetty, Mark would drive four hours north, back into Gojjam province, and spend the night with Paula in Debre Marqus.

"How's Hetty?" The question was predictable. Mark found himself waiting for it, just to have it out of the way.

"She's fine."

"Are you still sleeping with her?"

"I am not sleeping with Hetty, now or ever."

"Room 311. Ras Hotel. Everyone knows."

"What the shit do I care?"

"I know you're fucking her."

"And I'm fucking you too." He sat up. "What does it matter?"

"It matters. She's a friend of mine."

"Bullshit!"

"I like her," Paula answered meekly. She turned away from him. Her body made a shallow mound, like the outline of a grave, in the narrow bed.

"None of you women like Hetty, because she has more class and style than the whole lot of you. Goddamn bunch of leeches!" Mark had heard a thousand remarks about Hetty; the other American aid workers always watched for her failings. Then he was disgusted at himself for leaving Hetty, for treating her so poorly, for driving out of Addis Ababa and racing up the northern road just so he could sleep with Paula. He got out of Paula's bed, put on his trousers, and stepped out into the cold night, needing to get away from her. She cried after him, telling him that she was sorry for making such a fool of herself.

○

"My wife, she thinks a goddamn camping trip is a great way to spend a weekend," Roger complained. He was feeling better. His headache was gone, and he had been able to keep down stale bread and tea. "You know where we are? We're two thousand yards from Sudan, that's where. There're warring tribes across the river. The Nuer cross the Baro and steal cows from the Anuak. They kill white people. Cut off teats and balls. Did you know that, Paula?" He was enjoying himself.

"Roger, don't! It only frightens me. Please don't tell me anything about this place."

For a moment he was quiet, and then he asked, "You up for a beer? This village must have a bar. Let's go celebrate."

"What?" she asked.

"Us!" he told her.

Holding Roger's hand and walking through the woods, Paula got excited. She was not interested in Roger, but she liked the idea of Mark and Hetty turning around on the shore and calling to them through the darkness and finding them gone.

Roger stopped in the dark woods and kissed her. It was a sloppy kiss, a fumbling of arms. Paula let him play a moment with her breasts, and hated herself for it, but she couldn't stop him. She was afraid he'd get mad and leave her there in the middle of the jungle. Mark would not have forced himself on her. He would have waited, gone into the village and drunk beer, let her get an edge on, and then, on the way back, he would have taken her down to the Baro, and there on the warm sand, he would have made love to her with the water lapping at their legs.

"What's the matter?" Roger dropped his hands.

"Nothing's the matter. You startled me, that's all. Let's go get drunk. I feel like getting drunk."

"They must have gone into the village," Mark said, coming down to the river's edge. "Do you want to go too?"

Hetty shook her head. He dropped down next to her and put his hand on her thigh.

"Leave me alone, please."

"Aren't you a little bitch tonight?" He stood again and went up the bank to the campsite, and from there through the woods, to the village beyond the thicket, leaving Hetty sobbing to herself.

They would have dinner at the Sheraton: cocktails, boeuf bourguignon or galantine of salmon, wine, and later liquor. Hetty would get herself drunk so she wouldn't think of her work at the hospital or all the starving children in the famine camps less than two hundred miles from Addis Ababa.

181

In their room back at the Ras Hotel, Mark would roll dope and they'd smoke a joint, sitting cross-legged on the narrow bed. Mark, intent on his task, would speak only occasionally, in just a few mumbled syllables. Hetty would light incense, and its fragrance mixed with the grass and took them away from Africa, from the sounds of sporadic gunfire in the streets and from the memory of the famine camps, filled with silent children, too hungry to cry.

Hetty would get off the bed and remove her dress, taking her time, knowing he liked to watch. She moved slowly. She took off her blouse and felt each of her weighty breasts, the rubbery nipples tensing. She kept moving, unwrapped her skirt and let it slip into a dark corner. Her panties were a patch of white. She stripped them off with a quick tug and turned to let him study her. Her eyes were brown and watery, complacent as a tamed animal's.

It was not a compelling body, she knew. Her breasts did not soar, her ass was not tucked tight. Yet she knew she was sensual for she had heard the sharp, almost painful intakes of breath men experienced when seeing her naked.

She moved to the edge of the bed and placed her hands around his head and pulled him forward. Outside their room a noisy couple went past, speaking in French, and she felt a shiver of vulnerability at her nakedness. Then she brought Mark's wet lips to her vagina and forgot about everyone else, the couple, her husband, the starving children.

The next morning they would eat breakfast in silence, like airline companions being careful not to glance at each other. They sat at one of the small tables near the open doors. A rose had been picked from the garden and placed in a thin glass vase on their table. Water still clung to the red petals. They could see the garden, lush with vegetation, growing in abundance, and above the trees of the courtyard Hetty saw the windows of their room thrown open, their bedcovers slung over the ledges of the windows by the hotel maid, airing, as if they had been contaminated during the night.

O

Paula and Roger, in the barren village, were drinking gin without ice in large tumblers. There was no electricity or refrigeration and the bar had no tonic. They sat against the wall at a table made from packing crates.

On the table was a blunt candle, waxed to the boards. A half dozen other candles were lit around the small room, and on the counter was a kerosene lamp. Its yellowish glow lit up a row of bottles on a shelf behind the counter. The gin they were drinking was homemade and poured into a Gordon's bottle. Someone had amended the label to read, "A Type of Gordon's Gin."

Paula had acquired a taste for gin. It was a sharp, cutting alcohol that burned her throat. She could get drunk on it without a next-morning blinding headache and nausea. Instead, she awoke with, at the base of her throat like an irritating itch, the need for another shot, taken neat in her bathroom. The gin purged her and left her trembling.

Then the nag was gone and she recovered, cleared her eyes with drops, brushed her teeth, gargled, combed her thin hair, and, with the practice gained from a thousand such mornings, pulled her face into order, never letting her eyes catch herself fully in the mirror.

Now, in the comfort of the dark bar, she relished the drink, positioned herself for a long night. Roger had quickly finished one glass, banged for another. She nursed hers. She let the alcohol work slowly. It was only the first taste that was truly enjoyable.

Afterward, she just kept drinking, pushing herself to catch again those few moments of equanimity. But they always eluded her, and she'd become loud and clumsy and then maudlin, weeping herself to sleep toward morning in the little house where she lived alone. She pushed those occurrences from her mind. She had only three more months in Africa. The thought warmed her. She sipped the gin to celebrate, watching Roger with a smile. Perhaps she should sleep with him. It didn't seem like a bad idea now, in the candlelight.

Paula had told herself she would not sleep again with Mark, but on Sunday she found herself listening for his Land Rover, and when it roared into the yard, all her breath escaped, as if he had physically assaulted her.

She sat up and lit a cigarette, listened to his feet grate across the gravel yard and to the front door. He didn't knock. He shoved the door open and came inside as if he owned the place, everything in it, including her. She hated herself for her ambivalence about him. For being so timid. He stood in the middle of the room and said nothing. He dominated the small house as he shoved his gloves into the pockets of his bush jacket and stared down at her.

He made love to her in the living room, disregarding her protests. His eyes did not flinch from her face, but held hers, like a threat.

"My wife is sleeping with Mark," Roger announced.

THE ECOLOGY OF REPTILES

"He's a son of a bitch," Paula answered.

"I'll get him." Roger nodded knowingly, then sat back against the barroom wall. "And I'll get her."

"How?"

Roger gestured that he had everything under control. He said, "They're down there right now on the river fucking, you can bet your sweet ass on that."

Paula stared into the dim candlelight, confused not by drink, but by what Roger had declared.

Roger leaned forward over the crate table and whispered, "Let me tell you something else about the ecology of reptiles."

Hetty could have followed the others into the village, but Roger and Mark had taken both flashlights and she was afraid of getting lost in the thicket. She heard noises, rustling in the bush, the crunch of sand on the bank. She peered into the dark, her eyes aching from the smoke of the campfire.

She had to keep busy to hold off the fear. She would make more coffee and clean up the cups. She took the pot and walked down the bank to the river's edge. Halfway to the water she stumbled in the dark over something. "Oh, damn," she swore, falling into the warm sand.

"Crocs sleep on the bank at night, you know that?" Roger said, grinning over the glass of gin. "They come up from the Baro and burrow into the warm sand at the river's edge."

185

Paula stared at him. People told her she was a good listener, but she never really listened. It was too much work, especially after she'd had a few drinks.

"And you know how they kill?" he asked.

Paula shook her head.

"They drown the victims. They seize prey in those immense jaws and pull the kill into the deep water. Then, in the river itself, on shelves up under the banks, they have secret dry beds. They leave their catch, you see, on the shelves and come back later to eat their victim. How about that?"

Paula sat up and tried to clear her mind. Roger was telling her something.

"They wanted a little party all by themselves. Well, let them." He sat back, downing the rest of his gin.

"Does Hetty know?" Paula asked, beginning to understand. "I mean, does Hetty know that crocodiles sleep on the bank? Roger!" She started to cry.

"Paula, it's all right. Paula, it is." He reached for her, to pull her into a drunken embrace, felt for her breasts but she slipped off the stool and ran from the dung hut bar and into the dark night.

She remembered the path, where it went into the thick vegetation, but once in the trees, she did not know what she was doing and she stumbled forward, crying hysterically, but kept running. Running from Roger and his fumbling kiss, running from his cold hands on her breasts.

She stumbled and fell forward and was caught by Mark.

She screamed.

"Jesus H. Christ, Paula!"

She could hear herself screaming and wanted to tell Mark that the crocodile had come ashore and would find Hetty sitting there by the fire, but she couldn't stop screaming.

THE ECOLOGY OF REPTILES

Mark hit her. He slapped her once, then a second time. She fell against him, sobbing and clutching his body.

"What the fuck are you talking about?" He had her by both shoulders and pulled her face up to his.

In the black night, she could not even see him.

"The crocodile! Roger says the crocodiles come on shore at night."

"Jesus!" Mark let go of Paula and, spinning around, ran back down the sandy path to the shoreline. Paula could hear his soft, sliding footsteps fade away.

"Don't," she whispered, not wanting to be left behind, and she stumbled after him. She could see only the wavering spot of his flashlight and she kept running after it, terrified of being left alone.

O

When she came out onto the shore, Paula realized she had taken the wrong path. There was no campfire blazing, no Land Rover parked in the acacia grove.

"Mark!" her panic took the strength out of her voice. "Mark!" she said again, whispering, "Oh, dear Mother of God, please help me."

She should never have come to Africa. It was all a terrible, stupid mistake. What was she doing here, with these people, in this strange place? She started to run along the shore in what she thought was the right direction, and through the palm trees, the scrub brush, and the thin thorny acacias, she saw the tiny blaze. It seemed miles ahead of her, flickering like the fireflies she used to catch in Mason jars as a kid. She relaxed. The light melted her fear, and she felt safe. She slowed, exhausted by her effort, and the ground moved under her.

She was hit by a fierce wedge and knocked sideways into the water. In swift silence a half dozen crocodiles slipped into the warm river and tore her limb from limb.

O

Mark had a flashlight, but he couldn't find Hetty when he reached the water's edge and moved slowly along the shore. The thin beam was helpless against the enormous black night. It angered him, seeing how feebly it lit the surroundings.

Without a light, he heard every sound in the dark, all of the jungle and the rushing river. He heard as he had never heard in the day. The forest, the river, the whole world of the game reserve. There were crocodiles here, he knew, and also hippos and lions. Mark had not said anything to the women. They would not have come if they had known the campsite was in the middle of a reserve.

It was not the wildlife that worried Mark, but the Nuer. The missionaries had told him to camp close to the village, warned him about tribal raiding, but he had kept quiet and let Roger pick the campsite, this cluster of acacias close to the water. "We don't want to walk too far for water," Roger had chimed, like a Boy Scout.

"Hetty!" Mark shouted.

Behind him, in the deep night of the woods, something moved.

"Hetty?" he asked again, his voice cracking. He could taste his own fear. He stepped back, away from the trees and underbrush. There was more movement and the swaying of thick palm leaves. Mark stumbled in the sand, regained his footing, and flashed the thin light back and forth, trying to see beyond its pale beam.

THE ECOLOGY OF REPTILES

"Hetty? Jesus Christ, where are you?" He had seen a group of local people earlier, selling handicrafts. They were tall and slim, with the passive eyes of the dying, eyes he had seen in thousands of starving children farther north. They would kill him for his flashlight and the dimming batteries. All that they had been waiting for, he guessed, was nightfall.

He felt the wetness of the river. He had stepped backward into the soft sandy shore. The water was warm, and he remembered the missionaries had told him there was a soda spring nearby where the water bubbled up from the roots of trees. It was something of a tourist attraction, the missionaries joked.

Through the thick growth of trees edging the river he saw huge shadows swaying in the darkness and moving towards him and the water's edge.

"Christ!" he said out loud, realizing it wasn't tribesmen at all. The elephants moved slowly like a leather wall, and in the night breeze he smelled their bodies. He shouted out, trying to frighten the herd, and a bull roared back in warning.

Mark tripped and fell. He would swim across the river. It was narrow there at the campsite, he knew, and he could spend the night at the missionary complex on the opposite shore. He dived into the mucky water.

A crocodile caught him less than twenty yards from the opposite shore. It seized his ankle and pulled him under the water in a swift plunge, drowning him in the depths of the river. He had no time to scream.

Roger, coming from the bar, heard elephants and circled through the trees to where the Land Rover was parked. He would be safe in the vehicle until morning, or whenever the elephants finished drinking.

He turned on the flashlight and aimed it at the darkness. The light picked out the water in the thicket. It surprised him, seeing how dark it had become. Earlier, there had been an ocean of stars, but now, after midnight, the sky had closed over. If it rained, they would have a hard time getting the heavy Land Rover off the bank. There was always something wrong in Africa. Nothing ever went right. Not the land. Not the people. Not even them, foreigners coming to help. The whole damn continent was cursed.

The Land Rover's high beams popped on. Roger raised his arm to cover his eyes.

"Mark! For fuck's sake!" He stumbled in the soft earth, trying to pick his way toward the vehicle, and then he heard the elephants roar, and he turned around and faced the herd.

In the bright headlights of the Land Rover he could see a half dozen still at the shore. Several of the bulls had moved into the shallow reaches of the river. He saw a hippo farther out in the swift river, and a dozen small hartebeests and reedbuck. It looked like a peaceable kingdom, lit by the bright beams of the Land Rover.

He grinned. It was that goddamn Paula getting him so excited. He shouldn't have told her about the crocodiles just to amuse himself. Shit, what a stupid woman.

The Land Rover moved forward.

"Mark, for God's sake." He tried to walk in the soft sand, but his body, tired from being sick, from the hike to the village, from too much to drink, from too many days in Africa. He waved his arms, seeing the big machine coming toward him, down the slight slope, forcing him ahead. "You'll hurt someone, you bloody fool!" he was trying to shout over the engine, waving at the blinding headlights.

THE ECOLOGY OF REPTILES

The elephants roared and spun away from the sound, moving in a slow, graceful dance, swinging their ten tons of weight, their giant and deadly tusks. The hartebeests and reedbuck bolted, and one small roan, stumbling into the Baro, was caught by a submerged crocodile and dragged into the depths of the river.

Caught between the charging elephants, the river, and the Land Rover, Roger raced for the trees, toward the safety of the dense underbrush, hoping there would be a low-hanging branch that he could grab to swing out of harm's way. When he reached the trees, the heavy clubfoot of the bull kicked him off balance, and a dozen others, all frightened by the noisy Land Rover, trampled him into the soft sand.

Hetty drove, following the riverbank for a couple of hundred yards to a narrow road through the thick forest of junipers and lush undergrowth of giant lobelia and groundsel. She swung right and drove through the village, lit only by candles and a few lanterns. She thought about stopping and telling the locals that there had been an accident at the Baro, but she thought better of it and kept driving north. In the morning there would be nothing left at the river's edge. The campsite would be stripped by the roaming tribes from Sudan who crossed the Baro and scavenged the landscape. They would take the sleeping bags, tents, and utensils, and in the morning no one would know there had ever been a camping party there down from the capital. As for her husband, lifeless on the soft shore, the crocodiles would have him. It was the way of nature, the ecology of reptiles.

She kept driving. In eighteen hours she would reach Jimma, and another day's drive would get her to Addis. She would drive for a hundred kilometers and then sleep a few hours to be ready for the long haul in the heat of the next day.

Hetty rubbed her knees, which she had bruised on a boulder. It was nothing to complain about. To come away from a camping weekend with only a minor bruise was nothing at all. She thought about the bath that awaited her at the Ras Hotel. The anticipation of it made her smile as she downshifted the Land Rover and, picking up speed on the dry road, raced across the lowlands, toward the warm water that would cleanse her.

THE ENEMY

The night the phantoms struck for the final time in the halls of Saint Philip College's freshman dormitory bringing down the wrath of their resentment on the long suffering head of Freddy Longshaw, Thomas Charters, second floor proctor, was quietly and completely drunk at the nearby College Inn.

Since five o'clock that afternoon when, angered and frustrated, he had stormed from Father O'Donnell's room to seek in the solitude of the bar a few hours of stolen freedom from his responsibilities as dormitory proctor, Thomas had come to the sudden realization that his long sought after and applied neutrality was slipping away from its moorings.

The cause of Paul's troubles was the bulky, sandy haired, ex-Army chaplain, Father Dan O'Donnell, freshman dormitory director, and Paul's immediate and only superior. Father had summoned Thomas that afternoon, as soon as he heard about it, to give an account of the latest outbreak on the second floor.

"Nothing at all to it, Father." Thomas hurried to comment as he settled uneasily into the chair opposite O'Donnell's desk. "Just some of the boys acting up. They're excited you know about Christmas vacation." He started a smile but faded it when Father continued to sit brooding.

"You don't think tearing the picture of the Blessed Virgin off Longshaw's door is anything to get excited about?" His charging voice jumped at Paul.

"Yes, Father, but...but under the circumstances I don't feel the boys intended any disrespect." He selected his words carefully, skirted away from any commitment. It was going to be another of those meetings. Father was out for blood.

"This is the fifth time isn't it?"

"Yes, Father, I believe so."

Thomas knew damn well how many times it had happened. Each time little Freddy, his face torn with anguish, had brought him the evidence. "Do you see this," he would say extending the fragments. "They did it again last night." And each time with his understatement, his failure to condemn or demand reprisal, he was blaming Thomas for letting it happen, until now, the fifth time, when he had by-passed him and carried the remains, like a sick child, right to the top, to Father Dan.

"I understand each incident is accompanied with a message: 'The Phantoms strike again.' Is that right?"

Thomas shifted uncomfortably in the chair, crossed his long legs. Father's unemotional voice bore down on him. It was getting around to the Phantoms now. He ran his finger, a nervous habit, along the brink of his large nose and answered vaguely.

"Something like that, Father. I'm not sure."

"You're not sure? Don't you patrol that floor?"

Thomas struggled silently under the attack. Father was going military again. There was nothing he could do. Perhaps the worst would be a new set of regulations. Thomas avoided Father's face and glanced around the room. In the far corner a small bunk bed was neatly made. His shoes were aligned at the foot, all polished, shining for inspection. Over the bed next to a crucifix was a large framed glossy picture of Father O'Donnell standing with a formation of soldiers. Across the top of the picture written in dark ink through a cloudless sky was the inscription: "To Fighting Father Dan O'Donnell...Good Luck...from your men of the 173rd."

"I check the rooms at Lights Out, Father, but I don't go out after that unless there's noise."

Father shoved a cigar between his lips, worked it around with his teeth to the right corner of his mouth, and lit it.

"They've got you mapped out, Chapman. You'll have to use some diversified measures if we're going to catch them." He leaned forward, dropped his elbows on the desk, and stared at Paul. "We're in charge here and things are getting out of hand."

Paul's eyes bent under the pressure and glanced guiltily away.

"Perhaps, Father," he began slowly. "If we eliminate the cause..."

"What cause?"

"It seems, Father, from what's happened and everything, that the boys resent Fred's actions."

"What actions?"

Father dealt the questions out coldly, like cards.

"With regard to waking them for Mass on Sunday mornings."

"Do you find anything wrong with that, Paul? I think we could use a little lay apostle work in this dorm, don't you?"

"Oh, yes, Father. It's just that the boys resent..."

"Discipline's the word. They resent the discipline. It's too damn bad! They'll get plenty in the Army. You weren't in the service, Paul?... That's right...something was wrong...4F?"

"Yes, Father, nervous tension."

"Well it doesn't matter. What I want you to know is that we have to run a dormitory with discipline. There's no place for trouble-makers. Now I want you to put a stop to all this mid-night prowling."

Thomas glanced up.

"But you always handle these matters, Father..."

"I know, but I think it would be best if we followed chain-of-command in this situation." He released the cigar from his mouth, held it out between his thick fingers, flipping ashes carelessly into a tray.

Thomas tightened under the announcement. He did not like this at all. Until now everything had been fine. He had left the boys alone and they hadn't bothered him; except for Longshaw, it had been a peaceful arrangement. Don't look for trouble and it won't find you. It was a maxim he always followed.

"Get the names of those Phantoms, Chapman. We'll deal with them individually. And don't let those young faces fool you. Students are always scheming. Keep them on defense; it's the best offense. Let me know when you have the names." He jammed out his cigar and dismissed Thomas with a nod.

Thomas hurried upstairs to his room. He was too agonized to protest longer. What he had feared most was happening. His intervention into disciplinary matters. For four months, since becoming dorm proctor, he had avoided, shifted, neglected, disciplinary actions. Now it was being pushed on him against his will. He swallowed two tranquilizers, grabbed a coat, and left the building.

THE ENEMY

For the next five hours in the quiet of the College Inn Thomas fought with his problem. There seemed no possible way out. He would have to take a stand against the boys. It was not the safety or involvement of the students that he feared, but rather the consequences of what would happen once it was known he had put the finger on the Phantoms.

However, while Thomas sat at the bar the real threat to his security (unknown to him) had already begun to form in the second floor of the freshman dorm he had abandoned. Bill Tighe, medical student and undisputed leader of the Phantoms, had been since seven o'clock that evening recruiting members for the latest and biggest attack on the common enemy of the freshman students: Freddy Longshaw.

Bill Vicar's personal feud with Longshaw had begun earlier that semester when Freddy primed him out of bed, with a half glass of water, to make the twelve o'clock Mass.

Tighe, groggy with sleep, had sprung from the bed, thrown a wide, round-house left hand that caught air before Freddy's startled eyes. Falling away Freddy escaped through the door into the safety of his own room across the hall as Tighe hotly pursued.

"What the hell you doin', Longshaw?" Bill shouted after him.

Doors opened on the floor and students stepped out to see the commotion. Several wandered down to get the story.

"I was stone dead...a hangover from last night, when...whammy...right in my goddam face a glass of water." Tighe glanced at his audience. "I could have killed him." He stepped forward and banged on Freddy's door. "You hear me, Longshaw? Don't go pullin' that stuff with me again...understand?" Silence answered him and standing dumbly a few minutes longer staring at the door he turned around and waddled back barefoot into his room, slammed the door, and flopped into bed.

197

In the sanctuary of his room Fred Longshaw contemplated the outbreak. This sudden and unexpected act of violence had left him momentarily tense. He eased into a chair and enjoyed the quiet.

Freddy Longshaw, a seventeen-year-old Latin major, was slightly built. His face, pear shaped and sad, floated always through a half dozen agonizing expressions. A long stiff neck connected it rigidly to a fragile body. For the past four months he had been a piercing thorn to the peace of the freshmen. It was his self-imposed habit to roam the halls on Sunday morning hunting students who had overslept or intended to miss Mass.

"You're Catholic aren't you?" He would declare standing firmly behind his dogma when they cursed him for waking them. Grumbling they would roll from bed, start to dress, as Freddy, satisfied, watched.

This morning, however, it had been different. Faced with his first serious opposition a wave of excitement stimulated his delicate body. Finally he was to have his first challenge—a chance to exercise his religion; to bring a soul back to God. He visualized himself a champion of the Faith and gloried in a hundred daydream acts of suffering.

Bill Tighe' loose fitting slippers slapped against the tile floor with urgent impatience as he hurried from room to room explaining his plan. The attack against Longshaw, which swept favorably through the hall, was to take place at eleven that night when Freddy came back from saying the rosary in the dormitory's chapel.

Time clicked slowly around to ten o'clock, as the Phantoms waited. Longshaw, unaware of any danger, picked up his rosary and left his room. Tighe, camped in his dark room across the hall, restrained a temptation to peep into the hall.

Outside on the walk Father O'Donnell, coming back to the dorm after an Army Reserve meeting, glanced at the dark windows of the second floor.

198

THE ENEMY

Thinking Chapman had already begun clamping down on the students he smiled and went into his room.

Two blocks away at the height of this activity Chapman ordered another round. The problem of the afternoon still stirred unresolved in his mind. The beer had left him both tired and sick. Gushes of self-pity washed through him. He had come to the sad conclusion he was everyone's victim. The thought brought him some comfort.

Yet his immediate problem centered on Father O'Donnell and the Phantoms. He would have to supply the names. What plagued him was that it was not his fault. Hadn't he left them all alone? It was not fair! He remembered bitterly how he had pleaded with Tighe to stop the raids.

"What are you after?" Chapman had asked sneaking down to Tighe's room one night.

"Who said I'm a Phantom, Chapman?" Tighe, already in bed, sat up and lit a cigarette. "Where do you get all these ideas? Is that what you've been doing in that room with the door locked?"

"Cut it! Do you understand I want this midnight crap stopped!"

"Listen, Chapman, if you tell me what you're doing in your room with the door locked, I'll tell you who the Phantoms are. A deal?"

Thomas thought a moment of how it would feel to jump forward and slap the hell out of Tighe. He watched him move an arm over his eyes noticing the muscles flex under his tee shirt.

"All right, Tighe, I've warned you. I'm not responsible for what happens, remember that." Then, helpless, he barged from the room.

The beer was sour on Paul's lips. It was now ten fifteen. He would have to leave. Lights Out was in another fifteen minutes. Stumbling off the stool he grabbed his coat, worked it onto his shoulders, and stepped outside.

The sudden cold of the winter night slapped his face. Turning against it he started up the hill toward the college. His mind whirling with a hundred disarranged and confused thoughts. Hadn't he told Freddy to quit hanging the pictures, he mumbled into the hostile air.

"Why do you bring me those pictures?" he had asked Freddy. "It's not my fault."

"You're proctor."

"What's with you, Longshaw?"

"What do you mean?"

"Why do you post those pictures?"

"I have my reasons."

"And waking guys for Mass?"

"They have an obligation."

"That's their problem."

"I'm just practicing my faith, that's all."

"Then practice it alone. You've caused me nothing but trouble since the year started."

"I haven't bothered you."

"The hell you haven't. Every time there's a disturbance in this hall I have to answer to O'Donnell."

"Father O'Donnell?"

"Don't wise off! Now get this straight, I don't want you bringing me anymore of those pictures, do you understand?"

"Why?"

"Because, Longshaw, I don't want to be bothered; I just don't want to be bothered!"

"You mean you're afraid...afraid of the Phantoms."

THE ENEMY

Thomas stared at the figure standing tensely in the doorway of his room. He searched the pale face for a glimpse of weakness.

"No, Longshaw, I'm not afraid. You're the one who's afraid of something...I don't know what...the Phantoms...yourself...me. And that's why I can't be bothered with you. Do you hear?"

"You hate me, don't you?" Freddy asked quietly.

"No, I don't hate you. Now get the hell out of my room."

Freddy Longshaw did not return to his room after saying the rosary. Instead he came up from the chapel, turned into the first floor hall, and knocked softly on Father O'Donnel's door.

"Who is it?"

"Fred Longshaw, Father, do you have a minute?"

The door opened and Father's big frame filled the lighted entrance.

"Come in, Fred."

"Is there anything I can do for you, Fred?" Father asked after they had sat down.

"No, Father...it's just that I have some information for you."

"What's that?"

"About the Phantoms."

"Oh, you won't have to worry about them any longer. Chapman's going to supply me the names of the ringleaders. I'll clean up that mess."

Longshaw watched Father a moment and then said, "Father, I think Chapman has been fooling you. He's one of the leaders...Tighe is the other."

Longshaw's indictment surprised O'Donnell. He slowly unwrapped a cigar and studied the passive looking boy.

"Are you sure, Fred?"

Longshaw nodded.

"I've overheard them plotting, Father. They want me out of the dormitory."

"This is a serious matter, Fred. Do you have any proof?"

"I've seen Chapman sneaking down to Tighe's room after Lights Out, Father."

Father wiped his face with a large handkerchief and tried to gain a perspective on the issue. He reviewed Chapman's recent statement searching for a conflict of interests. The boy could be lying. This was a new problem for him. He could handle the trouble-makers, the students coming in drunk, or getting involved with girls, but this was different.

"There really isn't much to go on, Fred. Let's sleep on this and tomorrow we'll have a meeting. I don't want things to get out of order."

"I wouldn't waste too much time, Father," Freddy answered, standing up. "You should act before there's more trouble."

"There won't be any trouble, Fred, you can count on me."

"Would it be all right then if I slept down here on the first floor tonight? I'm expecting trouble in my room. I think they're out to get me again tonight."

Annoyed at Freddy's attitude, Father pulled a key from his desk and handed it to Longshaw.

"You can sleep in 112."

Freddy, smiling faintly, took the key and said goodnight. Father watched him leave realizing that he did not like that boy.

Thomas Charters entered the dormitory and climbed clumsily up to the second floor. Under the exit light at the landing he leaned against the doorway waiting for his head to clear and debated whether to see Freddy Longshaw.

There was something he had to tell Longshaw. Something in the isolated and cold night he had finally admitted to himself. It was the realization that he was afraid. Afraid of all those who opposed him. He knew he would have to give up his proctor's position, but before he did he wanted Longshaw to know it wasn't because of him. He did not want Longshaw to gain any satisfaction out of his resignation.

In Longshaw he saw something worse than his own cowardice, something worse than the pranks of the Phantoms. He saw in Longshaw the corrupting force lurking behind the facade of religion.

Thomas gathered himself together and started down the hall toward Freddy's door. He did not bother to knock, but using his pass-key opened the door and stepped inside. The room was empty. He closed the door and sitting down on the bed waited for Freddy to return.

Across the hall Bill Tighe waited anxiously. He had heard Freddy's door open and close. Waiting ten more nervous minutes he then stepped into the hall and listened at Longshaw's door.

Inside, a steady, heavy sound of breathing filled the silence. Tighe signaled for the Phantoms. Quickly they tied the door shut with a rope and taped the split between the door and floor. Then pulling the fire hose off the wall they dropped the nozzle into the mail slot and turned on the water. A steady stream of water poured into Longshaw's room. On the bed Chapman slept peacefully. Outside in the hall the Phantoms shambled back to their rooms.

Thomas slept for three hours before the annoying sound of running water awoke him. He blinked his eyes open in the dark room. His mind whirled with dizziness. Moving his right foot across the bed he dropped it to the floor. The splash of water against his foot drew him fully awake. He stood up and stared down at the water. Over an inch deep it slapped against his feet.

Chapman waded to the door. When it wouldn't open he banged against it and shouted for help.

Tighe, wide awake across the hall, listened to the commotion. The shouting voice was not yet distinct; he strained to hear what was being said. Then it was not Longshaw's voice he heard, but Chapman's. He jumped up and hurried into the hall. Chapman's voice, loud, frightened, belligerent, called from behind the door. He couldn't understand how Chapman had been caught in Longshaw's room. Quickly he cut the rope that held the door and jumped back into the safety of his room.

Chapman jerked the door open and blurted into the hall, his feet wrapped in the escaping tide. He stood in the hall for a moment and then started toward the stairway, his walk faltering from drunkenness and cloudy with sleep.

At the stairway his stomach heaved from the abuse of beer and nerves. He reached to secure himself. His hand, reaching for the railing, missed; his feet, wet and slick from the tide of water, slipped on the concrete, and Thomas Charters fell forward, graceful as a stuffed animal, into a crashing heap at the bottom of the stairs.

BURN THIS FLAG

Marsha puckered her glossy lips at the bathroom mirror. "Not bad," she whispered. Her valentine-red fingernails slowly cruised over her body and her black leather push-up bra. "But not too bad." She returned her focus to her hair, penciling in a washout violet shade on a honey blonde strand. Vickie had told her not to dress "downtown," which was why she was now wearing leather underwear. She was making herself look outrageous, the type a girl any john would lust after in a New York downtown club.

She liked this part, being made up, living another life, being on stage. She thought of herself as Georgette, the Paris prostitute that Jack Barnes had picked up on the terrace of the Neapolitan. Or Elizabeth Taylor in *Butterfield 8*. Pretending to be someone else always took her mind off of herself. Usually she did it with music. She had, in fact, been on her way to buy the new Pixies album when she checked her service and heard Vickie had called.

"He's having a party and he wants a couple hot girls around," Vickie told her when she telephoned from the booth outside of the Lincoln Center.

205

"He's not a regular, you understand." Marsha knew the tone. It was Vickie registering her disclaimer. "He told me he got my number from a friend; a client, but he won't say who. Boys are like that." Vickie was in her chatty mood, which also meant she had gotten a nice piece of change on this one. Cash, Federal Express.

Marsha took a deep breath and looked up Broadway at Tower Records, remembering the CD, and remembering, too, that she had a tuition payment due at Columbia University.

"Do I have to fuck him?" she asked.

"My, Marsha, your language has certainly deteriorated since you started college. I told him the fee was two-fifty. Six hours. Cab Fare. The usual. Anything extra is between you and the boy." Vickie always called them boys.

"Okay, I guess," Marsha finally said, sighing. "I was going to work on a Brit Lit paper tonight, but money is money. Where's the place?" She reached into her Banana Republic bag for a pen and a scrap of paper. "That's Alphabet City!" she exclaimed, when Vickie told her.

"I said it was downtown!"

"I thought you meant the Village." Marsha stuffed the scrap of paper into her bag.

"No one, honey, lives in the Village. You're so dated, Marsha. Oh, one more thing! The boy wants you to wear leather."

"Shit, not again!"

"Sorry, Marsha, you're the only girl I got that looks great in leather."

"If he hurts me, you're paying the medical bill."

"The pleasure will be yours, Marsha. The bills will be mine. Bye."

Marsha hated leather. She was convinced it was the cause of her rashes, being that it was so close to animal skin, but pulled on her black tights,

206

then a black turtleneck, and shook out her hair, violet-streaked and tumble dry. She glanced in the mirror for a final look. I shouldn't be doing this, she thought. I'm too nice a girl. I'm too pretty. I'm too smart. I don't need to do tricks for a living, even if they are all rich, married, and harmless.

Still, she couldn't be too careful. She was a woman on her own, and now she was going down to Alphabet City, New York's new wild side. She opened the medicine cabinet door and took out two Light Days pads, and then, just to be careful, she grabbed her can of mace and slipped it into her black leather bag.

As she stepped out the door, she promised herself: Nothing kinky! Nothing she couldn't tell her mother. She smiled wryly, thinking how her mother thought she was paying her Columbia tuition by working at Zabars. She would never understand that her daughter wasn't the first girl to buy a college education by working horizontally.

$$O$$

He was a boy, Marsha saw, sizing him up as he opened the apartment door. A kid, like herself. Her whole body relaxed.

He grinned and his smooth white face flushed.

"You're cute," she told him, following Vickie's standard advice: tell the john whatever he wasn't—cute, funny, rich. But glancing at him a second time as she stepped into his apartment, Marsha thought that he was actually kinda cute. He looked like a college student. Short, but cute. She shouldn't have worn spikes, she thought next, slipping smoothly from her heels to give him an extra inch.

"Whoa! This is your place?" she exclaimed, taking in the huge room. She spun around, pretending to look at the apartment while letting him check

her out, giving him a chance to see what he was paying for. She decided that
if he wanted sex, it was okay with her. She wouldn't mind spending time in
this place. She then thought to herself how bad she was.

"Is this all yours?" she asked, knowing it made her sound young. She
blinked her lacquered eyelids.

"Yeah, all mine." He kept grinning, following her through the foyer.
"Josh Goodman did it."

"What?" She looked at him, widening her blue eyes, knowing it made
her look innocent.

"The interior designer, Goodman." He kept staring at her.

This is going to be easy, she thought.

"Do you have anything to drink?" she asked next, sensing it was time to
start giving him orders. "A Perrier?"

"Yeah, sure! What?" He was hurrying. "Perrier, right?" He went to a
teak cabinet and opened the double doors with a flourish, showing off.
There was already champagne being cooled in a silver bowl.

"Perrier, yes, thank you. I don't drink. It's bad, you know, for your
skin." She smiled, wanting to pinch herself at her good luck. She scanned
the living room again. It glittered with brass and chrome, white throw
rugs, a black leather couch. Everything smelled new but was put together
with bad taste. A thought flashed through her mind: this guy is gay. And
she was immediately tense. Then he was beside her, holding her Perrier in
a champagne glass.

"Do you want to dance?" he asked, like a date.

"Sure! I love to dance." She widened her eyes over the rim of her tall
glass, flirting.

"Shit, you're really something," he said, shaking his head.

"Oh, aren't you nice." She reached out and touched his cheek. His flesh was cold to her fingertips, and he jumped back away from her hand. "Do you mind if I sit down?" she asked quickly, made nervous by his abrupt behavior.

"Oh, no, hey, what did I spend five big ones for if not to enjoy it. Right? Straight from Denmark."

He told her about his furniture then, and the co-op, and how much money his kitchen had cost him, and she kept smiling, not really listening, but watching him, thinking of what he might look like in bed.

He was too small for her, she decided. His hands and fingers were doll like, and she didn't like his eyes. They were dish watery in color and too close to his nose. But it was the feel of his flesh that upset her. She didn't like cold skin. Whatever had happened to hot-blooded boys?

"What's that?" she asked, breaking into his furniture monologue. "What's that on your neck?"

She spotted the tiny tattoo beneath the collar of his shirt when he leaned forward to pick up his drink.

"It's cute," she added, embarrassed now that she had brought it up. Tattoos on johns made her edgy.

"Nothing. Just our logo."

"Logo?" It looked like a bird with wings extended.

"Yeah, my club. We all have them." He pulled at his collar, as if made uncomfortable by her question. "What do you want me to do?" he asked quickly, not looking at her.

"It's your call, sweetheart," she continued to smile with her eyes.

"How 'bout hitting a club? How's that?" He kept glancing over, still unsure of himself.

"Sure! As I said, I love to dance."

"Great!" He slammed his knees and jumped to his feet, talking fast again, telling her the club was nearby, just across the park. He was like a kid on his first date, she thought again.

"Hey, what's your name?" he asked.

"Starr," she said, standing, "Starr Brite." She tried to imagine making love to him, but that thought unnerved her and she pushed it from her mind as she said quickly, "let's go dancing," forcing enthusiasm into her voice.

The man was on fire. Bright golden flames consumed his shirt and burned his arms, yet he kept dancing. At the other end of the long, under the low ceiling of the basement room, he flared away, dancing to Soul II Soul.

"Look!" Marsha shouted, grabbing her john's arm.

"It's just Smithie," he replied, pushing her into the crowded room. "He lights up on weekends." He grinned at her.

Marsha glanced away, annoyed by his grin.

She looked across the barroom basement to where the burning Smithie had been dancing. He was no longer on the makeshift stage and a huge ball game shout and whistling applause signaled the end of his performance. Marsha searched for him in the swarming crowd, and was stabbed with the realization that she was the only woman in the downtown club.

Marsha stopped walking. "Hey, what is this? Some kind of gay joint?"

"What are you talkin' 'bout?" her john answered back, flashing anger.

Marsha saw she was wrong. She spotted a few women at the bar, and others lost on the crowded dance floor.

BURN THIS FLAG

"What is this place?" she asked, pressing her feet against the stone floor and not budging.

"They're friends for Christ's sake." He grabbed her arm.

"They're skinheads!" Marsha declared, focusing on the shaved heads of the men, dozens of them, all wearing leather sprinkled with brass studs.

"Yeah, sure. Some." He pulled at her arm but she slipped loose.

"What is this?" she demanded.

"It's my club! I told you." Again his anger surfaced.

"You're not a skinhead!"

"They're not, either." He pointed toward a back table.

Marsha followed his gaze and saw three men sitting together. They were dressed like her john, wearing similar jeans, Banana Republic cotton shirts, no ties, and short jackets. They all had short, spiked glossed hair and they were staring at her.

"Okay," she said after a moment, still wary, but finding some reassurance in seeing more guys like her date. There wouldn't be trouble, she thought, with all the Wall Street types around.

"You want to dance?" her john shouted over a Bomb the Bass song.

"Is the show over?" she asked, nodding toward the platform stage. She could now see the man who had been on fire. He was holding a beer bottle and talking to a woman who was wearing leather jeans and nothing else. Her breasts were painted red, like stoplights.

"Jesus!" Marsha exclaimed.

"Hey, its downtown!" Her date grinned, watching her reaction.

She nodded. The year before she had gone to an AIDS benefit at The World with her friend Steve, and half the crowd there, men and women, had taken off all their clothes. "They must be professionals," Steve had

211

suggested. Marsha guessed they were, too, but she didn't tell Steve that she was a professional herself. Nor did she take her clothes off.

"Hey, loosen up," the john said, cupping her bottom with his palm and angling her onto the small wooden dance floor.

Marsha gave him a look and shouted over the music, "Easy with the hands."

He raised his hands, gestured, and concentrated on the house music. They danced in silence.

Marsha closed her eyes and let the music carry her away. She didn't know what she'd do if she didn't have music in her life. It was only when she opened her eyes again that she spotted the other men, the three investment banker types, staring at her from across the crowded room. She glanced at her john. He, too, was watching her, still grinning.

"What is this?" she asked, stopping on the dance floor.

"Hey, come on, what goes?" her date said, reaching for her.

Marsha pushed his hands away, telling him, "I don't want to dance." She was about to say also that she didn't like his creepy friends. This had been a bad idea, she thought, regretting that she had picked up Vickie's call. She was too old for this stuff. It was no fun balling a bunch of adolescent Wall Street types.

"What the fuck?" her date swore, grabbing at her.

Marsha didn't react. She had learned the hard way not to try and be tough with a john. She had been beat up once too often.

"Okay," she said quietly, backing him off. "Just let me get a breath of air; I'll be fine." She faked a smile.

He nodded and said something, but she missed it in a sudden push of people.

BURN THIS FLAG

When she spun around, she saw that one of the young women she had seen earlier standing at the bar was now struggling with a man. The crowd had pushed back to give them room.

"What is this?" Marsha asked, alert at once to trouble.

"The entertainment," her date shouted in her ear. He was moving her away from the push of people, trying to get her outside the circle and back to the table with his three friends.

They made room for her at once, helped her stand on a chair so she could see the show.

That was nice of them, she thought, jumping up.

The music had stopped and the dance floor was given over to what Marsha guessed was the entertainment her date mentioned. Another song started. They were playing Jane's Addiction, and she kept thinking of the fact she had the same album at home.

She watched the male on the dance floor and saw he was slowly and deliberately taking off his clothes, pulling down his jeans. She saw his erection bulge his red shorts. He kept stripping, facing a woman.

Christ, she thought, it was just another silly strip act.

"I'll bite off your joint if you come near me," the woman warned, keeping her distance. The girl had orange and green hair, and was wearing a short, short skirt and black tights. Her thighs were too fat for a short skirt, Marsha thought, but then remembered no one downtown knew how to dress.

"Take off your clothes," the male ordered.

"You're going to fuck me here?" The woman glanced around, tried to catch a face in the crowd.

But she was a good actress, Marsha saw next, catching the flash of fear in the woman's eyes. She already knew what was coming. She had seen plenty of home videos of S&M acts, and for several years had a customer who just liked to sit and hold her hand while watching such shows.

"We're *all* going to fuck you, girl," the man told her. He pulled off his shorts and his erection bounced into the bright colored lights of the dance floor. A roaring ball game cheer thundered through the small club.

The man stepped closer, still not taking his eyes off the woman, nor recognizing the cheering crowd which now, having seen him naked, picked up the rhythmic clapping to match the acid music.

He would fuck her, Marsha knew, and then half a dozen more would also do the girl. It was a stupid act, she realized, feeling sorry for the girl, and thinking, sadly, that she was just another whore trying to make a living. Marsha felt embarrassed, watching her.

Turning to the crowd, she scanned the faces of the skinheads and yuppies, searched for a woman's face, some friendly face. She was looking for anyone who might share her feelings and help get her out of this place. She didn't want to see what might happen to the girl. But the faces of everyone, all the men and the few women, were grinning, watching the action on the tiny dance floor.

The man had grabbed the woman's right arm and instead of pulling back, she had moved forward and raised her knee to catch him fully between the lights. When he doubled over, she grabbed his short hair and tossed him away into the crush of people. Then she bolted for the back door, toward the dim exit sign beyond the bar.

Marsha grinned. This was good, she thought, caught by the unexpected twist.

The woman never made it off the dance floor, however; she was lifted up by dozens of arms, caught above them. She was screaming, trying to reach down and scratch their faces, as if to pluck out their eyes with her long red nails.

Her fingers finally did catch one face and her nails quickly raked his smooth cheek. Blood blossomed on the young boy's face.

Marsha's heart caught in her throat.

Then, someone hit the woman. A fist punched through the air, hitting the woman on the side of her face. As if in slow motion, Marsha saw the woman's cheek crumble under the blow, saw her long hair fly, and she heard the smash of bones and skin. It was like a balloon busting at a birthday party.

She was dead, Marsha realized. The woman was dead. They had killed her. Marsha was screaming, shouting to stop this. She thought of Jodi Foster, and what had happened to her in the movie. She kept trying to remember the name of the movie as she watched the makeshift stage. This was not an act, Marsha realized. This wasn't just some sort of weird, sick entertainment.

The woman had now been stripped and swiftly tied to dog chains hung high on the back brick wall.

"Stop this!" Marsha demanded, swinging her fists against the shoulders of the man beside her. A half dozen men had mounted the stage and were going at the naked woman, raping her in quick succession, like a warren of rabbits.

The few women joined in next, shoving dildos into the victim to the cheers of the skinheads and Brooks Brothers yuppies.

Marsha tried to get down off the chair, to escape the bar and run for help, but when she tried, her john and his buddies grabbed her, seized her by the legs. She swung at them with her elbows, but they wouldn't let her go, wouldn't let her stop watching the show.

More men had jumped onto the stage and were painting the naked woman with bright colors.

Marsha tried to scream, but couldn't move her jaw.

"Don't let the bitch die!" her john shouted, still with his arms wrapped around Marsha's legs.

She would kill this john, Marsha promised herself. She would grab his balls and squeeze the life out of him.

Marsha squeezed her eyes closed to block out the scene and when she opened them again, she saw that the painting was finished. The woman was covered in broad strips of red, white and blue. Her breasts were clustered with tiny white splashes that resembled stars. She looked like a crude American flag.

"Happy Fourth of July!" her john shouted, trying to be heard over the deafening beat of music, the screaming crowd.

"What?" Marsha uttered, and then remembered it was July 4.

"The birthday girl!" Her date shouted, and finally let her go.

He was moving forward, surging with the others toward the stage.

Marsha couldn't run. She knew she should escape now, while she had a chance, but she couldn't leave the helpless painted woman. She had to save her from this madness.

The crowd had circled the small stage, but Marsha could see over their heads, see that the woman had been cut down from the dog chains and was standing alone on the small platform, flailing at the crowd of men, kicking out, fighting back.

BURN THIS FLAG

Do it! Marsha thought. Kill them! She jumped off the chair and rushed to help. She saw now the flashing of matches and the bright flames from big butane lighters.

"No!" she shouted, realizing what was happening. "Stop!" she demanded, trying to break through the packed crowd. She kept shouting, but her voice was drowned out by the heavy militant music. She saw that the woman's dance partner had mounted the platform again. He was wearing a jock strap and nothing else. Everyone was cheering him on, screaming over the music. The basement lights dimmed, then flashed into a pulsing stroke.

The man kept grinning, circling the painted woman, who kept trying to reach him, to kick him in his balls. He had a paper bag crumbled into a torch in one hand. Someone reached up from the crowd and lit the end. A brief orange flame blew up as the bag caught fire. The naked woman screamed, dancing away, trying to escape the stage. But the crowd raised their arms and pushed her back onto the stage where the man jabbed at her with his flaming, homemade torch. In the strobe light her body glistened and gleamed, wet with bright paint.

The paper bag flame caught the wet strips of paint on her thighs and licked her body as it ran up her flesh. She danced away, screaming behind the flame as the fire caught her face. Her dyed hair sizzled when it was touched by the flames.

The crowd fell away from the stage in an effort to escape the blaze, but the music never stopped.

Marsha was screaming and then began to vomit. She spun away from the sight of the burning woman and saw two skinheads rush the stage with red fire extinguishers. The white chemical foam was already spraying the room. Marsha glanced back and saw the burning woman tumble off the edge of the stage, falling like a charred log onto the dance floor. The white chemical foam swamped the body, dousing her and keeping the downtown club from bursting into fire. From across the room, Marsha could smell the burning flesh of the dead woman.

She turned away from the body and searched for an exit to the street. She had to get the cops. She had to get help for the woman.

They were crazy, she realized, and remembered having once heard whispered talk of a downtown cult that got it off by burning women.

She spotted the exit light, and the door to the street, and then she realized her life now might be in danger. Of course, she thought. They wanted a woman. They wanted a whore. They wanted someone whom no one gave a shit about. She ran.

They caught her before she reached the dimly lit exit. Her john was the first to seize her, and he dragged her back to the makeshift stage that was pulsating with the chest-beating music.

She tried to struggle away but already her wrists had been strapped with leather. She gasped for breath and sucked in more of the paint fumes. They would kill her. She looked into the face of her john, the nice little Wall Street investment banker. His eyes were bright with pleasure.

This was better than sex for him. This was better than a leverage buy out on Wall Street.

And that was the last clear thought she ever had.

THE DEVIL YOU KNOW

It began with Father Sweeney leaning into Matt's face, with both hands braced against the desk, speaking in his deliberately condescending way, telling Matt once, and then again—never raising his voice, letting his words work like a butcher's knife across the boy's sense of self—that he wanted what Matt Garrity was hiding between his legs and he wanted it *now!*

Matt was aware of the others in the classroom giggling behind their hands, their eyes darting from one to the other as they watched and waited; eyes wide with anticipation. He slipped his hands beneath the desk and squeezed his thumbs inside his fingers, the way he always did whenever he was frightened or angry or about to lose control of himself.

Again the priest asked in his patronizing voice for what Matt was hiding, adding the adjective *please*, making the word sound like a scrap of sarcasm.

Without looking up, still staring at the top of his desk, Matt slowly reached between his legs, seized the iPhone tucked under the crotch of his pants and handed it over, thinking all the while that he wanted Sweeney to fall on his fat ass.

The math teacher snatched away the phone, stood to his full height, and sighed a deep sigh, as if to demonstrate to the other students that this encounter had been a tiring, troublesome ordeal. As he walked towards the front of the classroom he declared that if he discovered another smartphone in his classroom, there would be dire consequences for this class of high school seniors.

Matt raised his sad grey eyes, without lifting his head, and watched the fat teacher squeeze sideways between the narrow rows of desks. Knowing it would provoke an outburst from the class, Matt resisted the urge to give Sweeney the finger.

The classroom was bright on this spring morning. The windows of the old brick building of Saint Ignatius High School stretched the length of the room, filling it with sunlight. Several of the lower sashes had been opened to the spring air. Matt could hear street traffic and occasional voices from the sidewalk.

Even as the morning eased back into routine, Matt felt another rush of fury, and once more he wished pain upon Father Sweeney. And as the priest cleared the rows of students, reached the front of the class, and just before he stepped onto his desk platform, his feet slipped out from under him as if he had stepped on a banana peel. He crashed to the floor with a loud and dramatic thump, landing on his big fat ass.

The classroom erupted in shouts and laughs and cheers, and Matt bolted from his seat and raced to the front, as if to help Father Sweeney. Instead he grabbed his phone out of the hand of the math teacher.

And so it began.

THE DEVIL YOU KNOW

Matt sat on the edge of the grassy playing field, desultorily watching a few undergraduates playing around with a soccer ball. He was daydreaming about girls, well, a girl. His mind and attention were only a thousand yards away and focused on a classmate. She was standing closer to the red brick school building, huddled there with a gang of girls.

"You got your fuckin' phone, Garrity?"

Matt jerked around to see Billy Smith and Davie O'Neill approaching. They had been in the math class. Normally, they wouldn't speak to him. Matt knew they thought of him as "Four Eyes," his nickname since elementary school. Mostly, however, he was just called dickhead, behind his back and to his face.

"Let me see!" Smith demanded, and, opening his palm, he jerked his hand impatiently at Matt to give him the phone. He was twice the size of Matt, heavyset, and with a round, fat, red face. After the long year, his school uniform looked the worse for wear. It hung on his bulky body, his tie was loosened, and several buttons of his white shirt were undone.

"I ain't got it," Matt answered, looking at neither of them.

"Shit you don't."

"Pussy Brannan has it," Matt lied, giving the schoolyard nickname for the principal.

Davie O'Neill reached over to search a pocket and Matt pushed his hand away, glared at him. He knew the football player wasn't afraid of him—none of the students were afraid of him, not even the girls.

"How come Brannan took it?" O'Neill asked.

Matt looked away, as if bored by the question. They all knew why the principal had taken the phone. They knew, too, that for Matt to get it back, his mother would need to call the school.

221

"Is that a new phone?" O'Neill asked next, sounding curious.

Matt nodded, still staring off.

"Fuck you," Billy Smith said, as if somehow everything was Matt's fault. "C'mon." He turned to O'Neill, adding, "He ain't going to give us fuck." With that, he shuffled off, shoulders hunched, head down, walking across the field to the main school building.

Matt watched the big oaf slouch across the yard. He hated his classmate, and he wondered why. It was not his way to be reflective about anything, but in that moment, he guessed that he hated Billy Smith and his kind, because they were bullies who picked on people. Without any deeper meditation than that, he reached for the side pocket of his blue blazer, touched his new phone, and imagined the football player falling on his ass. At that thought, Billy's feet swept out from under him, and he flipped up and onto his back and hit the ground with a thump, in much the same way Father Sweeney had done earlier in the day.

O

Matt stared at the empty Coke can on his desk. He had locked his bedroom door, as always, so he wouldn't be surprised by his mother. He wasn't sure why he was so careful as his mother was studious in her observance of his privacy—"his own space," as she called it. And since his father had been killed in the car accident, she treated him as the man of the family.

He knew, too, that it pleased his mother that he could always be found in his room. He rarely went into the other rooms in the house, not even the finished basement with the pool table, now that his father was gone and couldn't play with him.

THE DEVIL YOU KNOW

He was a thoughtful child, his mother said; she said he did well at school and was well liked by his teachers. He suspected these were her excuses for the fact that he had so few friends. The truth was he had *no* friends, certainly not girlfriends, though he spent his days in school watching one girl, seeing if he might catch a glimpse of her between classes, in the cafeteria or near her locker—not that he ever spoke to her.

He waited. He lingered. He hung around until sometimes, miraculously, she became aware of his presence and smiled, her whole face brightening like the flash of an exploding light, and he'd be greeted not only by her magical smile but also her voice saying his name: "Matt! Hi!"

He would duck his head and mumble something, then scurry away, furious at himself for his awkwardness and not having the courage to talk to her.

He understood and accepted, even with a certain amount of satisfaction, that he was considered strange. An oddball. A weirdo. At least in this way he stood out from everyone else. He took pride in that he knew he was smarter than anyone in his class, than anyone in the whole goddamn fuckin' school.

He also knew his life had magically changed. He knew it in every bone of his body. He smiled, immensely satisfied with his good fortune, not understanding or knowing nor even questioning the reason why it was happening. He stared at his new small silver phone reassuring himself by the sight of it that he had been given some strange new omnipotence.

He looked next at the empty Coke can on the corner of his desk, an arm's length away. He had finished drinking it earlier that afternoon, but he did not now reach over, pick it up, and toss it in the wastebasket. Instead, he carefully took the phone, typed in the passcode, then gently placed his open palm on the device and simply thought, *I want the can to rise up and toss and turn and dance around the room.*

The can lifted immediately off his desk like a miniature drone and turned and dipped in the air, soared higher, and bounced about the room, above his bed, his desk, and himself.

"*Holy shit!*" Matt couldn't stop grinning. He reached up with his right arm, beckoned the soda can to him, and grabbed it out of the air as if it were a high fly ball.

He stared at the can clutched in his grip and realized his hands were trembling. His *body* was trembling. He shifted positions in the chair and sat up straight, took a deep breath, and focused on pulling himself together. He flattened his palm on the smartphone, thinking, *Calm down.*

His body relaxed. His heart stopped racing. He was again in control.

For the longest moment, he stared at the phone—not touching it, only thinking of what he'd done and how he'd done it. He thought about Father Sweeney and Billy Smith, how the two of them had landed on their backsides simply by his wish and command.

He cautiously picked up the phone again, held it as if it were a sacred object. He turned it over carefully, reverently feeling the smooth device in his palm. Now it felt lighter and delicate to his touch.

He didn't know much about the phone. His mother had given it to him the night before, an eighteenth-birthday present. That way they could always be in touch, she had said, smiling and with tears in her eyes, when he went away to college.

He had hugged her, sadly thinking how he wouldn't have his dad to drive him to college in the fall.

THE DEVIL YOU KNOW

Surprising himself, surging with a confidence he had never possessed before, he again placed his hand on the silver phone. With a few taps, he had opened a video chat with Cathy Dempsey. There she was, sitting at the computer in her bedroom. When she saw his face, she broke into a bright smile and said, "Hi, Matt! What's up?"

She was not startled or alarmed by his sudden appearance, or by the fact that it was him, Matt Garrity. It was as if she had been waiting for him to call her all night, all because that was what he wanted.

"I got a new phone," he managed to say.

"OMG!"

"Yaaasss!" He grinned into his computer screen.

"From the fam?"

"Birthday."

"Well, here's my present for you." She leaned forward into her computer and kissed the screen.

Her spontaneous, unexpected, unimagined response stunned him. She was acting as if she *really* were his girlfriend only because, moments before, while touching the device, he had wished that she were.

"Is that the phone you had in math class? Stephanie told me what happened with Sweeney, how he fell on his behind. I wish I'd seen it. Do you have a name for your phone?"

"A name? No. Why?"

"You should name it. *I* know...you should name it Isidore, after Saint Isidore. We were reading about Isidore in religion class."

"Isidore?" Matt asked again.

"Cute, don't you think? The pope made Saint Isidore the patron saint of the Internet and computers. You're supposed to say a prayer to the saint every time you turn on your computer, Sister Pat said." Now she was laughing. "But you would never go to those porn sites, would you?" She cocked her head, smiling wryly, and staring at the screen.

Matt looked away from the computer, rested his hand lightly on his phone, and decided what he wanted Cathy to do. Without a word, in her bedroom across town, she stood and stepped back from the computer so he could see all of her.

She was wearing a big, loose jersey as pajamas. He recognize it as Bob Senese's old football jersey from the number, the large black block letters against crimson, the colors of their school. Without pausing, she crossed her arms, reached down, and grabbing the bottom of the shirt, pulled it straight up and off her slender body in one swift, smooth motion.

She was not wearing a bra. Her breasts were soft pink globes. Her panties were thin and pink, and while he watched and thought about seeing her fully naked, she smiled sweetly into the screen, slipped her thumbs under the elastic waistband, and peeled the panties effortlessly to her ankles. She stepped free and, widening her legs, dropped her arms and turned her palms toward the camera, as if beckoning him to come and take her. And then, lifting herself up on tiptoes, she spun around in a quick pirouette, and he saw a tiny pink butterfly tattooed on the right cheek of her buttocks.

Matt swallowed hard, his eyes focused on the patch of blond pubic hair. He had never seen a vagina.

"Matt?" She tilted her head sideways. "Are you okay?" The worry registered in her voice. "It's just me," she added, sweetly.

THE DEVIL YOU KNOW

She stepped closer and slid into the seat in front of her computer. Now he could see only her face and bare shoulders. She crossed her arms on the desk and leaned closer to the screen, filling it with her face, still smiling, her head cocked. Her blue eyes showed her concern.

Get dressed, he thought and squeezed the phone, and then mumbled. "Gotta go."

"All right," she answered with regret.

Out of the corner of his eye, he saw her reach for Senese's old shirt.

"'Night, Matt." She slipped the jersey over her shoulders and down her body, covering herself as her image and voice faded.

O

Matt wondered first if Bob Senese had ever seen her naked, seen Cathy Dempsey's fuzzy blond pubic hair. He should have taken a photo of her standing there, he thought. He could have e-mailed the photo to that ass-hole. That would have blown his goddamn mind! Or he could have printed a color photograph and pasted it on Senese's locker.

He realized that his hand was still resting on the phone, and he jerked it away, thinking frantically, *No, no, not Cathy.*

He would do nothing to hurt Cathy, even though she had unknowingly hurt him by being Senese's girlfriend, for wearing his old football shirt to bed.

He touched his phone again and immediately took his hand away. He was afraid of the phone now. He was afraid of its power—*his* power—and what he might do. He didn't want to hurt anyone. Then he grinned and thought about how he could get even with all the bastards at his school and in his life.

Then again, he knew he didn't want to hurt anyone, not Senese or Billy Smith, not even Father Sweeney. It made him feel hollow thinking of what he had done already, what he had done to Cathy, having her take off her clothes, strip in front of a computer screen.

O

Apprehensive, Matt stood and walked to the window. His bedroom looked out on a quiet intersection of two neighborhood streets, and through the branches and spring leaves he saw a half dozen kids playing touch football at the corner. He knew the kids. They were boys who lived on his block and played games on the street most afternoons. They were too young for him to play with, but he knew them by name and had even babysat for the McCauley twins.

The nine-year-old twins were the smallest players, on the same side with Toby Olson, an eighth-grader. Toby easily dodged the Frankford brothers and tossed a spiral to little Drew McCauley, who was wide open but fumbled the catch. The ball slipped through his grasp as if he had holes in his hands. Matt smiled, thinking, *That's what I did at his age.*

On the next play, Toby again danced away from the Frankford boys and, just before he was touched, flipped the ball underhand to Tommy McCauley, who briefly seized and held the pigskin before it, too, slipped through his fingers.

They were hopeless, Matt thought, and he realized what he could do.

He went back to his desk, grabbed the smartphone, and returned to the window. He watched Toby receive the hike and sprint back from the line of scrimmage. Both Frankfords rushed him, but Toby dodged them as the twins ran up the street, looking back, shouting for the ball.

228

THE DEVIL YOU KNOW

Matt pressed his hand over the phone and thought of what he wanted, imagined the result as Toby heaved the ball a dozen car lengths. The football floated gracefully down the center of the street, and Drew, the meeker of the twins, raced after it, arms up, head turned, eyes focused on the flight. He plucked the football out of the air and crossed the imaginary goal line for a touchdown.

Through the open window, Matt heard the shouts of triumph. He raised the silver phone and, reverently, as if it were the Holy Chalice itself, tenderly kissed the screen.

O

Matt decided to be discreet. That was the word. *Discreet.* Thinking of the word made him feel better. He liked the sound of it: *discreet.* He said it aloud as he walked down the hallway toward his locker. It would be best that way, to simply not draw attention to himself, to operate under the radar. He liked that. He wanted to be invisible and unnoticed. He had learned from childhood that it was safer that way. And now, because of his magical phone, he could do whatever he damn well pleased. He would never be harmed again. His whole body tingled.

But why this phone, he wondered? Or were there other phones with the same awesome powers? Did he have to worry about some kid from another school having the same phone? Was he imagining things? If he wasn't going crazy, then what the fuck was going on?

He had seen a YouTube video about a Chinese tech company: thousands of anonymous uniformed people hunched over tables. Had one of those people written a line of code, something like: *Do whatever the user wants?* A new kind of Aladdin's lamp.

229

He stepped again to the side of the hallway, up against the wall of lockers, and looked closely at the device. He wondered if it'd be possible to remove the back and look at the inner mechanisms, but he knew he wouldn't. As his dad used to say, "Let sleeping dogs lie."

"Hey, Garrity! Whatcha got?"

Cornering him against the lockers were Davie O'Neill and Billy Smith. The first bell had rung, and now he had less than five minutes to get to his locker and to his first-period class. Matt slid the phone into his pocket and turned it on, just in case.

"C'mon, I wanna see." Smith reached for the phone, tried to slip his hand into Matt's gray uniform slacks. Matt jerked away and dug his left elbow into Smith's chubby gut.

"Hey!" Davie O'Neill called out and wrapped his arms around Matt in a bear hug. He spun Matt around and slammed him against the lockers. Matt had his right hand in his pocket, clamped around his phone, as he wished for all the locks on all the lockers on all three floors of the building to fall off and smash against the cement floors.

And so they did.

The crash of hundreds of metal combination locks echoed down the school's long hallways, accompanied by shouts and screeches and a roar of voices from students. The locks bounced this way and that, like metal hailstones.

O'Neill dropped his grip on Matt, more from surprise than fear, and he and Smith turned and ran for their lockers.

Behind him, up and down the long corridor, kids were still shouting and screaming as they scrambled to retrieve their locker locks. Matt pulled himself up, straightened his tie, and turned to his own lock, the only one in the long row that was still in place. He cupped the Master Lock in one hand, spun the dial, and opened the metal door. Turning his face to the shelves, he removed from his backpack the newspaper photograph he had cut out of the sports page of the local paper. It was a photo of Cathy playing ball in the first game of the season. Cathy was on first base, handling a pop up and jumping high like a ballerina dancer to make the catch. He pasted it inside on the metal door, the first time he had ever put a girl's photo up in his locker.

O

Matt kept his mouth shut and drifted silently through his morning classes, listening to and nodding at the stories and theories from students and teachers about what had happened in the halls. By the middle of the day, there were dozens of explanations, from cosmic shifts to the wild rumor that decades before, back in the Sixties—on that very day, in fact—a Jesuit had hung himself in the basement and thus wasn't allowed in heaven. Now, on the anniversary of his suicide, he must be haunting the hallways of Saint Ignatius, they said.

Father Brannan made an announcement on the loudspeaker. The incident had been reported to the chief of police and the fire department, and their parents had been sent e-mails. He wanted the students to know they were safe and secure in the building. "Very soon, this strange physical phenomenon will be understood by the authorities," he said.

He added that any student who had seen anything "strange or curious" that morning should come to his office immediately. He told the students also to offer up a prayer to Saint Ignatius that they would soon know the answer to the question of the falling locks.

In science, Matt's last class before lunch, Father Thompson turned the entire period over to discussing the "Lock Drop," as the incident was quickly called. The class spent the period, drawing graphs and formulas on the blackboard, sharing theories, until Carol Barowitz said, "I believe it was God telling us the end of the world is here." At that, she broke down in tears and fled.

No one laughed. Matt found that impressive. But given the uproar, he'd begun to feel bad about what he had done. Carol Barowitz was silly, but also deeply upset. It was his stupid fault. He slid down lower in his seat in the back row and, hiding the phone from the eyes of everyone else, shut it off.

"Mr. Garrity!" Father Thompson's booming voice reached to where Matt sat in the far corner of the room. "What do you think, young man, given your interest in science? What would our young Spock suggest?"

The science teacher had walked to the far side of the room, the window side, and was working his way down the aisle. Matt glanced up at Father Thompson, but he couldn't keep his eyes on him. He looked away and saw a half dozen others had turned in their seats to stare at him. They were waiting too. He knew they thought he was a dork, but they also know he was "the smartest kid" in their school.

Matt pulled himself up in the seat and said confidently, "Metal fatigue?"

The science teacher nodded and smiled and leaned against the windowsill. He held a piece of chalk in his hands. His fingers were white from the dust. He gestured with the hand holding the chalk and asked,

"Do you think, perhaps, we have seen the work of a supernatural power today? We all believe in supernatural powers, don't we?"

THE DEVIL YOU KNOW

The teacher was giving him a way out, Matt realized. He could just nod and agree and let it go, but that wasn't how Matt did things. His dad was always warning him that he didn't know when to keep his mouth shut, to leave well enough alone.

"I don't think it's supernatural, Father," Matt kept his voice low, so that his classmates had to strain to hear what he had to say. Let them work to learn something, he thought.

"Oh?" Thompson crossed his arms, keeping his eyes on Matt, giving him the respect he might give an academic colleague, and let Matt take his time to explain himself.

"It's cosmic," Matt said.

"Cosmic?" Thompson frowned.

Matt nodded, keeping his grey eyes on the priest. He heard a few snickers from his classmates and, as always, that pissed him off. He had a fleeting moment's thought of reaching into his pants pocket, grabbing his phone, and silencing them.

Instead, he replied calmly to his science teacher, raising his voice now so the students in the front row could clearly hear his answer, and knowing they wouldn't understand a word of it. He began, as he always began when he had no idea what he was going to say, by building the answer from scraps of information he had heard or read about in science class or had learned from his library of comic books. He spoke about cosmic shifts and global warming and gravitational pull.

And then, with an ecclesiastical coup de grâce that he guessed would impress the Jesuit, he added how the big bang theory, the pillar of modern cosmology, was the brainchild of a Catholic priest, and how that priest, Georges Lemaître, using Einstein's equations of gravity, came up with his theory of how the universe began.

The class fell silent at his fusillade of scientific terminology. He spooled it out with conviction and authority, as if he were the weatherman with the local forecast. The other students, he knew, were baffled by his big words and his theory about the explosion of locks. His explanation had the appeal of a theatrical performance, a Shakespearean soliloquy. When he had summed up his theory, in a cadence of authoritative declarative sentences, the class burst into applause and pounded on the tops of their desks in appreciation and awe. None of them, he knew, had understood a word of what he had said.

Father Thompson stepped forward and jokingly shook Matt's hand, as if to declare him the winner, then walked slowly up to the front of the class. He waited a moment until the room settled down and announced, "Ladies and Gentlemen, now that we have heard from Mr. Garrity about cosmic shift, I want you all to articulate your own theory on what caused the "Lock Drop." It will be the question on next Thursday's quiz."

The classroom erupted in cries of protest and banged books on desks as the bell rang. Father Thompson scooped up his papers and strode from the room, beating the rush of students out the door.

Matt didn't move. The next class was filing in before he extracted himself from his seat, collected his books, and headed for the door. It was time for lunch.

He was opening his locker when Cathy startled him with a big, bright "hello," as if she were bringing him good news.

"Were you here when the locks fell off?" Her voice was excited.

THE DEVIL YOU KNOW

Matt pulled his head from his locker and shook it without looking at her.

She launched into a detailed explanation of how she had been walking down the third-floor hall, heading to French class, when everything went crashing.

"It was an earthquake for sure, and I texted my mom and she said I should come home, but I have my French test. I can't go anywhere." She rolled her eyes. "I just ran into Phil, and he told me you told Father Thompson and everyone in Science what it was, but Phil said he couldn't understand you. It was crazy brilliant, he said."

Matt locked his locker and headed down the hall toward the cafeteria. Cathy fell into step beside him. She was carrying a stack of textbooks, hugged against her small breasts. She was several inches taller than Matt, almost five-eight, and to make eye contact, he had to look up, as if at an older sister.

"I was just making stuff up," Matt mumbled. "Father Thompson was laughing at me. He knew I was completely bullshitting."

Cathy stared down at him, her face frozen. "Don't use such bad language; it's not nice."

"Sorry. It's been a weird morning."

"I know." At once she was consolatory, her voice softened. "I got called into the principal's office, too."

Matt stopped walking.

"Father Brennan asked about what happened in math class with you. Everyone thinks..."

"Everyone thinks what?"

Cathy shrugged. She wouldn't look at him. She turned away, and her eyes swept the walls, as if seeking somewhere safe to look.

235

"I don't know. That you did something to him, I guess, to make him fall down."

"What bullshit." He started walking. Cathy followed him in silence.

When they reached the entrance to the cafeteria, Matt stopped. Cathy, he remembered, would be heading to the library and her study period.

"Will I see you later at Sally's Place?" he asked nicely, mentioning the ice cream shop where the kids congregated after school. He never went to the local student hang out, let alone with her.

She cocked her head and looked concerned. "Of course. I'll see you there," she added, as if it was what they always did after school.

"Okay, good." He recovered and glanced into the cafeteria. O'Neill, Senese, and a half dozen other football players were crowded around a table too small to comfortably seat all of them.

Coach Nutley stood nearby. He was talking to Mrs. Penn, the cafeteria manager, but kept his eyes on his players, as if he half expected trouble.

The players, seeing Matt standing with Cathy, laughed and whispered among themselves. Matt could guess what they were saying.

He turned back to Cathy and asked boldly, "Do you want to study together tonight?"

"Of course. I want to study with you." A huge smile filled her face.

With that, she stepped closer to him and said, "I want to tell you something."

Glancing around her, she added quickly, "I had this really weird dream last night, and you were in it."

"I was?" Now his heart was pounding.

"I can't tell you now."

"Well, what was it about? Give me a hint." He was grinning, relaxed, realizing she had not understood what he had done to her. He was safe.

THE DEVIL YOU KNOW

She didn't say anything, just rolled her eyes in that way he found so endearing, blew him a kiss, and started to walk away. Turning back for a moment, she tossed off, "Oh, by the way, you haven't yet *actually* asked me to be your date for the prom."

Then she spun on her heels and rushed off, raising her right hand and waving goodbye.

O

The cafeteria had thinned out by the time Matt went through the line and carried his tray into the main dining area. He looked around for someone to sit with— another kid from the debate team—but most people had already eaten and gone outside to spend the rest of the period sitting in the sun.

On any other day, Matt would have avoided the table of football players, preferring the corner near the cafeteria office, where he knew he would be left alone. But now, with his smartphone, he felt emboldened, so he sat down alone at a table within sight and hearing of the football crowd.

They were talking about girls. He could hear them trashing one after the other, making fun of how they looked or what they wore, and confessing or speculating on who had gotten head from this one or that one.

Still, it took them only a few minutes to notice that Matt Garrity was seated at a table nearby.

Billy Smith started it, tossing a plastic cup across the room. It hit the long table where he was sitting and bounced off, just missing Matt. For his part, Matt never looked up.

Another kid threw a cup that bounced and stayed on the table. Again, Matt didn't stop eating his hamburger.

It was only when half of a hot dog landed on the table and sprayed him with a splash of ketchup that he looked over at the football players, saw them watching him, grinning, having a good time at his expense. Slowly, as if reaching for a handkerchief to wipe the red blot off his face, he pressed the palm of his right hand over the new smartphone in his pocket, felt the surface and, made his wish.

Nothing happened. The football players were laughing. He pressed harder and thought again what he wanted the players to do: jump up, dance the Doggie, and strip off their clothes as if they were a chorus line of teenage strippers.

They stood as a group and, grabbing their trays, walked across to Matt's table in single file. Without a word, each dropped his garbage on top of Matt's unfinished lunch.

It was only when Davie O'Neill, the last in line, had dumped his lunch and stepped away that Matt remembered he had shut off his phone in science class, and he pulled the smartphone quickly from his pocket, typed in the passcode, and made his wish again.

It came just as Jimmy Drummer reached the exit. He stopped, as did the others. Jimmy pulled his own phone from his pocket, tapped the screen a few times, and held it up in the air as music began to play from its speaker. Moments later, he and all of the football players ran back together to the open space in the room, as if it were a stage. Together, they began to lip-synch "UpTown Funk!" as they formed a line and systematically began to strip out of their clothes, tossing their blue blazers, striped ties, and white shirts into an imaginary crowd of screaming girls.

Coach Nutley rushed away from the wall, circled the edge of the room, shouting at his players as he hurried to the entrance of the cafeteria.

THE DEVIL YOU KNOW

All Matt could think was, *This is the best ever.*

The coach kept shouting and the football players kept stripping and singing.

Guys grab your bitches
Guys grab your women
'Cause we're going downtown now
'Cause we're going downtown now

They stripped off their undershirts, kicked off their black school shoes. Hobbling on one foot, then the other, but still dancing, they pulled off their gray slacks and underwear: boxers and briefs.

Out of the corner of his eye, Matt saw girls fleeing the cafeteria, ducking out behind the chorus line, shielding their eyes as they ran from the nude boys. Not everyone was running from the cafeteria. Several tables full of juniors and seniors, Matt saw, were on their feet, yelling, doubling over in laughter as the big, clumsy players tried to dance and keep in rhythm with the tinny music blaring from Jimmy Drummer's phone.

Coach Nutley reached the chorus line and grabbed Charlie Gifford, the closest to him, and spun the teenager around. The senior was stark naked, laughing and singing as he tried to keep dancing with the others. Nutley wrestled him to the floor. It wasn't until he hit the ground that Gifford stopped dancing, as if sense had been literally knocked into him.

The coach grabbed Billy Smith next. His Jockeys were caught at his knees, and he hobbled into Nutley's grasp. Seizing him, the coach tripped and fell forward, shoving Smith sideways into two of the other boys, knocking both of them over.

A roar went up from the gallery of students still in the cafeteria.

Matt reached into his pocket and ended the football players' striptease with one simple wish. Then he leaned forward and, placing his elbows on the table, folded his fingers together, rested his chin on his hands, and innocently sat and waited to see what would happen next to the football players, all flat out naked on the school's cafeteria tile floor.

"You were there?" Cathy looked up from her dish of ice cream.

They were sitting in the back booth of Sally's Place, the ice cream shop a block from school and crowded with kids. Matt had wished on his phone for the red rear booth to be empty when he arrived, and it was.

"So did they really, you know, do it?" she leaned closer, as if sharing a secret, as if what had happened at one o'clock in the cafeteria wasn't already known by all the students. Her eyes were sparkling.

"Do what?" Matt asked innocently, forking his apple pie, enjoying himself,

"You know..." She glanced away so as not to be looking at him when she added, "Do *it*."

"Do *what?*" He took another bite of pie.

"Matt! You know what I mean and I'm not going to say it." She was laughing and, to keep herself from saying more, turned back to her ice cream.

"No, they didn't do *it*, as you say."

"Sally Conroy told everyone in study hall that she saw them do *it*."

"She wasn't even there!"

"So, they were dancing?"

Matt nodded and kept eating.

THE DEVIL YOU KNOW

"And they took off *all* their clothes?"

He stopped eating the pie to nod in agreement.

"Oh my God!" Cathy grabbed her napkin to smother her giggles. "That's so bad. I wish I had been there."

"You probably would have run out of the room. The bare asses were not a pretty sight."

"I don't know. That would have been kinda fun." Cathy rolled her eyes. "What were they thinking? What could have possibly possessed them?" She paused and waited for his answer.

Matt shrugged, not looking up. He didn't trust himself to keep what he was thinking out of his expression. Cathy might be good at spotting that he was hiding something. Girls were pretty good at that sort of thing. He knew he could never get away with anything with his mother.

"You don't have any idea?"

"They're jocks. They think they can get away with anything."

"Not stripping!" She shook her head. "No way."

Matt pushed his dish away and leaned back in the booth.

"Maybe they wanted to show off their tattoos."

"They have tattoos? *Who* does? Kevin does, I bet." Cathy smiled at the thought.

"Yeah, a little pink butterfly tattoo on his right butt." Matt was annoyed by her sudden interest in Kevin Young.

Cathy paused, watching him. He tried to shift her attention off his slip of the tongue, his mention of the pink butterfly, by reaching for his backpack, as if to find something, and asked her if she had taken her science exam.

Cathy didn't respond. She kept watching him, pinning him with a steady, cold stare.

"Why did you say *a pink butterfly?*" she finally asked.

"I don't know." He shrugged, as if uninterested, and kept busy with his backpack. "I don't know anything about tattoos. I would never get one."

"I have a pink tattoo," she answered, silencing him. "All of us—Kathy, Barbara, Ellen—we all have pink tattoos on our bums."

He tried to look incredulous. He raised his eyebrows, faking a look of wonder.

"No one knows about our tattoos, and you just announced it as if everyone should." She kept her eyes on him. "Why?"

"It's a 'fashion statement' or something for girls? What's so secretive about a butterfly tattoo, anyway?"

"A *pink* butterfly tattoo."

"Okay, a pink butterfly!" He tried to sound annoyed, to silence her by showing that he was upset.

"No one has them at school but *us.* How do you know I have one?"

"How would *I* know?" He pointed his fingers at himself, kept up his outraged tone.

Cathy stared at him, watched him, judged him. She slowly shook her head and said softly, "I don't know. But..."

"But what?" he pushed. Seeing he had backed her into a corner he displayed sudden confidence. He was the captain of the debating team and he knew how to marshal an argument, as Father Shane always said, using Matt's performance as the example for the other debaters.

"Everything is so weird." She shook her head. "All this stuff at school, and last night..." She stopped talking and stared down at her dish of ice cream.

Matt kept quiet, watching her. He wanted to know, but he kept quiet. Girls were good at knowing what boys were thinking. Still, he needed to know what she knew.

THE DEVIL YOU KNOW

"What happened last night?" he asked innocently.

"Oh, nothing, I guess."

He kept quiet; he didn't rush in with another question. He guessed she was debating what more, if anything, to tell him.

"I had this weird dream, as I told you. I dreamed you and I were talking and you asked me to take all my clothes off and I did—right in front of the computer—and you must have seen the pink tattoo." She glanced at him and turned immediately away, looking guilty and small and ashamed.

"Oh, wow, that would have been great!" he grinned.

"Shut up!" With that, she grabbed her jacket and backpack, slid from the booth, and walked out of the ice cream parlor without waiting for him. She walked straight to the bus stop at the corner of the avenue and never once looked back to see if he was following her.

O

Having paid the tab at the register in the front of Sally's, Matt followed Cathy out to the street. When he reached her, she warned, "Don't you tell *anyone!*" She still wouldn't look at him.

"What am I going to tell?" he asked. "*Who* am I going to tell?"

"You know who!"

The bus had made the light at the corner and was slowing as it approached.

"Don't you dare tweet what I told you about my tattoo. Don't you dare put up anything on Facebook." She glanced his way as she pulled out her bus pass, adding, "Get it?"

He nodded.

"Say so," she demanded.

"I get it! I get it! I won't do *anything*. I won't say *anything*. I don't know nothin'."

"Good!" As the door hissed open and she mounted the steps, she added without bothering to look at him, "And don't Skype me later. I don't want to study with you tonight."

With that, she ran up the steps and disappeared into the crowded bus.

When he got to school the next day, he saw a notice on the entrance instructing students to go directly to the gym, not their first period. Something was wrong, Matt knew, and he was thankful that he had left his phone home at home.

Matt hesitated at the double door entrance of the gym and checked the wooden bleachers, swept his glance from one end to the other, looking for a safe spot to sit, someplace away from the jocks.

Usually he sat near the far exit door, up high, giving himself a panoramic view of the gym. He liked it there, alone and with a full view of the crowd. From wherever he was, he wanted to see Cathy, and she was always with the girls on the bleachers on the other side of the basketball court. That was the school rule: the girls sat on the left side, the visitors' side; the boys on the right side, the home team side.

He tried to spot her in the crowd of three hundred girls. It gave him something to do, watching her. It always had.

Also, he always brought a book to any assembly. By sliding it down between his legs and leaning forward on the bleacher, he could read while it appeared as if he were diligently listening to and watching what was happening on the stage beyond the basketball court.

THE DEVIL YOU KNOW

He didn't have a book today. He hadn't expected an assembly, but when he spotted the notice, he knew it was because of the "dancing jocks," as the football players had already been labeled in Tweets and on Facebook pages.

Matt circled the gym and found a seat near the freshmen who sat together in the far section of the benches, covertly texting each other and keeping out of trouble. He wondered how much they knew about the "dancing jocks."

At 8:30 on the dot Father Brannan, the principal—who considered it a venal sin to be late for any class or event—pushed open the main double doors of the gym and marched straight out onto the middle of the basketball court. He was wearing his Jesuit black suit and collar and even with his leather shoes he walked across the shiny waxed floor. It didn't matter to him that he was breaking the unwritten rule of the gymnasium—never step onto the court wearing dress shoes. That wasn't a sin to him, Matt guessed.

He was carrying a rolled-up stack of papers like the handle of a hammer. Nervously, he swatted the papers against the palm of his hand while he scanned the packed bleachers.

He did not speak. Instead he slowly turned and took in the crowd of students and teachers. The faculty—priests, nuns, and more than a half-dozen laypeople—stood together in a cluster near the entrance to the gymnasium.

Matt studied the teachers. He knew their expressions would reveal how serious the assembly was. They weren't smiling or whispering to one another. Matt knew it wasn't going to be good news from Pussy Brannan.

The principal was an impressive-looking priest, Matt thought. In his forties, the Jesuit was in great physical shape. He looked tough, even in his Jesuit black clergy suit. He never wore a cassock—no girl's dresses for him. Over six feet tall, he had played football and basketball at Notre Dame before he joined the priesthood. Matt had often seen him jogging on the track when his dad would drop him off at school on his way to work.

"Good morning, everyone," Father Brannan declared, stopping the students' conservations. It was suddenly absolutely quiet. Matt could hear water running downstairs in the boys' locker room.

"There was an incident yesterday at school. Actually, there were several unexplained and mysterious occurrences yesterday, as you know." He spoke slowly, pausing, and looking at both sides of the court, taking in all the students. "I need not mention what you are well aware of."

Matt thought Pussy might make a joke about the locks—he often started assemblies with a joke to ease the tension—but he didn't this morning. He continued in the same serious tone. They were all in trouble, Matt realized.

"I want to say that the incident involving the lockers is being investigated by our police department. Detective Sullivan was at school yesterday afternoon. Some of you might have seen him and his partner, Sergeant Hebert.

"We unfortunately also had a disturbing incident yesterday in the cafeteria." He paused once more.

This was odd, Matt thought, keeping his eyes glued to the principal, and thinking how Brannan always knew exactly what he wanted to say and said it quickly, forcefully. Why was he measuring his words today?

"The football players behaved in the most egregious manner," Brannan continued.

Matt frowned. *Egregious*. Jesuits always used fancy words when there was trouble coming.

"Those boys are no longer students of Saint Ignatius Loyola High School."

There was a sudden, loud, and uniform reaction from the girls' bleachers.

246

THE DEVIL YOU KNOW

The principal did not hesitate, silencing the assembly by stating that such lewd and ill-mannered behavior would not be tolerated at any high school, especially a Catholic Jesuit school.

Matt spotted O'Neill's girlfriend, Kathy Handley, burying her face in her hands as the principal explained how he had telephoned the parents of the boys that morning to tell them their sons had been expelled, and why.

Brannan explained that the boys' parents had been asked to attend a meeting that afternoon, when they would be shown a video of their sons' actions.

A video!

A video camera in the cafeteria? Of course, Jesuits were that underhanded.

But had they seen him?

He had a vivid recollection of slipping the smartphone out of his pocket, setting it carefully on the cafeteria table, placing the palm of his right hand over its silver face.

What would they have seen? He knew he was being ridiculously over concerned but he couldn't help wondering. *What would they know?*

Again, he refocused his attention on Pussy Brannan, but it wasn't easy. It was what he hated most about himself that he was always worried he would get into trouble. He remembered how, in the eighth grade, Sister Elizabeth had asked the class to list their best and worst qualities. He had put "worrywart" as his biggest problem.

He slipped his hands into his trousers and nervously squeezed his thumbs inside his fingers.

"Something is terribly wrong here at Ignatius," Brannan was saying.

The principal turned around in the center of the gym floor, making a complete circle so that he was looking briefly at all of them as he kept talking about the behavior of the football players and the locker locks cascading onto the floors. He mentioned, too, how Father Sweeney had taken a fall while teaching math the day before and that he'd had to see a doctor and was now wearing a brace.

"None of this is normal," Brannan intoned, as if delivering a homily. "We asked Detective Sullivan to look into all these matters when the police began their investigation yesterday afternoon."

He unrolled the papers in his hand, then rolled the pages back up.

"You have heard or learned about the term *poltergeist*." He paused again before raising his voice to add, "Strange phantoms, apparitions, and mischievous spirits. In other words, the devil himself. As Catholics we know the devil is daily with us, tempting our souls."

He paused a moment, then added in the same serious voice, but softening his tone, "I have also spoken to our Cardinal, and he suggested that Monsignor Robert Caifano, who is currently in the United States, visit our school.

"Monsignor Caifano is from the Vatican. Some of the seniors, I believe, were assigned by Father Delaney to read his book, *The Devil We Know*, the monsignor's study of terrorist organizations such as ISIS in Syria, Al Qaeda in Afghanistan, and al Shabaab in Somalia. How they have become tools of Satan."

The principal paused, then added in a burst, "But we don't have to worry about terrorists here at Saint Ignatius, so don't go home and tell your parents that is what I'm implying. I receive enough telephone calls, emails, and text messaging from your fathers as it is—and that's just about your grades."

He smiled, and there was a brief cheer from the senior boys' section, but the younger students and girls did not respond to the priest's humor. He wasn't, as Matt's dad always said, a lot of laughs.

THE DEVIL YOU KNOW

"What I do want you to tell your parents, however...," Father Brannan raised his voice so that he could be clearly heard and understood. "...is that Monsignor Caifano will be at Saint Ignatius to help us find an explanation for these recent strange occurrences.

"Meanwhile, I request that you be alert for odd incidents or strangers in our school and that you report them immediately to any faculty or staff member. We need you to be watchful in the corridors and on the grounds. And now, before dismissal, let us say a prayer to our Heavenly Father and ask for His protection, here at our beloved Saint Ignatius and wherever we go in life.

"In the name of the Father, and of the Son, and of the Holy Spirit..."

With all the students, Matt scrambled to his feet and blessed himself, thankful again that he had left his phone at home. He might be able to fool the cops, he guessed, but not a monsignor from the Vatican.

"Mom, where did you buy my new phone?" Matt asked innocently, coming into the kitchen to get a Coke while his mother was making a pie.

He glanced up at the clock and saw that he had been home from school for only an hour. He had been upstairs doing homework, and, thanks to the phone, he was already done. He had finished a ten-page book report on *The Catcher in the Rye* simply by turning on the device, placing his palm gently on its face, and thinking that he needed a two-thousand-word essay—thinking that it needed to be smart but not too smart, with a couple of typos and misplaced punctuation, so Father Shane wouldn't think he had plagiarized the assignment.

The paper appeared on his laptop instantaneously, filling out sentence by sentence, line by line, paragraph by paragraph. It was magic. It was mesmerizing. It was all written in sixty seconds.

He was at first afraid to read what the phone had written and sat slumped in front do the laptop staring at the text. Knowing he had the power to create something out of nothing by thinking what he wanted written drove a wedge of fear through him as much as it made him giddy with delight.

He finally leaned forward and read the opening paragraph. The sentences were simple, declarative, nothing he couldn't have done if he had written it himself, and yes, there was a word here and there used incorrectly, or so he thought. He didn't think that *presumptuous* really meant "unwarrantedly self-assured," but he wasn't positive. He could change it, he thought, but then realized he shouldn't. Let his pixie be his muse.

He kept reading, enjoying the essay as if he had written it himself, because, in truth, it was everything he thought about Holden Caulfield but would never have been able to put into words.

His mother looked up from her baking and interrupted his thoughts by asking, "Don't you like your phone?"

Matt slipped onto a counter stool and popped open a Coke can, shrugging his shoulders as he answered, "I think it's cool. Really cool. I was just wondering where you got it. Cathy Dempsey asked me," he lied.

"Does Cathy have one?" his mother asked.

"Sure."

"All the kids have them, right?"

"Yeah. Some of them have Kindles or small computers that they take to class and take notes and show off." He sipped his Coke.

250

THE DEVIL YOU KNOW

"You can go on the internet with it, right?" She stared at him, looking puzzled.

"Didn't you know that?" He was surprised by her question.

"Your father bought it off eBay shortly before the accident. It was almost the last thing he did." Her voice caught in her throat, and she turned away to wipe her eyes with the corner of her apron. Recovering, she explained, "I thought it was best to get a second hand phone so you could, you know, practice on it before college. Your father agreed."

"It's great, Mom. Thanks for getting it for me."

"I didn't know what's what. There are so many different types of smartphones. You have to be a genius or very young to understand them. The seller did say this phone is special. I think." She returned to her cooking with determination, asking, "What does this phone have that's so special?"

For a second Matt was tempted to say everything, but in the end, he only shrugged. "It's just a phone."

"It takes photos, right? That's pretty special. I'd say."

"Yes, it takes pictures, Mom."

"Take a picture and send it to my computer. Take one of Cathy. Are you two, as we used to say, 'an item'?" she smiled.

"We're friends." He thought of the photo he didn't take, the one of Cathy standing naked in front of her computer screen. What would his mother say if she saw *that*?

"Is that okay?" She asked, watching him, waiting for his reply.

"Yeah, it's okay. We had ice cream yesterday after school at Sally's."

"You're good friends then?" She asked, seeming to push for more details.

"She's in my year, Mom. She's on the debating team. Jeez." He slid off the stool. "I see her every day." He tried to sound exasperated, but in fact, his mother had never asked him about girls before. Maybe because he had never had a date.

"I know, but..." Her voice faded as she picked up the pie pan and turned to the oven. She opened the oven door and said over her shoulder, "Oh, I have some booklets that came with the phone, instructions or whatever." She placed the pie in the oven, then stepped over to the small desk in the corner of the kitchen. Opening a drawer, she said, "Here they are!" Smiling, she handed a small packet to Matt.

Finally, he thought. Finally he would have an answer.

O

It was only when he had the small instruction book in his hand that he realized his phone wasn't made by any company he had ever heard of. It was the same size as all phones, but it wasn't Apple's silver phone or any other company he knew of.

This phone had Force Touch, "a pressure-sensitive haptic system," he read. Matt skimmed the pages, searching for anything that might explain why the phone was so powerful, but all he found was more information about the wrap-around display—made of sapphire (more powerful than Gorilla Glass!)—and the Liquidmetal frame. The phone also had a two-lens system that "allowed DSLR-quality imagery," state-of-the-art processors, and 150-gigabyte capacity.

He carefully set the phone down on his desk and stared at it, now afraid to touch it, afraid he would inadvertently cause another calamity for someone if he had an angry thought. He could get rid of it, he thought, bury it in the backyard and save himself from doing more harm. He could tell his mother he had lost it on the bus or someone had stolen it from his locker.

THE DEVIL YOU KNOW

He could tell her he really didn't want a smartphone, that it was a waste of money. He could say he didn't deserve it. Sitting alone in his room, he thought of a dozen reasons he shouldn't have a phone. He was good at that, thinking of what a terrible son he was. It made him feel better.

To distract himself from more worrisome thoughts, he reached over to check his phone. There was a new message on Skype. He clicked the icon and there was Cathy. She was sitting at her computer, typing seriously, not looking up, not realizing she had left the video on, and he paused for a moment and watched her. Her newly washed hair was wrapped in a towel. She was wearing the white bathrobe that she had gotten for Christmas from her older sister. He had heard her tell the girls in the debating club what gifts she had gotten when they came back to school after the New Year. He wondered whether she was naked under the robe.

He clicked the video call button, and she looked up and smiled into the screen.

"Hello, Mr. Difficult To Talk To." She kept smiling.

He grinned. "Why? What do you mean?"

"You didn't say one word to me all day," she pretended to pout. "And then after class, you just split without a word or a text or anything."

"You know, you should be an actress, the way you make faces."

"I only make faces at you. Because you pretend you don't even know me. Yesterday we went to Sally's, and today you were invisible. I couldn't find you. I wanted to ask you what Pussy Brannan was talking about. It was all so weird. I figured you'd know. I thought you were my boyfriend." She sounded heartbroken.

"I am your boyfriend. But you're the one who told me not to Skype you."

"Is that why you had the police talk to me?"

"What are you talking about?"

"After school today. Mrs. Murphy was waiting for me when Betty Ericson and I were headed to baseball practice. She said Father Brannan wanted to see me. When I got to his office he was there with that monsignor from the Vatican. And Detective Sullivan. I know Mr. Sullivan—he plays golf with my dad."

Matt moved closer to the computer screen. His heart was racing as he asked, trying to be as nonchalant as possible, "What did they want?"

"They asked about you."

"Me?"

Cathy nodded.

"Why did they ask *you* about *me?*"

"Because you're my boyfriend. Everyone knows that. Even the Jesuits."

"So?" He tried to sound dismissive as he slipped his hands out of the sight of the Skype camera and squeezed his thumbs inside his fingers to calm down.

"Mr. Sullivan wanted to know if you were acting 'strangely' lately."

"Oh, for Chrissake!" Now he could feel himself getting furious.

"I told them you always acted strangely," she said, laughing into the computer screen.

"Yeah, sure, what did you tell them?" He was terrified again.

"I told them the truth. I told them you were the nicest, sweetest boy at Saint Ignatius High School."

Matt watched Cathy for a moment, swept up by her remark, and then he said, "thank you."

"What I didn't tell them was what happened to me." She kept staring at Matt as she spoke.

THE DEVIL YOU KNOW

"What do you mean?"

"You know what I mean."

"Did you fall down too?"

Cathy sighed.

"I don't know what you're talking about," Matt stated.

"Yes, you do! You know exactly what I'm talking about," she shot back, looking straight at the screen. When she was mad, he saw now, she always had the same fierce expression—all the soft sweetness disappeared from her hazel eyes.

"How I took off all my clothes just so you could see me naked," she blurted out.

"What are you talking about?" he protested, leaning back from the computer, as if to hide.

"Matt Garrity, don't give me that innocent act. The other night, when you Skyped me, I saw you had that phone in your hand, and the next thing I knew I was taking off my clothes. I couldn't stop myself. I knew it was wrong. I knew it was a mortal sin letting you see me naked, but I couldn't stop. I wanted—I needed—to do it. I told you it was a dream, but that was just to see if you would tell me the truth. And then you mentioned my tattoo! You saw me naked!"

"You've been watching too many *Star Trek* movies," Matt tossed off, thinking fast. "Every kid in school has a phone in his or her hand, and all the time."

"I didn't tell anyone what you did to me, but I'm telling *you*."

"Cathy, I didn't do anything to you!" He lowered his voice, trying to sound sincere and serious.

"No? Nothing but make me strip naked."

255

"I didn't *make* you do anything!" He let his voice register anger, hoping she would back off.

"No, *you* didn't! Your phone did!"

"Cathy, you're crazy!" He threw up his hands, feigning frustration.

"I'm not crazy, and I'm not stupid enough to tell Mr. Sullivan and Pussy Brannan or that Vatican monsignor what you did to me with your weird phone."

Matt dropped his shoulders, letting her see his weariness, and then blurted out everything, confessed to her, telling her he had had no idea about the phone's powers, and that it was all his fault, everything bad that had happened to her and at school.

"You okay, Matt?" Her voice softened hearing his long confession. She leaned closer to the computer, as if she wanted to embrace him.

He shrugged, warmed by her sweetness.

"What's happening?" she asked, frowning, looking frightened.

"I don't know." He told her all he knew, how the phone wasn't an Apple. He held up the instruction book. "It doesn't say anything about what it can do, you know, like have all the locks fall off the lockers."

"Oh my God! Matt, this is scary. How did you make the locks fall off?"

He picked up the silver phone, made sure it was turned off, and demonstrated how he held the phone and made the wish about the high school locks in the school.

"That's not possible." She was shaking her head, protesting his explanation.

"You told me you took your clothes off because I held the phone and wished that you would."

"Well, maybe I just wanted to do it for you," she looked away from the screen.

THE DEVIL YOU KNOW

"Okay, I'll do it again."

"Don't you *dare!*" Her hand reached for the computer.

"I can touch my phone and, whoosh, you're naked walking down Broadway." He was grinning, teasing.

"Matt, that isn't funny."

He heard the fear in her voice.

"I'd never do that to you."

"This is scary, Matt." She looked directly at the screen, "You won't do anything bad to me, will you? You like me, don't you?"

He leaned closer to the screen, seeing tears wash down her cheek. Now he felt cheap and sad, as if he had physically hurt her.

"Cathy, I love you!" he blurted out, surprising himself with his declaration.

She beamed and answered, "I love you, Matt."

He gushed out everything he had been thinking and feeling since he'd unwrapped his birthday present. He told her how his dad had gotten the silver phone from eBay and then died in the car accident before giving it to him, and how his mother had given it to him on his birthday. He'd had no idea the phone had such powers. He'd only discovered its powers by accident. Now, he told the story of wanting Father Sweeney to fall on his ass and how, moments later, he watched the fat priest drop with a thump to the floor. He told her what had happened with Smith and then the football players in the cafeteria.

"So you did tell me to take off my clothes?" She skipped the details of the football players in the cafeteria and came back to what had happened between the two of them.

"Yes," he admitted, growing embarrassed. "I'm sorry Cathy."

After a moment of reflection, she asked why.

"Because I wanted to see you without your clothes on," he answered directly, realizing as he spoke that he was getting an erection. "I love you." Having said once that he loved her, he wanted to tell her again and again. It made him feel grown up, telling her.

"You aren't going to tell anyone what you did to me, are you?"

"No, I'm not. I'm not a girl!"

"Boys are just as bad as girls."

"Not me."

"Well, I think that's true. If you were like other guys, I wouldn't tell you anything. In fact, you wouldn't be my boyfriend. You *are* my boyfriend, aren't you, Matt?"

"I told you, I love you," he said, smiling, taking pleasure in his admission.

"You can love a person and still not like them. Girls do it all the time."

"And are you going to tell your girlfriends about this?" He held up the silver phone.

"Oh my God, no! I would never...Matt, you believe me, right?"

"Yes, I believe you," he answered softly. His devotion registered in his voice. He felt wonderful knowing she was his and would be his for the rest of his life. And all because his new strange smartphone made her fall in love with him.

"I've got to go, Matt. Mom's calling. We're going shopping for my prom dress."

She was on her feet, stepping away from the screen. She turned and shouted, "*I'm coming, Mom!*"

Turning back to the screen, she leaned closer and whispered, "Bye, honey. I'll Skype you after dinner. We can do our homework together, and if you want I'll do whatever you would like me to do." With that, she winked and tapped the keyboard and the screen went blank.

O

When Matt got to school the next morning, a man was leaning against his locker, reading from what looked like a thick prayer book.

He wasn't dressed like a priest, and he looked too old to be a new student. Matt guessed he might be the new baseball coach. Whoever he was, why was he waiting by his locker?

Seeing him, however, scared Matt, and he had a sudden impulse to bypass his locker and head straight for class. That's when the man looked up, spotted Matt, and smiled.

"Hello, Matt," he said nicely. "I'm keeping your locker company."

He stepped forward with his hand out, as if Matt was someone important.

"I'm Monsignor Caifano. I believe Father Brannan mentioned me yesterday." He covered the side of his mouth with his hand, looked around, and said, in a theatrical whisper, "But actually I'm from the U.S. I just work at the Vatican." He smiled.

The priest had blue eyes, thick black hair, and a dark face with a wide mouth and bright teeth. As his dad would say, "He looked like a million bucks."

Matt saw then that the monsignor was sort of dressed like a priest, in dark pants and a white shirt. There was no Roman collar, however, and no dangling rosary wrapped around his waist, No bare feet and clergy sandals.

Monsignor Caifano kept smiling, as he asked, "Do you have a few minutes, Matt?"

"I've got class, Father. I mean *Monsignor*." He dropped his right hand down by his side and squeezed his thumb inside his fingers, frightened by the thought of being interrogated by the Vatican envoy.

"Oh, I spoke to your teacher earlier. He said it would be fine if you skipped class. He told me you e-mailed him an essay last night and he was very impressed. You're his best student, he said."

Monsignor Caifano casually reached over and placed his hand on Matt's shoulder in a friendly but tight grip, as if he half expected Matt to bolt.

"Good," Matt answered weakly. "I mean, that he liked it." He was trying to appear pleased by the praise, but his heart was racing, and he wondered if the monsignor noticed how scared he was as he fumbled with his locker lock.

"What you need is that magic moment when all the locks fell off, so you don't have to remember your combination, right?" the monsignor tossed off. He was still smiling and watching as Matt spun the dial and started over, trying to control his panic.

"Were you around when the locks dropped off the other day?" the monsignor asked next, as if he were just making conversation.

Matt almost shook his head no, but then he remembered hearing that there were not only video cameras in the cafeteria but also in the hallways. His father had always warned him he couldn't get away with anything when it came to Jesuits.

He told the priest then what he guessed the monsignor already knew, that he had just gotten to his locker when it happened.

He unlocked the lock and open the metal door. There was Cathy's photo on the back of it, the newspaper photo of her snagging the fly ball.

"Is that your girlfriend?" Caifano asked.

THE DEVIL YOU KNOW

Matt nodded and hurriedly dropped his backpack inside and shut the locker door.

"Isn't that Cathy Dempsey?"

Matt slipped the lock into place, thinking, *He knows everything about me.* Now he was pissed at the priest for acting as if he was just curious about the strange happenings at the high school. The Jesuits were always in your face about how much more they knew about you and everything else.

"Very nice young woman. I met her yesterday. Father Brannan introduced us."

Matt grabbed his books and notepad and looked up at Monsignor Caifano, waiting for him to say what was happening next.

"Ready?" The monsignor gave him another friendly smile.

Still Matt didn't respond, not even with a nod.

Monsignor Caifano gestured down the hallway and said the library was likely to be quiet early in the morning. He joked how when he was in the seminary in Rome, he never could bring himself to study before noon. Matt didn't respond. He let Caifano go on about his high school days, trying, Matt knew, to create a bond between the two of them.

Cathy had prepared him last night, recalling the questions she had been asked by the monsignor and the detective. They knew about Father Sweeney; they knew about his fight with Billy Smith; they knew he was in the cafeteria when the football players stripped.

He worried only that they had made a connection between him and Sweeney and Smith both falling on their asses. Or had they spotted the phone on the cafeteria video? If they did, he knew, Pussy Brannan or the dean of students, might call and talk to his mother. His mind kept spinning with conspiracy theories.

He sighed thinking how the smartphone had started all his trouble, but even so, it had given him Cathy.

O

The library was not empty.

"Freshmen," Matt explained, seeing a cluster of kids at the far end of the room.

"No problem." Monsignor Caifano pointed to the opposite corner of the room, away from the students and the librarian's desk.

Sitting down, Matt made sure he was opposite the monsignor, keeping the library table between them. His back was against a shelf of books.

Caifano didn't bear down on what had happened. He didn't back Matt into a corner with questions. Instead, he asked him about his family and said he had heard about the death of his father and that he would pray for his dad.

Matt nodded and thanked the priest. He knew he should talk more, fill in details about his father and provide useless information and long narratives in order to let the hour slip away without the priest getting around to what he really wanted to know.

But Matt wanted it over. He was on the monsignor's radar, and next, he guessed, he would be questioned by Detective Sullivan.

And then Monsignor Caifano stopped his random "get acquainted" questions and surprising him, said directly, grabbing Matt's full attention, "I know you have it."

Matt stared at the priest, keeping his expression blank, if not slightly bored. It drove Jesuits nuts, he knew, when they thought you couldn't care less what they said.

THE DEVIL YOU KNOW

"Have what?" he responded innocently.

"The smartphone." Caifano kept smiling. Kept his eyes on Matt. "You and Father Sweeney had a disagreement about the phone. You were texting in class, is that right?"

"He thought I was, but I only wanted to find out how much longer class was. I had to go to the bathroom. I had a case of the runs," he lied.

The monsignor studied Matt for a moment, then he leaned forward, placed both of his elbows on the table, and lacing his fingers together, lowered his voice, though they were isolated in the long library, and said, "Matt, we need your help." The smile was gone, his eyes were darker and serious. "The Catholic Church needs your help. In truth, all of mankind needs your help."

O

Matt slipped his hands beneath the tabletop and squeezed his thumbs in his fingers.

"Do you know about exorcism?" the monsignor asked. His voice softened, as if they were in a dark confessional.

Matt nodded, alarmed by the shift in Caifano's attitude. Now he knew he had to be on guard.

"You have been taught, I'm sure, that the devil traditionally goes after the damaged souls of troubled creatures, those among us unable to withstand the onslaught of his power and sinful allure. You saw *The Exorcist* movie? Read the book?" The monsignor raised his thick eyebrows.

"Once," Matt whispered, thinking of the nightmares he'd had for a week, believing the devil lived in his bedroom closet.

"I understand you've been accepted by Georgetown. Congratulations. That's a great college. That is also the setting of the *The Exorcist*. It was a Jesuit priest who battled and defeated the devil. You might need the wisdom of those men." He smiled for a moment, then his manner and tone shifted, and he went on gravely, "Matt, we know Lucifer is always in our midst, and today his menacing power is in evidence in the Middle East with those ISIS soldiers. All of them, unfortunately, are under his evil power, and here we are facing similar acts of evil. The recent shootings in movie theaters, and a few years ago, all those innocent children being killed in their classroom in Connecticut."

"And those guys who flew their planes into the Twin Towers?" Matt tossed in, needing to say something.

The priest nodded solemnly, saying, "Pope John Paul II said in 1999 that, while only one in every five thousand cases is an actual demonic possession, nevertheless the devil *does* exist in that one wretched person. That means, in the world today we have thousands of such persons possessed by Lucifer."

The monsignor paused and, reaching inside his shirt pocket, pulled out an iPhone.

"Is your phone anything like this one, Matt?" He held up his iPhone, saying, "I call it Jebby, you know, after the order. What's the name of your phone?"

"Isidore."

"After Saint Isidore?"

Matt nodded. "It was Cathy Dempsey's idea."

"The protector of the Internet, right?"

"I guess."

"May I see your phone, Matt?"

"I don't have it with me."

THE DEVIL YOU KNOW

"You don't? Isn't that the purpose of these phones? I don't leave my room without making sure I have mine in my pocket." He was smiling, but kept his dark eyes on Matt.

"I got in trouble with Father Sweeney for having a phone in class..." He shrugged, tossing the school's rule back at the Vatican envoy.

The monsignor leaned forward, "Matt, I have come to America because our Holy Father is concerned about the power and influence of devices like these smartphones and the internet and everything we call "social media." These devices have become instruments of the devil. The devil is using them to lead young people into temptation, taking them to sites which are occasions of sin. There young people—teenagers and younger—are sharing information, sexual photos and videos, committing mortal sins. Adults, too, are using the corrupt devices to seek out victims. These images and illicit meetings are causing the spread of deadly sexual diseases and the corruption of immortal souls."

Caifano gestured, as if helpless before this onslaught of evil.

Matt squirmed in his seat, then he shrugged, saying, "But everyone has a computer or phone and they text and share information and do good things." He kept shaking his head, baffled by the Vatican envoy's claims. "You have one, Father! You just said you won't leave your room without it."

The monsignor leaned forward and stated. "My phone has been blessed by the Holy Father, as have all the phones and computers and other devices in the Vatican, because the devil is constantly trying to corrupt the good people working for our Holy Mother Church."

Matt pulled himself up in his chair, his mind swirling with what the monsignor had just said. "You think the devil is inside *everyone's* computers and phones?"

Caifano was shaking his head before Matt finished, and raising his hand, gesturing with his finger, pointing at Matt, he answered swiftly and directly to him.

"No, I don't think that all social media devices are possessed by the devil, Matt. But I do think that your phone is. In Rome we learned that a cell phone—such as your own—had been corrupted by an evil spirit. I was sent here to seek it out and destroy the phone before harm was done.

"The Vatican, like any nation, has an intelligence service very much like the FBI and CIA. They uncovered information that a cell phone, possessed by the devil, has been sent to the United States by Middle East terrorists trying to cause destruction in America. I believe you have that phone."

Matt was stunned into silence. His thumbs bit into the palms of his hands.

Caifano glanced around, as if making sure he was speaking in confidence, and continued in his soft voice.

"It isn't just me, Matthew, who is trying to protect you and everyone else from terrorists using the devil on their behalf. It's our Holy Father and all of Christianity.

"In the Middle East today Catholics are being killed by Islamic terrorists. ISIS soldiers are marching Ethiopian Christians onto the beaches of Libya and beheading them."

"What if one can do *good* things with the phone?" Matt asked, thinking of how he helped the little kids win the touch football game on his street.

Monsignor Caifano smiled wryly. "Beelzebub succeeds through deception. These 'acts of kindness' are his way to lead us into mortal sin. He's seeking to claim our souls for all of eternity. Be aware, my son, be very aware."

THE DEVIL YOU KNOW

Matt looked away from the priest. The freshmen were gathering books and papers. The period was over, and he had American History with Father Martin. Cathy was giving an oral report on the causes of the Civil War. He didn't want to miss her presentation.

"I've got to go, Father," he said. "I've got class." He shrugged, as if he was a hopeless victim of his own hell, high school.

Monsignor Caifano nodded, then said, in the tone of a cop and not a priest, "Bring your phone tomorrow."

"We're not allowed to have phones at school," Matt answered quickly, sticking it to the Jesuit again about their rules and regulations.

"I'm giving you absolution."

"If you say so." Matt made it sound as if he was unhappy breaking the school rules. "May I ask why?"

"You may." The monsignor flashed another smile. "I want to provide you protection from menacing Lucifer. I realize many young people no longer believe there is such a phenomenon as the devil, but the existence of Satan is at the heart of Catholic faith and doctrine. *Your* Catholic faith, Matt."

Matt attended Monsignor Caifano's morning Mass in the high school chapel the next day. It wasn't yet eight o'clock, and when Mass was over, he didn't file out with the other students. Instead, Matt walked up on the altar, through the sanctuary, and into the side sacristy.

The monsignor was still wearing his vestments. He paused in changing, leaving on his alb and stole. Taking the phone from Matt, he turned it over carefully in his hands, then said softly, "Come with me."

Matt didn't tell Caifano that the phone was turned off; that now, because of what the monsignor had said, he was afraid to use the phone. He followed the Vatican envoy, but kept his distance. The pews were empty. The monsignor genuflected in front of the altar, then stepped forward and set the phone down on the altar.

Matt stepped away, thinking, *If the devil really was in the phone, there might be an explosion or something.*

The monsignor blessed himself and placed both of his hands on the phone and, looking up at the crucifix hanging from the ceiling in front of the stained glass windows, spoke as if the chapel was filled with worshippers and he needed to be heard:

Depart, then, impious one, depart, accursed one, depart with all your deceits, for God has willed that man should be His temple. Why do you still linger here? Give honor to God the Father Almighty, before whom every knee must bow.

Matt dropped to his knees on the altar steps and quickly made the Sign of the Cross.

Monsignor Caifano turned toward Matt and asked him to respond to his prayer.

"Lord, we have sinned against you: Lord, have mercy."

"Lord, have mercy," Matt said.

"Lord, show us your mercy and love."

"And grant us your salvation."

"May Almighty God have mercy on us, forgive us our sins, and bring us to everlasting life."

"Amen."

THE DEVIL YOU KNOW

Genuflecting again, Monsignor Caifano picked up the phone and, with a smile, handed it to Matt and said confidently, "Your phone is without sin, Matt. Go with God."

Matt took the phone and held it carefully, as if afraid he might damage the blessing. It was only when he slipped it into his pocket that he realized the phone had been turned off. What good would an exorcism be, he wondered. But as the nuns always said, God works in mysterious ways.

He turned away from the altar and walked down the main aisle and out of the chapel, his phone tucked into his back pocket. Leave well enough alone, is what his dad always said, Matt thought, and headed for class, realizing as he glanced at the hall clock that he was already late for History.

O

The devil! Christ Almighty. What would they think of next?

Even as Matt thought that, he wondered what was giving his smartphone such supernatural power. But everything was so weird in the world, he thought next. They had automobiles that could drive themselves, robots that served food, drones halfway around the world that could kill people with a push of a button.

He shook his head, thinking, maybe it wasn't the devil, as Caifano thought, but just an ISIS computer terrorist in the Middle East reading his mind and causing chaos.

The devil! Christ Almighty. What would happen next?

Matt glanced again at the hallway clock as he skipped down the stairs, hurrying to get to history, but he didn't make it.

O

Pussy Brannan and Detective Sullivan were at the first-floor landing, in front of the administration offices, waiting for him.

"There he is!" Father Brannan declared, as if Matt Garrity was a desperate fugitive.

Matt slowed his descent down the staircase, giving in, knowing he was in more trouble.

"Matt, come over here." The principal waved him to where he was standing with the detective.

Matt tried to look annoyed and put out, but that didn't stop Brannan.

"Matt, this is Detective Sullivan. He wants to examine your phone." The principal was smiling, as if it was just a favor. That was Pussy Brannan's MO. If you were in real trouble, he acted as if you were his long-lost friend.

"I have class, Father. Father Martin doesn't like it when we're late."

"You can leave the phone with the detective. He'll take good care of it." The principal ordered and kept smiling.

Matt guessed Pussy Brannan knew Caifano had performed an exorcism on the phone. Jesuits shared information and gossip. It was their way to keep tabs on students.

Matt reached into his trousers' pocket, turned the phone on and quickly made a wish of what he wanted to happen next at Saint Ignatius, then he turned off the phone before handing it over to Father Brannan. The principal immediately gave the phone to Sullivan who slid the device into a plastic bag, telling them both he'd take it down to headquarters and have it examined by the department technicians.

270

THE DEVIL YOU KNOW

"Good!" Brannan declared and said to Matt, "You'll have the phone back later today, son, if everything checks out. Right, Joe?"

The cop nodded, and added, "Don't worry, son, I'm sure your phone is perfectly fine."

"I'm late, Father," Matt looked up at the hallway clock.

"Yes. Yes. We don't want Father Martin upset. Off with you." He tapped Matt on the shoulder and gave him a little shove in the direction of the class.

Matt took off, rushing now, but not to class. He needed to reach the broom closet on the first floor before the fire alarm sprinklers went off in all the classrooms and hallways of the high school.

And that is exactly what transpired. So much for the power of exorcism, Matt thought, ducking into the tiny broom closet just as the deluge of water soaked the students and teachers in all the classrooms on the three floors of the old building.

O

Now they were scared. The kids. The teachers. The administration. The janitors. Even the parents were scared. They had gotten urgent calls and texts from their children saying the sprinkler system had malfunctioned and everyone and everything was soaking wet at school as half a dozen firetrucks and police cars arrived at the scene.

"Structural engineers," Pussy Brannan announced over the loudspeakers "will be on the school property this afternoon to evaluate the situation. School is dismissed."

Matt cautiously opened the broom closet door and checked the hall. The sprinklers had been turned off, water now just dripped from the ceiling

271

sprinkler. The last of the students were leaving school. They were all soaking wet. The girls looked especially wet, with their hair dripping, and school blouses clinging to their bodies.

Matt thought of Cathy then and took off for the second floor, where her locker was, realizing that what he had done to everyone in the school, just to get even with Brannan and Sullivan, he had also done to the girl he loved.

"You!" She raged as he arrived panting at her locker.

"Are you okay?"

"Another of your stupid tricks?"

She slammed the metal door and locked her locker, then turned and headed for the stairs.

"Wait!" Matt implored as he fell into step with her. There were other upper classmen on the floor cleaning out the mess inside their lockers. Everywhere he looked there were pools of water and drenched classmates.

"I'm sorry."

"No you're not." She answered back, not bothering to look at him.

She raced down the flight of stone stairs, then out the front double doors of the school and into the bright spring morning where the street was crowded with trucks and police cars.

THE DEVIL YOU KNOW

The students were gathered in clusters away from the building. It looked almost like a routine fire drill, Matt thought, except that everyone was soaking wet. It was warm in the sun, and the students were taking a certain perverse delight in their disheveled looks and appearances. The girls, especially had taken the situation into hand and were busy combing each other's hair, using the wet conditions to create hair-do styles.

"Cathy, please...wait! Let me explain." Now Matt was begging.

That caught her attention and she stopped on the sidewalk that circled the school and led to the next block over where, he knew, she could catch a cross-town bus and head home.

"What?" She demanded.

"I did do it, yes, but I didn't mean to hurt anyone."

"You didn't hurt anyone, Garrity. You just soaked us all down to our underwear, that's all. I'm sending you the bill for dry cleaning my uniform. Look at me! Look at the mess you have caused."

Matt smiled sheepishly. Now that she was yelling at him, he felt relieved. He could tell by her tone that she wasn't still furious.

"Well?" she asked, sighing. "Explain yourself."

"I had a meeting with that Vatican monsignor."

She nodded slowly.

"He performed an exorcism on my smartphone."

"WHAT!"

It was only because they were isolated on the far side of the school that her shriek didn't draw everyone's attention.

"Shhhhhh." Matt glanced around.

Cathy stepped closer. "An *exorcism?*" Her eyes were bulging. "Where? How?"

He told her, whispering what had happened earlier that morning and what Caifano had done and said.

He told her everything, even how he had secretly made his wish before handing over the phone to the principal.

"But what about the exorcism? Didn't that get rid of the devil?" The shock in her eyes changed to fear.

"I didn't have the phone turned on when I gave it to the monsignor. I don't think the exorcism worked. It would be like talking to a dead person." He shrugged, looked helpless, and now his sad grey eyes showed his own fear for what he was causing to happen.

Seeing his reaction, Cathy seized his arm, as if taking part ownership of what was happening.

"What am I going to do!"

"I want to help you."

"You can't. I don't know what I want to do."

"Get rid of that phone, that's what you want to do."

"I don't have my phone, remember? Sullivan has it. He is going to have it checked out by the cops."

Cathy covered her mouth with the palm of her right hand. "Oh, God." Fear registered on her face and in her eyes.

"What if they do something with it? Say something? What if they wish that all of us drop dead or *something*?" Panic registered in her voice.

"They can't. There's a passcode."

"Is that true? What's the code?"

"Your name."

Hearing that, Cathy relaxed, but then immediately asked, "What are you going to do?"

THE DEVIL YOU KNOW

Shrugging, Matt looked off at the turmoil around the school, with fire trucks and firemen and crowds of students still milling around the front entrance and lawns of St. Ignatius.

"I'm going up to Father Martin's class. I want to find him and ask for his help."

"I'm going with you."

"No, go home. You're sopping wet."

"I don't care. I want to be with you." She stepped closer and took his hand and nodded towards the side entrance of the school. As they headed back into the building, she said, "But first I have to comb my hair."

Father Martin stopped cleaning the mess of waterlogged papers and books on his desk as Matt and Cathy opened the door and stepped into the empty classroom.

"Well, well, well," he exclaimed, smiling at their surprise appearance. "Actual living students!"

At 60-years he was distinguished looking with a mass of white hair and physically strong. It was agreed by everyone that Father Martin was the best teacher at St. Ignatius. Upperclassmen also knew that while Brannan was the principal, Martin was the real authority in the hierarchy of the Jesuit school.

"Survivors!" He stepped around behind the desk and sat down. "And to what do I owe this pleasure, Ms. Dempsey?"

Cathy grinned and glanced at Matt and waited for him to rescue her with a reply.

"Wow!" Matt exclaimed, taking in the empty room cluttered with discarded books and backpacks and scattered paper that the students had abandoned when the sprinkler system went off.

Father Martin gestured for the two students to sit and asked how they were allowed in the school.

"We snuck in the side door," Cathy grinned, pleased with herself.

"Ahhh!" The Jesuit, cupping his palm to the side of his face, proclaimed, "I'll tell them I never saw you two. Now what's up?" He glanced from one to the other and leaned back in the chair and got comfortable, as if he expected they had a long story to tell.

Cathy looked at Matt and, as she did, she slipped into one of the front desks, ready to hear what he had to say.

Matt didn't sit down. Instead, he kept looking around the cluttered room, as if still shocked by its condition.

"You're not worried that the building might fall down next, given all that has happened?" Father Martin asked.

"No, Father."

"I think we all should call it a day," He swept the two of them with a quick glance. Then he gestured toward the board. "Don't worry about *that* assignment. God knows, we might not have a building to teach in come next week." He forced a smile.

Matt felt bad. Father Martin was favorite teacher, and now the priest was worried about the school, and it was Matt's fault.

"Maybe we should say an extra novena, Father...you know, to help keep the building up." Matt gestured with both hands, as if to support his attempt at humor.

"We'll need more than a few novenas, Matt." The Jesuit kept his eye on him.

THE DEVIL YOU KNOW

"Father," Matt said, surprising himself as he asked, "do you think the devil is with us at all time, tempting us to do bad things?"

Cathy was startled by Matt's question and sat back in the desk chair and looked at the teacher, waiting for his reply.

Father Martin said nothing, studying Matt. He crossed his legs under his cassock and finally replied, "Isn't that what the good nuns taught you in second grade, Matt?"

It was so like the history teacher to reply that way, Matt thought. It was how he taught his class, always lobbing back a question, never exactly answering, forcing all of them to come up with some sort of answer, some defense for whatever they said. He was like a tennis player, always on defense, always knocking the ball back to the other side of the net, never going for the match point.

"Well, they taught me that the devil because of pride, did not return God's love, and that God did not destroy him, or other fallen angels, but allowed them to live."

"And they told you, too, that all of us have a good angel on our right shoulder and a bad angel on our left, trying to steer us to do evil," added the Jesuit.

Matt nodded and being very serious, went on, "Monsignor Caifano, the Vatican envoy, told me yesterday that my cell phone is possessed by the devil. He made me bring it to school so he could perform some sort of exorcism."

Father Martin uncrossed his legs and sat forward. His arms were braced against the desktop, and he had clasped his hands together as if in prayer, Matt could see, though, that his fingers were squeezed tight. "An exorcism," he whispered.

Matt explained how he had taken his phone to the chapel after morning Mass.

Father Martin nodded, then asked, "Was the north door open?"

"The north door?"

"You know about the devil's door? The good sisters taught you that, right?"

"About baptism?" Matt was still not sure what he meant.

"That's right. In the Middle Ages it was held that the devil resided in an unbaptized child's soul, and at the baptism the devil is driven out of the child. Because the devil has to leave the church, the baptismal font was always placed opposite the north door, a door too small to have any real use but was there to let the devil escape. Check it out the next time you're in the chapel—you'll see a tiny door in the north wall."

"Is that actually true? About the devil in a baby's soul?" Cathy exclaimed.

The priest shrugged, "Well, that's what they thought in the Middle Ages."

"And now the Pope believes the devil is in phones?" Cathy sounded more incredulous with each of her questions.

"I won't say it is so farfetched, Cathy, given what I'm told goes on today in social media, what with the language and photographs being shared on-line, especially among high school students." He glanced at the two of them, as if he knew their secret.

"The monsignor wasn't baptizing the phone!" Matt said, pulling the topic back to what had happened in the school's chapel.

"The door is also left ajar during an exorcism, to allow the devil to flee," Father Martin replied. "Where's your phone?"

"I gave it to Father Brannan and he gave it to Detective Sullivan."

"Are you waiting to get it back? Is that why you're still here?"

"I offered to get the phone for him," Cathy piped up. "I know Mr. Sullivan."

THE DEVIL YOU KNOW

"I don't want Cathy, or anyone, touching the smartphone," Matt cut into Cathy's statement, then realized how rude he sounded and fell silent.

He knew he had alarmed Father Martin, that there might be something more involved than just a simple cell phone. Then, to justify his comment, he added, "My mom would be mad." It was always wise, he knew, to appear as if you were trying to be a perfectly obedient child.

"It's a new phone?" Father Martin asked.

Matt nodded, saying he had just gotten the smartphone as a birthday present, and that it was the last thing his father had gotten for him. For that reason, he hoped that Father Martin would talk to Pussy Brannan. Matt knew it was always a good ploy to play one Jesuit against another. They always wanted to outdo one another.

"I nicknamed it Isidore, you know, after Saint Isidore of Seville, because he's the patron saint of the Internet." Matt nodded towards Cathy, saying that she told him about Isidore, having learned it in Sister Patricia's religion class.

He kept smiling and went on to say how he had read up about Isidore, trying to impress the Jesuit.

But Father Martin wasn't buying it, Matt saw. The Jesuit was watching him with an amused look as Matt went on and on about Saint Isidore, everything that he had gathered from reading Wikipedia. Still, he kept talking as if he were one of those cable news commentators who couldn't shut up, another Chris Matthews on MSNBC.

Finally, Father Martin raised his hand, as if he were asking for relief, and said quickly, "Let's go see Father Brannan."

The priest stood. The discussion was over. Matt and Cathy followed the priest obediently from the classroom. Matt knew he had made a mistake. Now, would he have two Jesuits after him?

"I didn't do anything, Father," Matt commented weakly, following Father Martin down the hallway toward the staircase. Matt could hear fear in his own voice. Cathy reached over, took his hand, and squeezed it.

"Aren't all phones alike?" Matt asked innocently.

"I don't know. I don't own one. I took a vow of poverty," the priest declared calmly.

Matt glanced over at Cathy who was shaking her head, telling him to keep quiet.

Matt stopped talking. He knew that when dealing with Jesuits, it was best to say as little as possible. They were good at taking what you said and turning it against you.

O

When they reached the first floor, they saw Father Brannan and Detective Sullivan pacing the deserted hallway, assessing the mess, the puddles of water on the cement floor, the abandoned backpacks and books scattered over the length of the corridor.

Matt knew he should be alarmed by what was unfolding, but he suddenly felt curious about it all. He felt like an onlooker in a drama that had nothing at all to do with him.

"You've brought the culprit?" the detective said, trying to lighten the situation with a bad joke.

Matt spotted his silver phone in Sullivan's right hand, still in the plastic wrapper. The phone was turned off. He saw no small shiny light, and he sighed.

"Our friend here, Mr. Garrity, tells me Monsignor Caifano this morning in our chapel performed an *exorcismus* on his smartphone." Father

THE DEVIL YOU KNOW

Martin's statement momentarily sounded like a criticism of the principal for letting such a thing happen on school property.

"What? Exorcism?" Sullivan stared at both Jesuits

"Yes, exorcism," Father Martin went on calmly. "The act of driving out or warding off demons. You must have learned about exorcism when you were a student here, Joe."

"Come on." Sullivan said, half grinning. He glanced from priest to priest, then shot a look at Matt, as if he suddenly realized the teenager was more dangerous than he had thought. "Exorcism!" he announced again.

"No sense being a Catholic, Joe, if you don't believe in the power of Satan," Father Martin commented. He gestured to the detective to hand him the phone, then holding up the plastic container, said to Matt, "Is this yours?"

"Yes, Father."

"Why don't you show us how it works, Matt?" Father Martin asked nicely, taking the device from the plastic bag.

"It's just a phone, Father."

"Well, the Vatican monsignor has expelled the devil. Let's see if it is now *just* a telephone." Father Martin kept smiling, speaking softly. His tone, however, suggested he only wanted to prove to the principal and the detective that the phone, and Matt, were harmless.

The principal raised his two hands and stepped toward Matt, reaching for the phone, but Father Martin blocked him, turned to Matt, and asked, "You said Monsignor Caifano performed an exorcism this morning, correct?"

"In the chapel."

Father Martin glanced at the principal and the detective and declared, "Well, I believe we are now in good hands." He kept smiling. "Monsignor Caifano has written a book on the topic. He teaches a course at Rome's pontifical university Regina Apostolorum on satanic cults and how they are making inroads in society. We know the influences of the devil are still real today—what is happening in the Middle East is evidence."

The Jesuit handed the phone to Matt, adding, "The Vatican believes that the devil now possesses such devices."

For a moment, all of them stared at the cell phone until Detective Sullivan asked, half whispering, "But doesn't the devil possess the souls of humans, not things?"

"That's what we first learned in school, Joe," Father Martin replied. "But Pope John Paul, ten or so years ago, issued *De Exorcismis et Supplicationibus Quibusdam*, or *Of Exorcisms and Certain Supplications*. That text replaced a seventeenth-century version and reaffirmed the existence of the devil. In this document the pope approved prayers and rites for driving devils out of people, but also for cleansing places and objects of demonic influences. Matt's cell phone, perhaps, is one such object."

"That's why we're having all this trouble," Father Brannan declared, reaching for the phone.

Then he stopped abruptly, as if realizing what he was doing and what harm he might face. Turning toward the detective, he said, "Joe, you're taking this cell phone into custody, right?"

"I know what we should do." Cathy announced, stepping up beside Matt. "Why don't I order us pizza? It's almost noon."

She grabbed the phone quickly out of Matt's hand typed...typed in the passcode—her name—and quickly sent a text.

To the group, she announced. "I'll order two large pies, with everything." Her smile was bright and impish.

THE DEVIL YOU KNOW

Down the length of the long first-floor hallway, the scattered litter of books and backpacks and pools of water disappeared and evaporated in a long whoop of sounds, as if the school had been hit with a reverse hurricane, sucking away all the debris. Matt and the others jumped back at the sudden violence of the scene.

Matt stepped in front of Cathy, as if to protect her from the sudden destruction.

Sullivan gestured impatiently for the phone, as if to take charge of the situation.

Matt looked at Father Martin and, widening his eyes, waited for the priest to help.

"Perhaps that would be best, students," Father Martin said firmly. "Let Detective Sullivan have the phone until we can talk to Monsignor Caifano." He was smiling, fatherly. "It will clear your name. You don't want your acceptance to college jeopardized."

The principal stepped around Sullivan and Father Martin, raised his hand and pointed his finger at both of the students, saying, "Give that phone to Detective Sullivan if either one of you expect to graduate from Saint Ignatius."

Matt turned to Cathy. She was staring at the three men as she slowly withdrew the silver device from behind her back. She held it up as if she were about to hand the phone to Detective Sullivan. He stepped forward and abruptly froze, with his hand outstretched, a kind smile on his big Irish face. Behind him, the two Jesuits were also locked in their footsteps, as if imitating statues.

Cathy slipped around them and stared at Matt, now stunned by the fixed figures of the two priests and the detective.

"Let's go, Matt." She rolled her eyes towards the exit at the end of the hall. The morning sun flooded through the open door. It was as if it was their own devil's door, Matt thought, their way of escaping everything that he had caused to happen.

"What I wished for was that they will wake in another ten minutes and have no idea of what happened, nor remember anything about your phone." She smiled at Matt, then added, "See, you should listen to me if you want to stay out of trouble."

When they reached the drive in front of the school, Cathy realized with a new surge of self-awareness that they did not have to hail a taxi or wait for the next city bus.

Instead she decided she wanted an Uber car to take them home, and a long black limousine materialized on the street, turned into the driveway, and eased to a stop in front of the high school.

Matt looked at Cathy, surprised by the car.

"I just summoned it." She shrugged, holding up the silver phone.

She waited and watched as the uniformed chauffeur hustled around to greet them. "Hello, madam, sir" he said, opening the limo's rear door.

Cathy nodded her thanks and ducked into the dark interior. Matt followed, slipping into the car. It was only when he sat down and the door closed behind him that Matt saw Monsignor Caifano was already in the car, sitting alone in the deep seat.

A smile filled the monsignor's face as he greeted them. "Welcome, Cathy Dempsey, to your boyfriend's world." His voice was full of smug satisfaction.

Without pausing, and as fast as any gunfighter in Call-Duty, Cathy raised the smartphone, pointed it at the monsignor and made her wish. She blew Caifano out of his mind, out of the limousine, out of existence.

Matt jerked back in shock.

"His *nomme de guerre* is Monsignor Caifano. His real name is Sami Al Oraidi. He was a member of Al Queda Jabhat al-Nusra, a terrorist group in Syria," Cathy stated clearly before Matt could open his mouth.

"How do you know all this? Wikipedia?"

"Social media."

"Social media."

"Well, actually, Facebook. That's how they communicate. Don't you watch the news? The talking heads on T.V. are always saying terrorists use social media to recruit mixed-up teenagers. Girls to marry their soldiers. Guess what? They thought you were a likely candidate. Your dad had been killed in a car accident. You didn't have many friends. No girlfriend." Cathy rolled her eyes again and smiled smugly.

Matt stared at Cathy, as if trying to comprehend everything she had just said and what it meant. Then he asked how she knew the Vatican envoy wasn't really a Vatican envoy.

Cathy grinned at Matt, pleased with her success, pleased that she had impressed him. "I found out on Facebook. This phone was made in Iran. I read on one of those sites that it was lost. Your Dad must have found it on eBay. How would he know it was an ISIS weapon?" She shrugged.

"Maybe it wasn't an accident," Matt said after a moment. "Maybe my Dad was killed because he had the phone. Maybe he was murdered by the Jabhat al-Nusra. Killed by this so-called Vatican envoy when they were trying to get it back."

He sank back into the limo seat as it pulled away from the curb. For a moment neither one of them said anything. Matt was exhausted from the long morning and everything that had happened, his mind whirling with the realization his father had been killed by mistake, for having bought him a smartphone on eBay, by the terrorists.

"We blew him away," Cathy nodded to the empty cushioned seat across from them, then added, "One less terrorist." With that, she reached across and took hold of Matt's hand.

"What are we going to do, Cat?" he asked, looking at her now with his sad grey eyes.

"Do? We're going to school on Monday morning as if nothing happened—and nothing has happened. No one will remember what took place this last week. We're going to graduate in three weeks and we're going to Georgetown University in the fall. I think I'll major in computer science." She sounded almost giddy, reciting plans.

"And me?" Matt asked. "What about my phone?"

O

Cathy slipped the silver device from the pocket of her school blazer, but instead of handing it to him, she held it up as if it were a Borromean Ring, saying "The Holy Trinity, Matt. You, me, and this phone which will someday..."

With that she paused, turned on the silver device, and typing in her name as the passcode, made her first wish.

ACKNOWLEDGMENTS

"Flight" © 1989. First published in *Stalkers*, 1989.

"A Cabin in the Woods" © 1976. First published in *Alfred Hitchcock's Mystery Magazine*, July 1976.

"Call Me" © 1981. First published in *The Berkley Showcase*, Berkley Books, 1981.

"Catholic Guilt" © 2015.

"Snow Man" © 1959. First published in *Fleur de Lis*, Spring, 1959.

"The Crazy Chinaman" © 1983. First published in *The Dodd, Mead Gallery of Horror*, Dodd, Mead & Company, 1983.

"Winter Morning" © 1982. First published in *Berkshire Magazine*, Winter, 1982.

"A Game in the Sun" © 1972. First published in *Ellery Queen's Mystery Magazine*, March 1972.

"Obscene Phone Calls" © 1991. First published in *Masques IV*, Pulphouse Publishing. 1991.

"The Ecology of Reptiles" © 1993. First published in *Predaters*, Roc Books. 1993.

A GAME IN THE SUN AND OTHER STORIES—JOHN COYNE